FAREWELL PERFORMANCE

Recent Titles by Tessa Barclay

THE CHAMPAGNE GIRLS
A LOVELY ILLUSION*
OTHER PEOPLE'S DREAMS
THE PRECIOUS GIFT
THE SATURDAY GIRL
STARTING OVER*
* available from Severn House

FAREWELL
PERFORMANCE

Tessa Barclay

This first world edition published in Great Britain 2001 by
SEVERN HOUSE PUBLISHERS LTD of
9–15 High Street, Sutton, Surrey SM1 1DF.
This first world edition published in the USA 2001 by
SEVERN HOUSE PUBLISHERS INC of
595 Madison Avenue, New York, N.Y. 10022.

British Library Cataloguing in Publication Data

Barclay, Tessa
  Farewell performance
  1. Detective and mystery stories
  I. Title
  823.9'14 [F]

ISBN 0-7278-5773-8

Typeset by Palimpsest Book Production Ltd.,
Polmont, Stirlingshire, Scotland.
Printed and bound in Great Britain by
MPG Books Ltd., Bodmin, Cornwall.

Author's Note

The first book I ever planned to write, years ago, was a documentary about an aspect of World War II. I needed funds for a tape-recorder and travel expenses so to earn the money I tried writing a detective novel. To my delight it was accepted. Ever since I've loved the challenge and the fun of writing mystery novels, the feeling of enlisting the reader in a game to solve the puzzle before I 'reveal all'.

Farewell Performance was on the verge of getting into print two or three times but mergers and buy-outs among the publishing firms got in the way. Here it is at last, featuring a detective from a background never used before – I hope you'll like him.

One

There was no foreboding of death or destruction on that special day in Edinurgh. On the contrary, Archibald Gower's antique shop in George Street, Edinburgh, was so full of happily chattering people that there was a policeman controlling the overflow on the pavement.

Inside, the longcase clocks by Christopher Gould, the Chinese porcelain, the Sheraton tulipwood table and matching chairs had all been carefully cleared away from the display area. On the fine old Turkey carpet, television cameramen planted their feet apart while their helpers directed the beam of light just so. Sound-men poked microphones out on long rods. Press cameramen looked through lenses, reporters held miniature recorders to their ears to hear the reassuring hum of the turning tape.

'Now, ladies and gentlemen, if you'll all just . . . That's it . . . Careful, now. We wouldn't want to harm this beautiful instrument, would we?'

Certainly not, thought the tall, rather angular man on the edge of the crowd – not after all the trouble he'd taken to get the cello, the maestro, the press and the money all together in the one place.

Cameras glared at the violoncello exposed to view in its case. The Emilio . . .

'Is she not beautiful?' said the maestro, Talik Edder, in his throaty voice, made more throaty by emotion.

Well, no. To the untrained eye, it was a cello like any other cello – larger than a violin of course but much the same shape,

1

with f-holes cut in the beautiful maplewood, which glowed with a varnish like honey.

The tall man who had brought them all here, Gregory Crowne, watched them with attention. People interested in music, he reflected, and even some who don't know Bach from Offenbach, have heard of Stradivarius. 'He made violins,' they say in quiz games, and gain two points if they can add that his name was really Stradivari and that he worked in Cremona towards the end of the seventeenth century.

The number of cellos by great makers is strictly limited. The cello hadn't really been invented when Stradivari, Guarneri and Amati were making stringed instruments. From time to time cellos are 'found' supposedly by great makers but then they're proved to be forgeries – very disheartening to a great maestro waiting for the instrument of his dreams. Crowne ought to know – he'd listened to the laments of the great cellist often enough.

His friend Talik Edder, presently appearing at the Edinburgh Festival, owned two cellos, a Guarneri and a relatively modern one by Abraham Prescott. But all his life he had longed for a Stradivarius, and one special Strad in particular.

'One day,' he would murmur when he was being interviewed, 'I shall clasp in my arms my great love.' The interviewer would quiver with excitement – for Edder's success with the ladies was well known. But his face would fall when Edder named his 'great love' – the Emilio.

Crowne, who had sent out a press release, had made it clear that almost all the instruments by famous makers have individual names, from the men who ordered them or played them during a famous career. The Emilio had belonged to Tomasa Emilio, cellist at the court of Frederick-William of Prussia, and had been brought by Boccherini from Prussia after the King's death. Its history was well documented from there on: in 1939 the instrument had been owned by Isaac Ziegler, who willed it on his death to the family who had helped him escape from Hitler.

The Kyles, mistakenly, had put the cello in their private museum of musical instruments. A rich and somewhat eccentric Scotsman, Hubert Kyle had felt it his duty to preserve rare specimens from damage, resisting all efforts to bring the cello into use. He had even resisted Crowne's persuasions – and that was unusual, for Gregory Crowne could be very persuasive when he put his mind to it.

But times had changed, death and taxes had taken their toll. Recently the collection had been put up for sale, and it was the best of possible luck that the agent chosen should be an Edinburgh man with a well-known shop in George Street. There was the Emilio, looking for a new owner. And there was Talik Edder, booked in Edinburgh for Festival engagements.

It was a heaven-sent opportunity for publicity, too. The tall, handsome Finnish player would hand over the cheque – a record price for a cello, which in itself was newsworthy. That it should be the cello he'd longed for for over twenty years added human interest. And his friend and concert agent Gregory Crowne had made sure every human was going to take an interest, through press, radio and TV.

There had been a short interlude of alarm when some rich Japanese had thrown his yen in the works. 'Top any offer,' his fax said . . . and a day of suspense had ensued. Crowne knew very well that the dealer had been tempted. As the memory stirred in his mind he gazed across the room, and Archie Gower's eyes were drawn to meet those of the thin, brown-haired man who had talked him out of it.

To his relief, Archie got a faint smile of encouragement. Thank goodness . . . It would never do to get on the wrong side of a man like Gregory Crowne.

So, thanks to that persuasive tongue, here they were next day, Archibald Gower, antique dealer, Talik Edder, cellist, and Gregory Crowne, well-known concert agent – well known against his will, that is, for being something more than just a concert agent – gathered in front of the press of several continents to complete the sale of the Emilio.

Edder opened a briefcase, took out an envelope and handed it to Mr Gower. Mr Gower accepted it though his gaze remained fixed on the TV cameras, smiled self-consciously, and shook hands.

'Let's see the cheque!' cried the reporters. They always got to see the cheque when a lottery winner received a record sum.

Sheepishly Gower opened the envelope to display the cheque. Cameras whirred, flashguns lit up the elegant shop.

'A few words from you, Mr Edder? Tell us how you're feeling, Mr Edder? Hey, Talik, you happy or what?'

Talik Edder was in fact close to tears. He took the Emilio from its case so as to hold it close against him – truly like a lover.

'What can I tell you?' he murmured. 'This is one of the most beautiful things in the world – a treasure that has been shut away from the world for years, like the Sleeping Beauty. Thirty years ago she gave what seemed to be her farewell performance, the Emilio. But now . . . now . . .'

'Now she's awakening to the kiss of her Prince Charming,' gushed Senhora Angeliza Kelly, who was never far away if Talik was around. She squirmed her way through the reporters, a plumpish figure in pastel mink, to present Prince Charming with a sheaf of red carnations. 'For you on this great day, maestro,' she whispered, gazing up at him with adoration.

Gregory Crowne fielded the carnations. He'd talked it over beforehand with the TV men: once Edder had said his little piece, the important thing was to get him to play. He handed the maestro his Nurnberger bow. Edder smiled, looked round for a chair. One was standing ready.

He sat, fixed the spike, bent his head to listen to the strings. He had tuned the cello earlier in preparation, but he couldn't resist adjusting the pegs just a little, for the mere pleasure of the wood between his fingers.

He looked up. His head took up its usual attitude, a little tilted to hear his tone. Silence fell. He played.

Inevitably he played 'The Swan' by Saint-Saëns. Well known, trite even. But the most hardened of the press-men felt tears spring to their eyes at the rich, liquid notes, the soft phrasing, the love in every stroke of the bow.

There were calls of 'Encore,' but the performer shook his head. 'You must excuse,' he said. 'The Emilio and I have waited long for each other. I must have an intimate talk with her in private before we know each other perfectly.'

What a card, the reporters muttered to each other. What an angel, sighed Senhora Kelly to herself. What a publicity star, thought Crowne, and shepherded him out to his car.

He was driven away to friendly cheers and demands for autographs from the fans who had been forced to wait outside. Mr Gower went back inside with Gregory Crowne to offer this important personage a last glass of champagne and to supervise the rearranging of his display area. With the Festival about to begin, the city was full of rich tourists who might very well step in and buy his Sheraton dining-set without batting a pocketbook.

The TV men were checking to make sure they'd been recording, and the reporters were drinking up the leftovers, when a short, square figure shoved the door open and erupted into the shop.

'Gower? Archibald Gower?'

The dealer came forward, straightening the lapels of his Savile Row suit. 'I am Archibald Gower—' He broke off. The man who had just shouted for him was a middle-aged Japanese with anxious black eyes and the worn look that comes from jet-lag.

'Takamasa Shige,' said the customer, with a brief bow that showed his estimation of their relative stations in life. 'I'd like to see my Emilio.'

'*Your* Emilio?'

'You got my offer, I assume?'

'Yes, but—'

'Then let me see the cello.'

'I'm afraid, Mr Shige . . . I'm sorry to tell you . . .'

'Sorry? What do you mean, sorry?'

'It's gone – I mean, I don't have it—'

'Gone? Where has it gone? Gower, what have you done with my cello?'

His manner was autocratic. He was clad in a suit of fine navy wild silk, beautifully tailored. His wristwatch was a sliver of platinum. The document case he carried looked as if it was made from the skin of the unicorn, it seemed so fine.

He had the air of being able to buy and sell Archibald Gower ten times over, supposing he had the least interest in buying and selling Scottish antique dealers. He glared at Gower with his angry black eyes, and Gower suddenly felt that he should have accepted his money and run, no matter what Crowne had said about artistic merit and rightful ownership of rare instruments.

Too late now to run. 'The Emilio has gone to its new owner,' he said with dignity. 'To Mr Talik Edder, the great cellist.'

There was an awful pause. Mr Shige's grey face went white. He closed his eyes and opened them.

'You've *sold* it?'

'It was already sold – as good as sold – when your offer arrived.'

'But I told you that I would give you a better price than—'

'I sent you an e-mail to let you know,' Gower said.

'I never got it. I have been in the air since eight o'clock yesterday morning. It never occurred to me that you—' He broke off. 'You sold my Emilio!'

'Excuse me, sir, it was never your Emilio. Mr Edder—'

Shige clenched his fists and hurled them into the air as if

he would beat Gower over the head. A torrent of Japanese poured from his lips.

The newsmen still in the shop were delighted. This little man, whoever he was – somebody rich, no doubt – well, he was behaving quite unlike the usual Japanese businessman. No suave, polite demeanour here. He was more like a samurai about to carry out the execution of a serf. All that was lacking was the sword with the curved blade.

Archie Gower looked positively terrified. He glanced about wildly for help. And, to his delight, Gregory Crowne stepped to his side. There, thought Archie with gratitude: you could always rely on royalty to do the right thing.

'Excuse me, Mr Shige,' said Crowne.

The Japanese millionaire paid no heed, except that the flow of words changed back to English. 'That was *my* cello! I ordered you to keep it for me!'

'Mr Shige,' Crowne insisted.

Something about him made the other man pause. He stared at him – and matters weren't helped by the fact that he had to look up by at least twelve inches to meet his gaze.

'Keep out of this!' he grunted. 'This is between this shopkeeper and myself.'

'You're wrong there . . .'

Takamasa Shige wasn't accustomed to being told he was wrong. All the years of his adult life, he had made decisions and given orders, knowing conclusively that he was right. The proof of the matter was that for thirty years he had been a millionaire industrialist.

'Mr Shige,' Gower quavered, 'this is Mr Gregory Crowne.' He said it as if he were invoking St Peter and all the angels.

'I am not concerned with anyone else—'

'But Mr Shige, Mr Crowne is—'

'I'm Talik Edder's agent during his appearance here at the Festival,' Crowne put in with some haste. He didn't enjoy it when others, eager to impress, gave away his identity.

'I don't wish to discuss this with a mere concert agent. I want to speak to Edder himself.'

'Mr Shige!' gasped Gower, greatly shocked. No one ought ever to speak to Gregory Crowne like that.

'It's all right, Gower. I don't mind,' said Crowne. 'You must understand, Mr Shige, Talik had first claim on the Emilio. He had always wanted it, had made the fact known, and put in the first bid the moment it came on the market.'

'Huh!' said Shige, his voice dark with anger. 'The market! I understand the market! Money talks in the market, and I sent this man a fax to say I would offer more than any bid he received. I came here in the certainty that I am the owner of the Emilio. How could this fool have sold it to Edder?'

'Because I persuaded him to keep to his original bargain.'

'You!' Once again the angry torrent of words, once again the fists came up. For a moment it seemed as if the unbelievable would happen, and this wild little man would actually hit Gregory Crowne in front of the television cameras.

'Shige!' Crowne said. His tone was cool and sharp; it caused Shige to draw back. Crowne indicated the cameras whirring and clicking all around them. 'Do you really want this recorded for the world to see?'

There followed a struggle for control that suffused the weary face with dull red, a hissing intake of breath. Then Shige gave a sort of aborted bow. 'You are correct. This is undignified. I must speak to Edder. What hotel is he staying at?'

'I'll take you there if you like. He's at the Hill Hotel, in Hill Crescent.'

'The *musicians'* hotel,' Gower put in pointedly. How glad he was not to have decided to hand over the Emilio to this barbarian.

'Thank you,' Shige said to Gregory Crowne. 'I regret my outburst. I didn't mean what I said.'

Which was just as well, for if anyone had been able to translate the Japanese they would have discovered that the tycoon had been shouting, 'I'll kill you for this, I'll kill you!'

Two

A rchibald Gower put in an urgent phone call to the Hill Hotel to warn Hector McVay, the manager, that Gregory Crowne was bringing an eccentric Japanese millionaire to see Edder.

McVay himself took over at the reception desk, so as to handle this unknown oriental. When Mr Crowne and Mr Shige stepped through the entrance doors, McVay came forward with an attempt at Scottish diplomacy.

'I'm very sorry, sir, but I can't tell you where Mr Edder is,' he said to Shige.

'Can't or won't?'

'Sir, Mr Edder doesn't tell me everything he's doing.'

'But I have to speak to him. It's a matter of life and death.'

McVay had heard tales like that before, particularly from autograph hunters. The fact that Mr Shige was a millionaire made no difference – McVay had known classical-music groupies who were multi-millionaires. Senhora Kelly, for instance – rolling in money from coffee or cattle or some such that her husband's Irish forebears had built up in Brazil, yet absolutely dotty over Mr Edder. He glanced at Mr Crowne. He had a great respect, almost amounting to awe, for Mr Crowne. A real gentleman, and clever with it, even if he did oddly choose to spend a good part of his life wet-nursing temperamental concert artistes. 'Ah, Mr Crowne,' he remarked. 'What should I do? This gentleman seems to have a particular need to get in touch with Mr Edder.'

Crowne stifled a sigh. He had a vital lunch engagement – the chance to talk an important A&R man into recording the special concerts he himself was promoting. But clearly Mr Shige ought to be attended to first, for he wasn't going to be put off by McVay's evasions. Yet Talik Edder had a performance to give tomorrow, and certainly wouldn't want to wage war with a contestant for the Emilio before it.

'It looks as if Edder isn't available at the moment,' he said.

'Not available? I think he'll see *me*. I'm prepared to offer him a fortune.'

'He can't be disturbed. I expect he's practising.'

'Where?'

'I'm afraid that's classified information,' Crowne said, trying to lighten the atmosphere. In fact, Edder was in one of the soundproof rooms in the hotel basement.

'Who are you to make jokes when I tell you I want to see Edder?'

'I told you before, I'm a concert agent. My name's Crowne. It's odd we've never actually met before – I've seen you in Salzburg and New York with your daughter.'

'You know of my daughter? Then you can probably guess why I have come a long way . . .'

Crowne had made it his business to find out more about Shige and his daughter when the faxed offer arrived for the Emilio. He'd taken Archie Gower out to lunch armed with what he knew, determined to prevent the cello going to the wrong buyer. He'd had to get the antique dealer sentimentally drunk so that he'd stick to his original bargain.

'Think, Mr Gower,' he had said over the third whisky liqueur. 'Think how it would look to the musical world if you back out now! That cello *belongs* to Talik Edder. He's been waiting for it all his life.'

'Och, I know that,' Gower agreed, wagging his head. 'I feel for the man, I truly do. But money's money, ye know.'

'Edder offered a more than generous price. You were

11

completely satisfied with it. Now, because a Japanese tycoon faxes a better offer, you're prepared to forget all about artistic integrity.'

'"Top any offer," his fax said. "Top any offer." Ye have to admit, Mr Crowne, he means business.'

'But I'll have to cancel the ceremony we had planned for tomorrow.' Crowne watched the dealer blinking at him over his cigar. He was swaying ever so gently in his chair. Probably it wasn't fair to take advantage of him in this way, but Talik Edder would die of a broken heart if he didn't get the Emilio.

'It'd be a pity to cancel the cer'mony,' said Archibald Gower through his cigar smoke. 'But I have my duty to my clients, y'see.'

'You have a duty to the Emilio too. It would be wrong to sell it to a non-player. The Emilio has been out of circulation far too long. A cello needs to be played on, Mr Gower. Any musician will tell you that – the more an instrument is played, the more it's *loved*, the better the sound.'

'Really?' Gower was taken by the romance of this concept. He was a dealer who specialised in antique musical instruments, but a musician he was not. 'But mebbe Mr Shige would love the Emilio.'

'I dare say he might, but not as much as Edder. With Edder, it's been a lifelong wooing. He tried and tried to get the Kyles to sell to him, and always the reply was the same – they didn't want to break up the collection. Now it's on the market, it's *intended* for Edder. He'll play it, every day. Every day it will be more and more beautiful.'

'More and more beautiful,' murmured Gower in a dreamy tone.

'Shige can't play. He's a music lover, but he's no cellist.'

'P'raps he wants it for someb'dy that will play it.'

Honesty forced Crowne to report the facts. 'He has a daughter . . . Suso, I think she's called. She's been studying cello and he probably wants it for her. But she's a teenager,

Gower. It hardly seems right that the rich little daughter of a millionaire should take precedence over a great artiste like Edder, does it?'

'No, that doesna seem fair,' Gower agreed. But with a snatch at commercial sense he added, 'Though it means more money.'

'Even that isn't so certain,' Crowne replied. 'You might find yourself involved in a court case. I haven't talked with Edder about this – I don't want to upset him unnecessarily – but you wrote accepting his offer. I think it would be regarded as a binding contract in law.'

'A court case . . .' said Gower in dismay.

'Oh, I hope it won't come to that.' No sense in dealing a blow from a cudgel when strokes from a feather would work just as well. 'Think how bad you'd feel if the press got hold of it – that you'd welched on a great player like Edder—'

'No, no,' groaned the dealer.

'And the TV and radio people would never forgive you if you cancelled tomorrow's jamboree.'

'But I could say it was going to a wee girl who's mebbe going to be great one day,' Gower said with unexpected shrewdness. 'You said yourself she'd studied.'

'Yes, at the Tokyo School of Music, but she left about a year ago. She's had a tutor since then, but not with any good effect, so far as I can learn.'

As a concert impresario of good standing, Crowne had friends where it mattered. A journalist had looked up the Shige family in the files, and a teacher at the Royal Academy had supplied a little personal gossip on the phone: the cello tutor hired by Takamasa Shige had thrown up the job because the father was so possessive and interfering. It seemed a case of a child with a small talent being forced to attempt the impossible for the sake of the father's ego.

A well-known syndrome. Mothers carted their daughters round to auditions in the belief they were presenting the next Makarova; men trained their sons to run in hopes of seeing them take the Olympic gold that had eluded the father.

'It's probably the father who's keen about music – the daughter's just doing what she's told. So you see, Gower, it would be an awful waste . . .'

'Aye . . . well . . . that does seem . . .'

'I don't know how you'd feel about releasing this latest turn of events to the press,' Crowne went on, 'but it would reflect great credit on you to have refused a larger amount from Shige so as to put the instrument in the right hands.'

Gower wasn't so much the worse for the whiskies that he could go along with that. 'I don't think the Kyles would like it.'

'No, I suppose not. But they were perfectly happy with what Edder was offering?'

'Oh, peffickly happy. Perhaps I ought to leave't at that, eh, Crowne?'

While his diplomacy was still working, Crowne paid the bill and got him outside. He drove Gower to his shop and stood at his elbow while he dictated a refusal to Shige.

So it was his fault, in a way, that this rich and important man was standing tired and at a loss in an Edinburgh hotel.

'You look as if you had a bad flight.'

'Exceedingly bad.' Shige's English slipped a little so that it came out 'etseedinry'. He glowered. 'I couldn't get a direct flight. I had to take the first available plane, and we had engine trouble and put down in Moscow. *Moscow!* I tried to phone the dealer but I could not get through . . .'

'It would have been no use anyway,' Crowne said. 'The cello was promised to Edder—'

'Promised? Promised? What does that matter? I told that fool he could have any price he wanted—'

'It wasn't just a question of money, Shige. The Emilio is a very special instrument—'

'Do you think I would have flown halfway round the world if it was not?' Shige's sharp black eyes took in Crowne – a tall, angular figure, well dressed in a faintly countrified way, more suited to this city than Mr Shige's expensive wild silk. There was an ease and an authority in his manner that was impressive. A concert agent?

'You're in the music business? And you know Edder. Set up a meeting for me—'

'Could we talk about this later?' Crowne interposed. 'I have an important engagement. Perhaps we could put this off to the afternoon?'

'No we could not! Do you realise who you are speaking to? Takamasa Shige, Chairman of Orient Chemicals Incorporated – and I am not accustomed to let myself be put off. I want to arrange this with you *now*.' It was said in the tone of one who is always obeyed.

'I'm afraid I can't oblige you at the moment,' Crowne said with calm politeness. 'And I think you'd be the better for a few hours' rest—'

'Keep your impertinent opinions to yourself—'

'Sir, sir!' McVay put in in agitation from behind the desk. 'You shouldn't speak like that, sir, really you shouldn't—'

'I'll speak any way I please! And as for you—' Shige turned back to Crowne – 'you'd better get your friend Edder here immediately if you know what is good for you—'

'Mr Shige!' cried the hotel manager in an agony of distress. 'Don't you know who you're speaking to? That's Crown Prince Gregory of Hirtenstein!'

Crowne cast a glance at him that said, 'Shut up, you fool,' but it was too late. The royal cat was out of the bag. And it had its uses, for Shige drew back in some surprise. Despite himself he was impressed. After all, he came from a land that revered an emperor. He made an effort to get hold of his temper.

'Oh . . . then . . . Your Highness . . . ah . . .'

'Mr Crowne,' supplied Crowne.

'Incognito? I understand. I hope you'll forgive me for speaking to you like that but the truth is I have stepped straight off the plane and I'm suffering from jet-lag and frustration and much disappointment.'

'About the Emilio. I'm sorry,' Crowne said.

'The Emilio,' said Shige thoughtfully. 'You seem to know all about it.'

'Edder is a friend of mine, so I shared his ups and downs over buying it. And I set up the publicity for the sale of the cello. It's part of my business.'

'Your business?'

'I told you, I'm a concert agent.'

'You mean that seriously? But being who you are . . . ?'

'There's no money in being an exiled crown prince,' Crowne said with some feeling. 'There are bills to be paid and things like bread and butter to buy.'

'You can't tell me there is much money in arranging dates for opera singers!'

'Not much, but enough.' Crowne shrugged, then glanced at McVay. 'Can you fix Mr Shige up with a room? He looks dead on his feet. I really have to go, Shige. I'm seeing a recording manager about a series of concerts here.'

'Just give me ten seconds,' Shige said, putting a hand on his sleeve. 'I need to sleep but I shall be unable to close my eyes until I know what to do about the Emilio.'

With a polite inclination of the head Mr Crowne asked permission to use that bête noire, his mobile phone. Those in the world of music hate the things, because they tend to ring during tense moments of rehearsal, or when the orchestra leader is giving the tuning note, or worst of all, during a performance. So in general they keep them switched off or leave them at home.

But now was a moment when the need justified the use. He rang his lunch date, apologised and asked for a delay of fifteen minutes, and then immediately returned the phone to mute.

He led Shige into the bar. It was deserted – too early yet for the pre-lunch drink – but as they entered, Tam the bartender appeared as if by magic.

'What will you have, Shige?'

'I'm in Scotland, yes? I shall have whisky.'

'Make it the Glenmorangie, Tam. And I'll have Byrrh.'

They went to the padded bench seat. Shige sank down with a sigh he couldn't suppress. He was clearly bone-weary.

'Did you say Edder is a client of yours, Your—I mean, Mr Crowne?'

'Only temporarily. I'm nursing along a special project here at the Festival – have you seen the programme?' Shige shook his head. 'Well, we're doing a tribute to Villa-Lobos, and one of the things I've had to provide is eight cellists.'

'For the Bachianas Brasileiras?' Shige said, glancing up with interest.

'You know them?' Crowne was pleased. The whole thing was his idea, and he'd grown used to people – even knowledgeable people – saying, 'What?' when he mentioned the Bachianas.

'My daughter . . .' Shige's voice trailed off.

Tam brought the drinks. 'Cheers,' said Crowne, sipping.

'Here's to the Emilio,' said Shige, and drank deeply of his Scotch. He came out of it after a moment, looking better. 'I am asking – what is this I'm drinking?'

'Glenmorangie. It means the Glen of Tranquillity.'

'I believe it. How does it happen I never tasted it before?'

Crowne smiled. 'Stay a while and you can try a few more. Tam will advise you.'

'I must stay a few days at least. I must catch up on some sleep, and then it is imperative to meet Talik Edder. Will you introduce me, Mr Crowne?'

'If it's about the Emilio, I advise you not to bother. No amount of money will get him to part with it.'

'But I've got to have it, Crowne! I've promised my daughter!'

It sounded absurd. Hush, little baby, don't say a word, Daddy's gonna buy you a mockingbird. As simple as that.

After a moment Crowne said, 'There are other cellos besides the Emilio, Shige.'

The other man stared into the light amber of his Glenmorangie. He had iron-grey hair and a small, bushy moustache of the same shade. His skin was almost as grey, from the fatigue of travel and the change of time zone.

He seemed unwilling or unable to respond to Gregory Crowne's remark. At last he said, 'The fact is, Suso is ill. You know how it is when one of your children is ill . . .'

'I'm not married. But, yes, I understand.'

'She saw a piece in the newspapers about the Emilio coming up for sale. She has set her heart on having it. I promised her she should have it. I cannot fail her.'

'That's a difficult situation, Shige. But, tender-hearted though Talik Edder can be on occasion, he won't part with the Emilio for your daughter.'

'But you could talk to him, couldn't you? You said you were his friend.'

The tone of appeal from the stern, square Nipponese face made the words touching.

'I'll talk to him,' the prince said against his better judgement, 'but I don't think it will have the least effect. Talik's just got the cello. He's like a man in the first stages of a new love affair.'

'Yes, but love affairs become less fevered, do they not?'

'That's true, but I wouldn't hold your breath waiting for it in this case. In a year or two, perhaps . . . If Talik got the chance of another cello, equally good . . . He might just part with the Emilio to raise the price of the other. But how many cellos are there of that calibre?'

'I don't know. How many?'

'Thirty? Not many. And they're mostly owned by great performers who aren't going to part with them, or by museums.'

'That's just why Suso wants this one! She knows how rare it is, how unusual to have it come on the market—'

'It's not on the market,' Crowne corrected him, but with

18

gentleness. 'You have to face it, Shige. Talik Edder owns it and he isn't going to part with it.'

'If I offered him half as much again as he paid for it?'

'That would come to an awful lot of money.' He was tempted to ask if Suso's talent warranted such an investment, but he thought better of it. Parents were touchy about their children's talent. 'Come back in a year and make that offer, Shige. But now I think it's too early.'

Shige bent his head. Then he swallowed the last of his whisky. 'Let me buy one for you,' he said, as politeness demanded, though his voice was weighted with the smoothness of whisky and the harshness of jet-lag.

'No, thank you, I really have to go or I'll lose that recording contract. Then I'll have all the artistes breathing fire at me. If you think they're temperamental about music, you should see them over money, Mr Shige.'

On that light note he meant to make his exit. But Shige spoke again. 'You *will* introduce me to Edder? You'll put us in touch?'

'He's practising, and then he's got a rehearsal.'

'Well, I have to get some rest. I'm exhausted. Have them page me here when you have arranged the meeting, please.'

Crowne agreed to do his best and made his escape.

Three

He had intended to walk through the lovely Georgian crescents of the New Town to his lunch date, but now time was short. He hailed a taxi at the corner and had himself driven to the Sheraton, being whirled dizzily round the leafy splendour of Moray Place and Charlotte Square to the toll of one o'clock on Edinburgh's myriad churches.

He thought about his concerts. He thought of them as 'his', because he had suggested them and done all the work for them.

Two years ago he had watched the rich South American tourists buying cashmere sweaters and tartan plaids in the Princes Street shops, and he had said to himself, Why can't we lay on something especially for them? Something that would attract even more of them?

Who, he asked himself, is the most famous composer of South America? Who else but Villa-Lobos.

He went to the Festival organisers proposing a 'tribute to Villa-Lobos', to run through the three weeks of the Festival. He had been able to promise at least one famous cellist – Edder – to be among the eight that would be needed if the most popular of Villa-Lobos's work were to be played: the Bachianas Brasileiras Nos. 1 and 5.

'Think of all the Brazilian millionaires who'll come,' he said.

The planners didn't give in all at once. They foresaw all kinds of difficulties. Eight cellists! How were you to get eight cellists?

'I'll see to it,' Crowne said.

In fact, it wasn't as difficult as one might think. Edder agreed to take part because he could take other engagements in Edinburgh and later in London. Then the Kamikura Quartet would be at the Festival, and their cellist Michiko Toshio was eager to perform the Brasileiras. There were four symphony orchestras in the Festival programme, to say nothing of the opera orchestra, the ballet orchestra and the various chamber orchestras. From among their ranks he was able to recruit the six other cellists.

That done, he had to find a soprano. The most famous of the Bachianas Brasileiras has a soaring, wordless song, and the voice that sings it must rise like a golden lark above the rich brown notes of the cellos.

There had been long phone conversations with artistes' agents and letters to some with whom he had good personal relationships. In the end he had engaged Anne Gleghorn. But she was hard to please.

'I'm not coming all the way to Edinburgh for two per-formances of the Bachiana,' she said over the phone from Houston, making it crackle with her long-distance indigna-tion. 'The money isn't worth it.'

'I know, I know. I'm doing all I can. Don't forget, Anne, *you* are the soloist. You're out there in front holding the centre of the platform—'

'I always hold the centre of the platform,' she said. 'You'll have to come up with a bonus, Gregory.'

The Festival had its shape by now. Anne was going to have to be fitted in around the fringes. Not *the* Fringe, of course – the Foolish Fringe – Anne Gleghorn wasn't a fooling kind of person. She was firmly in the mainstream of modern music.

But there was always a kind of tidal flow around the three weeks of big events: recitals given in churches and big private houses and even bank entrance halls.

'What have you been learning recently?' he enquired, expecting her to say he ought to know.

21

She talked for a few minutes about operatic roles. He wished she would be more realistic. No one was going to put on Vaughan Williams' 'Riders to the Sea' or Samuel Barber's 'Vanessa' for Gleghorn. When she began to mention the seventeenth-century oratorios of Schütz, he brightened. There was a growing fashion for Schütz, and it was always easier to get a recital of church music organised – a local choir and local soloists with one visiting voice, that was the way to handle it.

Anne kept saying she wasn't sold on it, but she wanted to sing Schütz. She'd discovered she had the voice for him. She allowed herself to be persuaded when Crowne held out the irresistible bait: 'I'll get you good publicity.'

Publicity is always of prime importance to musicians. Although the average concert-goer would never believe it, the concert circuit is a rat race, where the performers are the rats. They run round and round, trying to make good music while at the same time earning a reasonable income and improving a reputation that has to be made early or not at all. If concert organisers didn't hear about them in their early years, they were doomed to end up as teachers. A fate worse than.

The crown prince had a plan to get publicity for Anne Gleghorn: he could offer her a chance to shine in Schütz. So she agreed to come and sing the Bachiana No. 5.

His taxi stopped for a traffic light. He saw a newspaper placard: ASSASSINATION ATTEMPT. His heart gave a little lurch. 'Stop at the next newspaper man,' he said. 'I want a paper.'

The driver nodded, then drew up a few seconds later by a vendor at the West End. Crowne leaned out, bought a paper and sat back to read the item.

Thank God, it was some faction leader in the Lebanon. Not, he was glad to learn, his father, ex-King Anton of Hirtenstein. That hard-working and kindly man was still alive and well and living in Geneva. Despite *glasnost* spreading everywhere like chickenpox, he hadn't been invited home to restore the monarchy. (Not that it would necessarily have hit the headlines if the former King of Hirtenstein had been made away with. In general the newspapers ignored King Anton, and that was the way the family liked it.)

To make sure of being ignored, His Royal Higness the Crown Prince Gregorius of Hirtenstein used an alias. In English-speaking territories he was Mr Crowne, in France he was M. Couronne, in West Germany he was known as Herr Krone, in Italy he rejoiced in Signor Corona. Elsewhere he was not known at all nor, alas, in his ancestral land, that little region of pastures and lakes between Switzerland and the Germanic states.

Hirtenstein had been taken over somewhat belatedly in 1970 by the people's revolution. His father and mother had been invited to leave and had very sensibly done so, since they were young and scared. Queen Luisa had also been pregnant with the future crown prince, who immediately on being born became the ex-crown prince. Queen Luisa had not lived to see her son reach his teens, but the rest of the family flourished in the kindly climate of Geneva. Hirtenstein gave up Communism when the Berlin wall came down, but didn't invite its royals to return.

Crowne didn't mind being in exile. He had been born and brought up in Switzerland, so that he spoke the three main European languages with equal fluency. English was spoken at home, by his father and by the real head of the family, his grandmother the ex-Queen Mother Nicoletta.

The prince had done well at school, his best subjects being mathematics and music. 'Well done, my boy,' said his father. 'The Greeks always thought those two should be linked together, and you've proved them right.'

'Did the Greeks think of a way for a prince to make money at either mathematics or music?' enquired Grandmama with irritation.

He didn't play well enough to make a career as a professional pianist. Besides, Grandmama wouldn't have liked it if he'd performed on a stage. It was necessary, however, to earn money, for, besides being young and scared when they left Hirtenstein, the King and Queen had been broke. Queen Luisa didn't even get to bring her jewels.

Ex-Queen Nicoletta was an interior decorator; Papa taught equitation and dressage – in other words he was a high-class riding master. Their son too must make his way in the world. So, since he had organising ability and a calm temperament, he took up the role of impresario for classical artistes.

It didn't bring him a fortune, but he did well enough. Besides, car companies were always glad to lend or hire the latest posh car at very low fees, just so as to have it said that Mr Crowne (you know who *he* really is) was driving it. And when he wasn't at home in Geneva he lived rent-free in a time-share apartment in one of Surrey's former stately homes, simply because it pleased the owners to have his name associated with them.

Rank has its privileges. It also has its drawbacks, among which are that some people simply won't like you because you come from a royal background. Some even dislike you so much that they take pot-shots at you. Not often, however. And not in nice civilised countries like Switzerland.

After the business lunch at the Sheraton he dropped in on Edder in the school hall where he was rehearsing – one of the problems in Edinburgh during the Festival was to find a place to rehearse, since all available space seemed to be needed for performance or exhibition.

The conductor of the Orchestre Savoie called a five-minute intermission. The crown prince took Edder a cup of coffee from a hotplate on a side table. 'God, that I should be reduced to drinking coffee two hours old,' the Finn grieved as he swallowed the drink in one gulp. He was drenched with sweat. He wiped his forehead and face with a rather grubby towel. 'Did you hear? Was she good, my Emilio?'

'All the better for having you as the player.'

'Flatterer. So . . . you lunch with Mittel? He records the Bachianas?'

'It's in the bag.'

'You are good, Gregory. Even though I am from a republic and don't approve of royalty, I have to admit you are a good impresario.'

'Flatterer. Well, now, I have a thing to ask you.'

'Please do not ask that I allow the Brazilian widow to my rehearsals. Already she asks and I have said no.'

'No, it's nothing to do with Angeliza Kelly. It's about the Emilio.'

'What about the Emilio?' Edder said in alarm, looking back to the spot where he had left the precious Strad leaning against his chair. 'She is mine! The cheque vill not jump!'

'Jump? Oh, you mean bounce. No, it's nothing to do with that.' He related the story of Takamasa Shige and the sick daughter who longed for a Stradivarius cello.

'Um,' said the cellist, tugging his Zapata moustache, 'very sad and all that. Poor little rich girl, she has the measles and she wants the Emilio as a get-well present. I'm sorry, Gregory, but the Emilio is not for sale. Clear?'

'That's what I told him; but listen, Talik, don't be sharp with the man. He looks tired and depressed, and has come a long way to buy that instrument.'

'And has wasted the air fare, *mi amico*. I'm sorry, but I am not going to waste sympathy on Shige. You tell me he is a rich man?'

'Very. Biggest maker of paints and chemical solvents in Japan, Mittel told me over lunch. He keeps up with that kind of thing in the *Financial Times*.'

'Good. Then he buys the sick kid a Versace dress or a Maserati.'

'Well, you know, Talik, though I've never met the girl I've seen her around at concerts, and she doesn't seem to me to be the Versace type. Don't you know her? A nice little thing – like a little doll—'

25

'All young Japanese girls are like little dolls,' Talik growled from his great height. 'I'm not going to sell the Emilio to her just because she's cute.'

'No, no, of course not, all I was trying to say was, I don't think she wants the Emilio for a whim. She really understands what it is and what it's worth.'

'Then she should know better than to think she has any right to it just because her father's got money. No, Gregory, I vill talk to Shige since you promised him I would, but he gets nothing out from me.'

Yet the prince sensed a relenting in him – not enough to cause him to sell the Emilio, but at least to respond with kindness to Shige's offer.

All might have gone well if Anne Gleghorn hadn't happened on the scene that evening.

If Crowne had known that she and Talik Edder had had something going between them in Venice earlier that year, nothing would have persuaded him to engage her for the voice part of the No. 5. There were other sopranos, plenty of them. But Anne knew the Bachiana Brasileira particularly well, had had critical acclaim for a performance in Sydney, and added one more aspect of internationalism to the group Crowne was forming for the performance.

She had arrived during the afternoon from Athens, where she'd been singing Strauss. After taking up the hotel booking made for her by the crown prince, and dropping her luggage in her room, she felt in need of a brisk walk. A great one for exercise, Anne Gleghorn: it helped counteract the toxins she ingested by eating airline meals. Airline meals, hotel catering, air-conditioning that spreads Legionnaire's disease – to Anne Gleghorn the world was full of traps to her health, her well-being, her voice.

The church in which she was to sing 'Eight Psalms of Schütz' was in a square not far from the Haymarket. Three hours later she came back in a fury.

'So!' she cried as she stormed into the lounge of the Hill

26

Hotel. 'You'll get me good publicity, huh? Two rotten posters about Schütz, and they haven't even got my picture on! And all the newspaper headlines are about Edder and his damned knee-fiddle!'

Edder, Crowne and Shige had just sat down together over after-dinner coffee. The comfortable armchairs seemed to enfold them. A less tense look had come into the features of the Japanese tycoon, and Edder was in one of his rather sentimental, friend-to-all-the-world moods.

Gregory Crowne stood up. 'Anne, I didn't know you'd come back – I left word with—'

'What's more, if you think I'm singing in that barn, you're crazy! When you said "cathedral", I thought you meant something like Notre Dame, but *that* place—'

'I know it's draughty, but they put heaters—'

'Heaters? Two kerosene stoves, I bet! My throat will seize up! *And* all the publicity for the Villa-Lobos is about Talik.' She shook a folded newspaper under the crown prince's nose.

Talik too had risen now. At this repetition of his name he came forward to take her hand.

'Anne, poor girl, don't upset yourself so much. All will go well.'

She snatched her hand away. 'Well for you, you mean! You've got it made! Top billing for the Villa-Lobos, extra publicity for the cello, and troops of women queuing for one of your swoony smiles.'

A faint gasp of distress came from the depths of another armchair in the lounge. Deep within in its maroon tapestry depths, Senhora Angeliza Kelly, Edder's devoted fan, crouched with her fist to her lips. She had recognised the angry voice at once – Anne Gleghorn, who had monopolised the beloved's time all through that stay in Venice . . .

'While *he's* hogging the limelight, where's the publicity you promised to lay on for me?' Anne demanded in her ringing concert-soprano voice.

In fact, her impresario *had* been guilty of a blunder. Busy as he was about the matter of earning a living, and for some part of the year tucked away in the quiet respectability of Geneva, he didn't spend too much time keeping his ear to the ground – a position, as his father was wont to remark, which invited a kick in the pants. So he was unaware that Anne and Talik had had a torrid thing going for about six weeks in the spring, which had ended abruptly in Venice.

'My dear friend,' Talik had said with a shrug when the subject finally came up, 'so boring, the keep-fit first thing every morning. And in front of an open window – in Venice, I ask you! With the mist creeping in off the canals and the grunts and puffs as she lies on the back kicking the legs. It is not even as if one gets glimpses of charming corners of femininity, for she wears the grey tracksuit with *Fit for Anything* across the chest. My women, I like them with nothing across the chest, or at the most a little silk and lace.' Talik, like the sailor, had a girl in every port. When he divested himself of one girl he easily collected another.

But Anne Gleghorn didn't want to be shed like last year's snakeskin. She'd believed that, if she got to Edinburgh with Talik, true love would burn again. She'd certainly never intended to begin a first conversation with him by crying out in public that he was hogging the publicity.

The knowledge that she'd started badly only made her angrier. 'It's a breach of contract,' she proclaimed. 'You promised me, Gregory, that I'd be the centre of the Villa-Lobos event. I'll sue you—'

'No you won't, darling,' Talik said. 'Please calm down. Everyone is staring at us.'

'Oh, will you listen to that? Are you pretending you don't like to have people staring at you?'

She took time off for a quick glance around and, sure enough, every other head in the elegant Georgian lounge was turned towards them. Particularly the head of a plumpish, dark-haired woman who was sitting up in her cushioned armchair staring at Anne as if she were the Gorgon in person.

Anne decided to make the most of it. If she couldn't outdo Talik with his Strad, at least she could make some kind of mark with her indignation. Her voice, as she knew very well, carried effortlessly.

'I saw your picture in the paper – drooling over that instrument like a baby over a lollipop. You looked an absolute fool.'

'Well, darling,' Talik said, stung, 'you don't look so marvellous yourself. When you are angry you're always very ugly.'

'Ugly? My God, you're a fine one to talk. While you're playing you make faces that would scare Rambo.'

That was dangerous talk. Every performer is afraid that when he plays some facial tic or mannerism will mar his endeavours. Talik responded in kind. 'And when you sing, you heave up your bosoms as if an earthquake was beginning—'

'Talik, Talik! That's enough! Don't be childish! And as for you, Anne, if you want publicity I'll see to it. As far as the church is concerned, I think you'll find it's better when there's a congregation in it—'

'Ha!' Talik couldn't resist it. 'Will a congregation of six make it warmer? Six is all you'll get for Gleghorn singing Schütz.'

'Shut up, Talik. Would you like some coffee, Anne?'

'I don't want coffee! I haven't eaten yet—'

'Oh, that's what is wrong. When she is hungry, always she is bad-tempered. Bad-tempered, and more than usually hypochondriac.'

'I am not bad-tempered,' shouted Anne Gleghorn. 'I have the disposition of an angel!'

Across the room, Angeliza Kelly hugged herself in glee. The love affair was clearly over.

And deserved to be. Angeliza, who made it her business

to know everything that concerned Talik, knew something about Anne that Anne herself thought was a secret. Anne Gleghorn had prevented Talik from receiving an honour for which he longed.

His country had a Conservatoire of Music whose reputation was deservedly high. Talik had been under consideration for the post of Director. But Anne, in the first heat of resentment when he dropped her, had put a decided black mark among his programme notes.

The Finnish Ambassador to Rome, an opera buff, had something of a penchant for American sopranos. He had come to Venice to hear Anne sing. At a little gathering he sought her out to congratulate her. And Anne, driven by a mean desire for revenge, had murmured to the Ambassador that Maestro Edder wasn't to be trusted around young women students of music.

'My dear man, he's famous for it! He only has to see a tempting curve – on a girl, I mean, not on a cello—'

'Miss Gleghorn! Are you sure?'

'Why, even I myself . . . and I'm not a teenager any longer . . .'

The Ambassador spent some time uttering the necessary compliments about Anne's youth and beauty. But he came back to the point. 'You really mean he . . . how shall I put it . . . attempted to . . .'

'I had a terrible time shaking him off. Ask anyone that's been around in the last month or so – they'll tell you.'

The Ambassador had asked around and was told that Edder and Gleghorn had been in some kind of romantic rumpus. He sent word back to the right circles in Helsinki, and Talik Edder was not offered the post of Director, causing him an unexpected hurt.

Anne had been pleased at the time. Now she wasn't so sure about her behaviour. But her comfort was, that no one else knew.

There she was wrong. For Angeliza Kelly had been at the

same party. Angeliza, who always made it a point to keep an eye on her arch-rival, had been hiding behind a potted palm to overhear what she said to His Excellency. Angeliza knew what Anne had done to Talik – and hated her all the more for it. Now, from the depths of her armchair, she watched Anne, happy to see her making a public fool of herself.

'Come along, Anne,' said the crown prince, putting a hand at her elbow to shepherd her to the dining-room. 'You must have some dinner. I'll sit with you, if that's all right. I've eaten already but we've a lot to discuss. I've got the Palladio Players as accompaniment for the Psalms, and the organist of St Mary's . . .' Talking diligently, he steered her towards the calming influence of food and drink.

Having had his temper ruffled by this encounter, it was almost inevitable that Edder should be tetchy with Shige over the Emilio. Shige offered money, then more money. Edder said no, and then a much louder no.

'It's not a question of money! Nor is it a matter of getting publicity, as Anne Gleghorn seemed to imply. It's a matter of making music in the most beautiful way, and with that cello I can do it . . .'

'But you're a master, an acknowledged master. And you have the Guarneri—'

'I'm going to sell that. I don't think it's fair to own two great instruments.' Edder paused. 'I'll sell you the Guarneri,' he said with too much abruptness. It sounded as if he was saying it just to get rid of the troublesome, mercenary bargainer.

'But Suso has set her heart on the Stradivarius—'

'Too bad for her. I had set my heart on it too, and you see – I got it. And I intend to keep it.' He got up and stalked out, to be followed immediately by that faithful if plump shadow, Senhora Kelly.

When they came out of the dining-room Anne Gleghorn and the crown prince found Shige still in his armchair. Anne had eaten little. She knew she needed food, but her anger had

31

given her an upset stomach. Shige, in the short time he'd been alone, had managed to swallow several whiskies of various fine brands, though he wasn't noticeably drunk.

The Kamikura Quartet now came back from their recital. They were a young foursome of diverse nationality, owing their name only to the fact that they had first met in Kamikura. Their cellist, however, was Japanese. They trooped into the lounge to tell their impresario how they felt things had gone. 'It's a nice little hall,' their leader, Henry Holt, began. 'The acoustics are great once the audience are settled. The great thing is the feeling of intimacy – that was grand.'

They were aglow with pleasure. Their audience had listened intently and responded with delight to the urgent, romantic tone they brought to the Schubert A minor.

'No problems?' Crowne prompted. There was always something to report, some minor mishap.

'Only a man with an unquenchable cough who had to go out.'

'And Michiko broke a string,' teased Shemnitzi, the viola player.

The little Japanese girl came forward into the protective arm of the quartet's leader. 'It was all right, it was at the last moment—'

She broke off. She was staring past the others to Mr Shige.

Shige was sprawled in his armchair. At sight of Michiko Toshio he sat up like a puppet whose strings are urgently pulled.

'You!' he gasped.

Gregory Crowne looked from him to Michiko. The young musician had gone deathly pale.

She turned and made as if to run out. Shige leapt up to grab her shoulder. A torrent of angry Japanese poured from the lips of the millionaire, the strange throaty sound falling upon them like a mesh to hold them transfixed.

Michiko's head was averted. She was shaking. No one seemed able to move.

It was left to a stranger to come to her aid. A young man from the next group of chairs left his friends to come and pull Shige away from the trembling girl.

'That's no way to treat the wee thing,' he rebuked him. 'What's got into you, man?'

Michiko took one moment to cast him a glance of gratitude, then she fled. For a second Shige struggled in the grip of the tall Scotsman as if to follow her, but he subsided, the drink perhaps weakening him.

'Let me go,' he said with dignity. 'You've no need to hold me now she is gone.'

'But what were you doing?' Henry Holt demanded. As leader of the quartet, he felt a responsibility for all its members. 'What did you say to her?'

'It was a reproach,' Shige replied. 'She has done me great harm.'

'Michiko?' Shemnitzi said in disbelief. 'Michiko never harmed anyone in her life!'

'You just don't know,' Shige said. His voice with its strange undertones of Japanese inflection was hoarse and heavy. 'That girl, gentlemen, is a dangerous revolutionary. She's got a death on her conscience.'

Four

T he words were not uttered loudly, but with force enough to make the crystals on the table lampshade vibrate. The soundwave scarcely reached to the Georgian windows and their sedate grey and crimson Regency stripes, but it left its spell.

Which was broken by the laughter of the tall Scotsman. 'A revolutionary, is she?' he said. 'That's good. I'm a revolutionary mysel'.'

'A terrorist!' exclaimed Isaac Shemnitzi, who had first-hand experience of them. 'Send for the police!'

'No, no,' soothed the crown prince. 'He's a comedian, not a Communist. He doesn't really mean—'

'But I do! My party stands for a revolution in the government of this country!'

'Oh, really, Duntyre . . .' This was the manager, Hector McVay, summoned by the receptionist, who from her place at the desk had heard what she described as 'a stramash' in the lounge. 'Don't begin on your idiotic politics, for goodness' sake. Politics are bad enough, but Scottish Progressive Party politics are the worst yet.'

'Spoken like a true dunderhead,' Duntyre rejoined. 'If there's one thing stupider than an English Tory, it's a Scottish one. I suppose you'll be asking the wee lass to move out.'

'What wee lass?'

'The wee Japanese lass. Hirohito here just accused her of being a revolutionary.'

'Miss Toshio?' McVay said in disbelief.

34

'Michiko Toshio,' Shige said, pounding one fist into the other palm. 'What is she doing in a respectable place like this?'

McVay was pleased to have his hotel described as respectable but didn't like the aspersion on Michiko. 'This hotel is renowned as a haven for artistes of all kinds,' he announced. 'Especially during the Festival – you'll find many of the big names here. And seldom any trouble, sir, if I may say so.' He bent a frown on Shige, but since his round face always appeared benevolent, even when he was annoyed, the effect was minimal.

'I think you must have got it wrong,' Crowne said. 'Michiko is too busy with her music to be a Maoist.'

'Oh, you think because she plays in this group—' Shige swept out a gesture that included the other members of the quartet – 'you think she must be a good little girl!'

'*Und* so she is,' said Joseph Klein, glowering at the tycoon. 'Who are you, to say unkind things about our little Michiko?'

'She never thinks about anything except music,' Shemnitzi put in.

'*Now* she doesn't. But I know her from before she began her career—'

'Mr Shige,' Anne Gleghorn put in, 'honestly, nobody on the international music treadmill has got much time for politics, what with practice every day, and rehearsals, and getting your hair done and your dresses made, and travelling, and—'

'I think we should all sit down,' McVay suggested. His hotel lounge was no place for a loud altercation. 'Let me order you a drink. Something special. Miss Gleghorn, what do you say?'

'Oh . . . thanks . . . I'll have a petit Armagnac, thank you.'

'Mr Shige?'

'Ah . . . well . . .' He allowed himself to be persuaded. He sat down. 'I'll try Glenfiddich this time.'

McVay summoned a waiter with a jerk of his head. He seized the opportunity to stoop by the crown prince as he took his own place. 'I hope you're not having a disagreeable evening, sir,' he muttered.

'Not a bit,' lied the prince politely. He rued the day he'd ever thought the Emilio would provide good publicity.

'Well, *I've* found it disagreeable,' said Anne, whose sharp ears often picked up remarks not intended for her. 'First I find Talik here holding court as if he owned the place, and now this gentleman gives us a big fright about terrorists.' She gazed at Shige, without any appearance of fright. Quite the contrary – after a moment she seemed to approve of his compact frame, his beautifully barbered hair, his fine suit.

He looked like money. And, though not mercenary, Anne Gleghorn liked men with money.

'Oh, this about Michiko is all rubbidge,' said Klein, leaning forward to wag a finger at the Japanese. 'You should be ashamed, to say such slender.'

'Slander,' murmured McVay.

'It's not slander! That girl was part of a group of revolutionaries who regularly picketed my office in Tokyo. One day they attacked my car as I was leaving. They turned it over—'

'Right over?' Henry Holt said in surprise. He was intrigued by odd facts about physical power, was always doing equations in his head about how much steam equalled how many men or horses or sleigh-dogs. His hobby was steam locomotives.

'Right over. I and my chauffeur could have been killed. We scrambled out through the shattered windscreen—'

'Oh my goodness, were you hurt?'

'Only cuts and bruises, Miss Gleghorn. But we could have been killed.'

'My, that's true!'

'Michiko did that? I don't believe it,' Crowne said.

'I don't say she actually did it, but she was there. And

before that she had talked my daughter into wrong-doing, all sorts of silly escapades to get publicity for "the cause".'

'Well, but – that sounds like student demonstrations—'

'I am proud to say,' Shige went on, disregarding Holt's comment, 'that the incident of the car brought Suso to her senses. She understood that it could have been extremely serious. So she gave up her friendship with that warped and wicked girl—'

'Warped and wicked, eh?' repeated David Duntyre. The disbelief in his tone was open. And to tell the truth, the idea of the ethereal little Michiko Toshio as either warped or wicked was hard to sustain.

'But in a way it was too late for Suso,' Shige went on. 'The harm was done.'

'Ah, you mean she'd got behind in her studies? That's why you wanted the Emilio – to encourage her to work up to what she was before?'

'Talik will never part with that Strad, Mr Shige,' Anne Gleghorn said, with a moue of annoyance. 'He's just obsessed with it.' She frowned into her Armagnac.

'You should get him to sell you the Guarneri,' Shemnitzi suggested. 'It's a lovely instrument. It's Gruber's Guarneri, you know – Gruber who taught Suggia—'

'He's offered me the Guarneri. I'm . . . I'm thinking about it. I have placed a call to Tokyo to see what Suso feels. But she had her heart set on the Emilio, and you know, the Guarneri might be snapped up by someone like Miss Toshio.'

'Michiko can't afford a Guarneri! And see here, if she were a revolutionary, would she be bothering about tradition and ancient values and all that – would she *want* a Guarneri?'

'It seems to me, Mr Shige,' David Duntyre put in, 'that you've built up a tremendous case against this wee Michiko on the basis of a very frail piece of evidence. She was present when you were attacked, and your daughter had run around with her and got into mischief. That hardly makes her a dangerous revolutionary, and as for saying she has a life on her conscience – you've just said you and your driver got out unscathed.'

Shige looked across at him. His dark eyes were like pools of doom. 'She is responsible for bad things,' he said. 'She is not safe to have in this place, Mr McVay. You should tell her to leave.'

McVay was intensely embarrassed. He certainly didn't want to have a Maoist demonstrator in his hotel. But on the other hand, Michiko Toshio had done nothing wrong since she arrived. She was one of the creatures he revered – a performing musician. She was a protégée of Crown Prince Gregory.

It was true that Mr Shige was very rich. But he was nothing more or less than a tourist, and though McVay made a lot of money out of tourists he didn't feel the same for them as for his 'artistes'.

'Come, Mr Shige, come,' he urged. 'Michiko has done nothing wrong here in Edinburgh—'

'Do you have to wait until she holds up a bank or causes a riot?'

'What, a' by her wee self?' sneered Duntyre.

'You have students here? At the university?'

'They're not back yet, Mr Shige—'

'But the place is full of them,' Shemnitzi pointed out, 'all here from all over the world, doing their thing for the Festival.'

'Whose side are you on?' said Klein. 'Michiko is doing nothink. She has no time to plot vith students. The whole idea is rubbidge.'

'How can you be so sure?' Anne murmured, turning to Shige with a troubled little smile. 'I don't say I go along with what you say, Mr Shige, but I think it would be wrong to shrug it off.' Anne had her own reasons for making friends with the millionaire. It appeared he was a thorn in the flesh of Talik Edder – and anything that could mortify that particular flesh was worth cultivating.

38

But the heat had gone out of the conversation. Shige's earlier anger had no power to continue against the recurring fatigue of jet-lag. Henry Holt went to sit on the other side of him from Anne, and ask him about how it felt when his car had been overturned. Had the engine been running? The brakes on or off?

Relieved to see the storm abating, Crowne made his way towards the lift. McVay went with him to the gate. 'I wonder if we should inform the police, sir?' he said.

'Inform them of what?' said Crowne. 'That an angry father accused Michiko of leading his daughter astray when she was a student?'

'I'm thinking of the political undertones, Your High – I mean, Mr Crowne. You know the Special Branch sends us a wee word to keep an eye open when such as yourself is a guest here. It's better to be safe than sorry.'

This was the slogan intoned by officials in yearly briefings about the dangers of attack. No one had any real reason to put a bomb in the prince's car, but then Sirhan Sirhan had had no real reason to shoot Robert Kennedy.

As he went up to his room Crowne thought it over. Should he inform the Edinburgh police about Michiko's alleged terrorist associations? He shrank from it. It was all in the past, a youthful misdirection of energy. He knew how official fussing could put a musician off his stroke, could bring on laryngitis for a singer. And running his events at the Festival was difficult enough without importing problems.

But there wasn't only himself to think of. The British were hospitable, as were the French and the West Germans and, above all, the Swiss. But wherever Prince Gregory went, there was always the possibility the host nation might find itself embarrassed by an attempt on his life. Some mistaken idealist might take it upon himself to rid the world of an unwanted remnant of the *ancien régime*.

But Michiko . . . She was too shy and withdrawn, too wrapped up in her music, too intensely devoted to her career.

Well, yes, intense . . . She *was* intense. She belonged to a nation that had only recently discovered Western classical music and had thrown themselves into it heart and soul, with a passion for excellence that sometimes put the rest of the world to shame.

He could just about bring himself to believe that her ardour for perfection might lead her to follow political leaders claiming to be making the world faultless by ridding it of the imperfect. But he couldn't imagine those thin, strong hands – hands that could bring a singing tone from wood and cat-gut – being used to handle explosives. That rapt face cradled against the fingerboard of the cello, that mind lost in a wonderland of melody and harmony – they had nothing to do with violence.

All the same, he could hear in his mind Grandmama Nicoletta: 'You and your girlfriends . . . You are too soft with women, Gregory, I've told you that before. You should look at them with a realistic eye, as your grandfather did.'

But Grandmama only said things like that because she disapproved of the girl of the moment in the prince's life. Ex-Queen Nicoletta took it as an article of faith that her grandson should marry a suitable princess and beget children, so that on the happy day when the Hirtenstein royal family was restored to its throne there would be a king and a queen and lots of little royals to amuse the citizenry.

This ignored the fact that suitable princesses were quite rare, and those that existed were the wrong age, or didn't want to marry into the Hirtensteins, who had no private fortune and almost no chance of ever ruling in their homeland again, despite *glasnost*.

Elizabeth Blair, the lady of the prince's heart, was a commoner. An extremely common commoner, in the view of ex-Queen Nicoletta. She could have forgiven Liz for being in the fashion business if she'd been a designer of *haute couture*: But Liz was a buyer for a downmarket wholesale firm that sold clothes on to shops in provincial shopping centres. And nothing is more common than fashion worn by five million teenagers.

Thoughts of Liz always distracted him from the matter in hand. He had spent the night with her before taking the plane for Edinburgh, and now in his mind's eye he saw her as he had left her in the morning. Long slender body rosy from the shower, string-blond hair plastered to her elegant skull, a towel held in front of her to prevent the dampness affecting his clothes . . . She had clung to him wickedly, twining one leg around both of his.

'Stay,' she whispered. 'Let those dozy musicians look out for themselves for one more day.'

He recalled with some pride that he had resisted the temptation. With some pride, but with much more regret.

Crowne walked down the corridor to tap at a door further on from his own room. At first there was no reply, but then a muffled voice said, 'Who's there?'

'It's me, Gregory.'

'Go away.'

'Open the door, Michiko.'

'No, go away.'

'Don't be silly, I must talk to you.'

'What about?'

'Open the door and you'll find out.'

A thin-faced chambermaid appeared further along the corridor. She gave a disapproving look as Crowne continued to plead in low tones through the door. She looked even more disapproving when the door opened and he slipped through.

Michiko's little triangular face was pale. She'd taken off her glasses so she looked more than usually short-sighted. To the prince she looked shy and vulnerable.

'Poor little girl,' said the prince gently, proving that his grandmother's view of him was correct. He took Michiko in his arms and patted her.

To his surprise she sprang away from him. 'Don't patronise me!'

Startled, he dropped his arm. 'I'm sorry,' he said, frowning. 'I thought you were upset.'

'Upset! I'm furious! That man – that hateful man!'

'Well . . . He's just been telling us he's not your favourite heart-throb.'

The short-sighted eyes flashed. 'He's been telling you his usual lies! He's a bad man, a bad father!'

'Michiko, calm down. Come on, sit down. Tell me about it.'

'He's . . . He looks so ordinary and decent here in Edinburgh talking about the Emilio. But, Gregory—! Truly, he's not like that. He's ruthless, he's selfish, he thinks only about money.'

'Now wait a bit, my dear. He's thinking about his daughter. That's why he's here – to buy—'

'He's changed, then! He never cared ten cents for Suso before! Except, of course, to call her an undutiful daughter and to warn her he'd cut her out of his will—'

'That's not the way he sounds to me, Michiko. I have to speak as I find. He's bothered about her – she's ill, he says.'

'I don't know . . . That must be recent. When I knew her she was a real firebrand, and a very promising cellist. But of course she took a lot of time off for demonstrations and stuff . . .'

'You persuaded her?'

She looked down, stubborn and grim. 'I guess I did. Yet, you know, she didn't need much persuasion. The things her father did were terrible. He let his factories pour out chemical smoke, and all kinds of things went into the local rivers—' She broke off, sighing. 'My country has an awful record where ecology is concerned, Gregory, and it's thanks to men like Takamasa Shige. Suso took it upon herself to be her father's conscience. And he hated her for it.'

'And hates you too, it seems.'

'Well . . . He thinks he has grounds.'

'And does he? Michiko, are you "political"?'

'If that means do I care about what the world is going to be like in fifty years' time, then yes, I am.' Her usually shy features were lit up with a fierce indignation, her black eyes glowed.

'And this life you have on your conscience?'

'What? What life?'

'After you ran out of the room, he said you had cost a life, or something like that.'

She stared short-sightedly at him. 'What can he mean? I never hurt anyone.'

'He says you turned his car over—'

'I went with the group . . . I was scared at first but then he crawled out . . . Oh, the great Shige-san, all crumpled and dishevelled! I thought he looked funny.'

'Michiko!'

She got up to wander towards her cello, which stood in its half-opened case, leaning against the wardrobe. She took it out, holding it close as if for comfort. She sat down on the chair by the window, holding the instrument as if to play it. But of course she wouldn't do so – if one wished to practise in the Hill Hotel one went down to the quiet rooms in the basement.

The pause, and the feel of her familiar friend in her hands, seemed to help her collect her thoughts. 'I expect that's why he's telling lies about me,' she said with faint apology. 'We all laughed when he came out of the car on his hands and knees. He hates anything like that – being made to seem absurd—'

'Losing face.'

'What?'

'It's a phrase the English translated from the Chinese, I think. It means being made to look small.'

'Well, that's what the scene downstairs was all about – he's never going to forgive me for being there when he lost face, and of course if he's really blaming me for Suso's political views . . .' She hesitated, then went on, 'Would you like me to check out of the hotel?'

'Why on earth should you?'

'Well, Shige-san is clearly furious with me—'

'Then if it bothers him it's up to him to move out, isn't it? McVay will make it clear to him – either he observes the rules of common courtesy or he's got to go.'

'But I'll feel scratchy every time I'm around him.'

'Then you'll have to get that gallant young Scot to act as bodyguard.'

She blushed. 'He's nice, isn't he? Do you know him?'

'We've never met, but I saw him in the Festival Club the other night. He's got a play on somewhere on the Fringe.'

'He said he was a revolutionary too.'

'I don't think he should be taken too seriously.'

'Is he staying in the hotel?'

'Looks like it.' He smiled at her then moved to the door. 'Good-night, Michiko. Don't let yourself be kept awake by Mr Shige and his outburst.'

'No-o. Good-night, Gregory.'

It was only as he was going into his own room that he recalled her phraseology: 'A revolutionary too'. He didn't like that 'too'.

He sat down at the telephone. Though it was late, he had calls to make. The tape in his office in Geneva would give him an update on the bookings and offers that had come in since yesterday, and then he ought to speak to Grossmutti. After that he would spend ten precious minutes on the phone with Liz.

There was nothing of great moment at the office. Bennitz had declined the engagement in Munich; Tolmaya was annoyed because he'd refused to handle a concert in a drug-trading country for him; there was an offer of a recital next Easter for Powers; Kingston, Jamaica, was asking if he would like to take part in organising a festival of Caribbean music. Nothing that couldn't be handled by his assistant for the moment.

His grandmother came on the line, yawning.

'I'm sorry, were you asleep?' he asked. She was after all well into her seventies and needed her rest.

'I was asleep in front of the television. It's good that you woke me up otherwise I'd have gone on snoozing and got a crick in my neck. Well, how did everything go with the Emilio?'

He related the day's events. She snorted. 'Buy a Strad for a girl who hasn't even made her musical debut? How old is she?'

'About twenty, I think – a year or two younger than Michiko, at a guess.'

'I don't think you should waste any sympathy on Mr Shige. He's what we used to call a *nouveau riche* – I wonder what it is in Japanese? Anyhow, don't trouble yourself about him. What he's really trying to do is bribe his daughter to be good. Any claim he's making for her musical ability is bunkum.'

'Rubbidge, as Joseph would say.'

'How is Joseph? And has Henry tried my method of framing his steam-engine photos?'

They went on to chat about those of his clients she knew. Anne Gleghorn wasn't mentioned; Nicoletta had never met her.

After a time she began yawning again.

'Off to bed, Grossmutti.'

'You too, *Liebling*. And Gregory—'

'Yes?'

'If you're going to phone that girl of yours, make it a short call.'

She put the phone down before he could reply. She was good at that, making a grand exit over the long-distance line.

Liz Blair was still up and wide awake. 'I'm battling with these stock sheets,' she said. 'Gregory, since you got all kinds of diplomas and certificates for mathematics, why don't you take on the job of sorting out my stock sheets?'

'So you only love me for my diplomas?'

'Who said I love you at all?'

And so on. He gave her a brief sketch of the evening, omitting McVay's alarms about Michiko's politics and whether the police should be told. Liz took that kind of thing seriously. It was no good telling her he was too minor a royal to be worth plotting against, she always got upset.

'I must go,' he said. 'I've got to be up early tomorrow to get into the hall where the Bachianas are to be performed, to see if there's room on the platform for eight cellos.'

'Why do you have to do that early in the morning?'

'Because the hall will be in use from mid-morning on, and I don't think the Orchestre Savoie would like me crawling about among their desks with a tape measure while they're rehearsing.'

She giggled. 'Oh, Greg,' she said, 'you are sweet.'

With which comforting thought he went downstairs to say good-night to Anne and the members of the Kamikura before seeking his lonely bed.

During the Festival a midnight buffet was always laid on in what was called the writing-room of the Hill Hotel. Because so many of his guests were performers or members of the Festival audience, Hector McVay had had the brilliant idea of offering them a choice of light food and drink to help them unwind.

The room was a pleasant venue. During the daylight hours it was a quiet lounge for those who wanted to read or write letters (it looked out on to the back lanes of the residential streets of the hill). The walls were covered in neutral beige silk, the curtains were misty blue, the carpet was beige and blue with touches of cream, the chairs were elegant but didn't invite surrender as did those in the main lounge.

The late-night service of food was not open to the public. McVay made sure to flatter important guests by putting on their favourite dishes. Tonight Isaac Shemnitzi was being honoured with cold salt-beef, latkes and various salads.

Shige had gone up to bed. Henry Holt caught Crowne's eye and beckoned to him. 'Did you speak to Michiko?' he asked. 'What did she say?'

'It seems Shige was telling the truth, after a fashion. Michiko did take part in the demo which almost ended in an attempt on his life, but she didn't know that was how it was going to turn out.' He reported Michiko's version of events. Holt munched his beef thoughtfully.

'In a way it doesn't surprise me,' he said at length. 'She's a deep little thing, our Michiko. We've found that out in rehearsal – haven't we, boys?'

The viola player nodded. 'She's never satisfied with first or second attempts at interpretation. Or even third attempts. Henry has to be stern with her sometimes or she'd go on for ever, trying to bring out something or other.'

'But you're speaking only about music.'

'Oh yes, only about music. I never imagined she was the least bit interested in politics. Henry says it doesn't surprise him but I'm astonished. I'm sure it was only a phase: one of those brief – I don't know the English word, what is English for *Schwärmerei*?'

'A crush, I think you mean. Perhaps you're right. Of course she's an idealist – you only have to hear her talk about the damage to the environment by Japanese industries . . .'

'Ever been to Japan, Gregory?' Holt enquired.

'Not yet.'

'It's not a land of cherry blossom, that's for sure. But the workforce don't seem to mind how the countryside is being damaged. I gather they've got this big loyalty thing – they say things like: "Mr Tanata looks after us, we're seldom laid off though times are hard, if we get sick we still get a pension, when we die we get a fine burial." I could understand if Michiko got upset about it when she was a student and tried to do something about it.'

'That, yes, I understand that,' Isaac Shemnitzi agreed. 'I wonder if it's true she led Suso Shige astray?'

Talik Edder walked up, bearing a heaped plate of assorted meats. In his wake came Angeliza Kelly. 'I hear you had quite a *clamore* after I walked out?'

'You missed a lovely chance for publicity, Talik,' Anne Gleghorn responded. 'You could have rescued Michiko Toshio from the wicked industrialist who was giving her a shaking.'

'Shige? Shige did something to Michiko?'

'Oh, how awful,' breathed Senhora Kelly.

'I don't know if it's so awful,' said Anne. 'I'm here to say I think she probably deserved it. Seems she's a member of the Red Brigade or something of the kind.'

'A terrorist?' With a gasp of alarm the *senhora* looked about for shelter, and found it close to Edder, who smiled down at her.

'Don't be afraid, little one,' he said in a comforting tone. 'I won't let the bad Japanese bomb thrower get at you. I shall face Michiko Toshio – bare-handed, if necessary – and save us all from death.'

There was a roar of laughter. Michiko was approximately half the height of Edder and might have registered a quarter of his weight on the scales.

Senhora Kelly gave a tinkling laugh. She gazed adoringly up at her hero. 'You can make fun,' she said, 'but I know you'd be brave enough to face a real terrorist.'

Senhora Kelly was one of a tribe which plagues handsome musicians and singers. Rich, unattached, genuinely fond of music though without any talent of their own, they fill their lives by being in love with the idol of the moment. There are tribes that follow Placido Domingo wherever he goes, there are women who say their prayers to photographs of Simon Rattle.

Talik didn't much mind being dogged by adoring women. From among their ranks he often found a bed companion. So far Angeliza Kelly hadn't achieved that pinnacle, and it was doubtful she would survive the bliss if she ever did.

The conversation turned to lighter matters. The crown prince took part with one half of his mind, but the other was considering Takamasa Shige.

He could understand the man's bitterness. From Shige's point of view, here was the girl who at college had subverted his daughter into the ways of violent protest, causing Suso to lose ground in her studies by perhaps a year or more. Inattention in the early years of a musical career is difficult to repair. The damage might prove permanent.

Michiko Toshio, on the other hand, had kept working at her music even if she sometimes went out on demos. By exceptional talent and the luck of meeting three congenial spirits at Kamikura, she had become part of a young string quartet that was beginning to build a reputation for itself.

Michiko Toshio was here at the Edinburgh Festival, winning applause for herself and her colleagues. Shige's daughter was back home in Japan, trying to catch up on her studies and being bribed with the promise of the Emilio if she would only work hard and regain the ground she'd lost.

Shige had had the disappointment of missing the Emilio by a few hours. He witnessed Michiko's arrival, glowing with success. No wonder he had exaggerated her crimes so as to take her down the required peg or two.

The prince came back to the present to find Shemnitzi at his elbow. 'You're not going to do anything about it then?' he asked.

'Such as what?' asked His Highness.

'Go to the police.'

'Of course not. What makes you ask?'

The thick-set Israeli jerked his head towards Senhora Kelly. 'She was a bit upset. In her country politics can break out in bloodshed.'

Crowne smiled. 'I think she's found all the protection she needs,' he said.

'You're not going to mention Shige's accusations to the authorities?'

'No.'

That, however, turned out to be a mistake.

Five

C rowne went out early next morning to view the platform that was to hold eight cellos and a soprano. He got back to the hotel in time for a late breakfast.

The sun shone in through the tall sash windows, making a rosy gleam reflect off the crimson silk wallpaper. The white tablecloths shone, and there was a pleasant aroma of crisp bacon, toast and coffee.

He found Shige enjoying a first acquaintance with Scotch marmalade and wholemeal toast. The man looked much better than at any time since the prince had first seen him. A complete night's sleep had obviously done him a lot of good.

'Good-morning, Mr Crowne.'

It was an invitation to sit with him. Somewhat reluctantly, Crowne did so, reflecting that Shige would soon get up and go – he was on the last slice of toast.

'Is your room comfortable, Mr Shige?'

'Oh, very. Better than I could have expected in a strange little place like this.'

'Please, Mr Shige,' said the prince, affecting a pained disapproval. 'This is one of the best hotels in Britain.'

'You make a joke?'

'Not in the least. Believe me, people queue up to get in here, especially during the Festival.'

'So how is it McVay gives me a room in one moment?'

The crown prince didn't say, 'Because I asked him.' Instead he said with a grin, 'Don't get too comfortable, you may have to turn out when the real occupant arrives.'

The waitress brought a Continental breakfast. Crowne poured coffee and drank off a cup. Now he began to feel more civilised.

'I cannot understand how anyone can drink that concoction first thing in the morning.'

'You drink tea?'

'Certainly.' Shige patted the teapot of white and gold which matched the breakfast service. 'Though whether what is in this thing can be called tea I feel unsure. It is nothing like what we drink at home, I assure you.'

He was clearly in a better mood than yesterday. Crowne risked touching on the matter of the Emilio. 'Are you going to ring your daughter today?'

'Already I did so. It's evening in Tokyo, you know.'

'You explained everything to her?'

'Hm . . .' said Shige, putting the last piece of toast in his mouth and crunching hard.

'What does she feel about having the Guarneri?' Crowne heard his own words and marvelled at them. How does she feel about the Guarneri? It was like saying, 'How does she feel about emeralds?' But to someone who'd set her heart on diamonds, it was a question that needed thought.

'She says the Guarneri is a great instrument but she wants the Emilio. I explained all over again and she says she'll call me when she thinks it over.'

Crowne wondered whether to say, 'She'd better not take too long about it or Edder will make up his mind how to dispose of his Guarneri.' But he didn't want to add to Shige's problems.

The day that had begun so well went on in a calm and pleasant fashion. Anne Gleghorn allowed herself to be taken on a tour of the church where she was to sing and agreed the acoustics might prove quite good on the night.

She even acted with cool politeness towards Talik Edder. The cellist would have been happy enough to be friends, but then it was easier for him; he was no longer in love with Anne, if he ever had been. Whereas Anne, who had been discarded, couldn't come to terms with her rejection and moreover had a bad action on her conscience. She'd hurried to Edinburgh convinced she was going to patch things up somehow but had made a mess of it.

But it was necessary to believe it was all Talik's fault. *She* was not to blame. 'His ego is absolutely enormous,' she muttered to Crowne. 'I simply don't know how you can be so long-suffering with him.'

'It's my job to be long-suffering,' said Crowne.

'And as for that Brazilian bushbaby who sits gazing at him with her enormous eyes—'

'Bushbabies are African—'

'Don't quibble. I tell you, it makes me long to do *something* to shake them both up.'

'Now, Anne . . .' Crowne knew that Anne had already done something to Talik. Angeliza had been unable to resist telling him about the conversation on which she'd eavesdropped.

Luckily things went well on the musical side. Anne gave two recitals with the choir, on the Wednesday and the Thursday, and was well reviewed. True to his promise, Crowne got her some extra publicity. He had unearthed a family connection between the Gleghorns of Connecticut and a line who had once owned a lordly estate in Scotland, friends of James II, no less. Scottish newspapers leapt to attention, the notice was picked up by American journalists. It was small-scale stuff, but it pleased Anne. She began to look happy, almost smug.

Looking round the writing room on the Thursday night after Anne's second Schütz recital, Crowne felt the occupants had shaken down into friendships that would last through to the end of the Festival. Angeliza, of course, clung to Talik Edder, who seemed not displeased – he was so busy most of his working hours that her devotion was like a pleasant cushion at the end of the day. Anne Gleghorn, as if in some kind of retaliation, had struck up a link with Shige: they

53

would sit together over wholefood meals, and even went out jogging together – 'fitness freaks', Edder called them.

But the most remarkable relationship was between Michiko and David Duntyre. After the occasion when he intervened to save her from Shige, Duntyre seemed to think he had some sort of claim on her – and she certainly did nothing to discourage him.

Quite the contrary. She would look for him when she came into a room, and make straight for him. It was amusing to see the two together – he stood over six foot, whereas she was only about five. She would gaze up at him short-sightedly through her glasses, her black eyes gleaming with affection and her usually pale cheeks touched with a flush of pleasure.

Duntyre, self-centred and conceited as McVay insisted, nevertheless gave up some of his time for her. Instead of attending every performance of his play, *Displenishin'*, and disagreeing with the slightest variation in the text, he went to hear the Kamikura play Schubert.

'Not exactly my tot of whisky,' he said. 'But mind, there were some good tunes. And the wee lass played very bonnily.'

'Is that English you're speaking?' the prince enquired, laughing. 'I wonder Michiko can understand a word you say.'

Duntyre looked unexpectedly coy. 'We don't need to say much,' he murmured. 'There's languages that don't need words, Crowne.'

Perturbed, Crowne asked McVay about the man. 'It has the look of becoming serious,' he explained. 'And Michiko can't afford to get bogged down in a love affair with a man who's so taken up with his own talent.'

'He's a boor and a lunatic,' McVay riposted. 'You ought to get that little girl away from him, even if you have to drag her bodily. Him and his nationalistic nonsense – artistic isolation, that's all he wants. To be a big frog in a tiny wee pool. And why, I ask you? Why?'

'I've no idea. Tell me.'

'Because nobody in the larger world would give him two minutes' attention. He writes in the dialect. Lallans, you know.'

'Lallans?'

'It's a way of saying Lowlands – it's the form of English spoken in the southern half of Scotland, as opposed to Gaelic, which is spoken in the north.'

The crown prince had heard of Gaelic. He was interested in languages, having added a few to those with which he'd grown up -- languages useful for business, such as Portuguese and Spanish for South America, elementary Russian for handling those performers who made it to the commercial West, and modern Greek. From time to time he came across Flemish or Basque or Breton while travelling. Likewise Gaelic, sometimes sung in a folksong recital.

'His plays must attract a very small audience then?'

'Plays, if you can call them that! Political tracts, I think they are. The BBC had a play of his on TV last year – my, was it dreary! All about coalminers down a pit. I ask you!'

'What's it like, the play that's on in the Festival?'

'I've no idea,' McVay said in a tone that implied 'and I don't care either.'

The title, *Displenishin'*, sounded like the name of a hobgoblin. But it turned out to be a term for a farm being sold up. It was, as McVay had foretold, 'dreary'. The production was rather good, put on by a group of enthusiastic youngsters who clustered round the playwright after the final curtain to hear his strictures. The theatre was a disused school hall down a close – the Scots term for an alley – off the High Street. The language was so obscure as to be incomprehensible.

Yet there had been an audience. Mainly hearty academics from the Scottish universities, and earnest types in brown cloaks and sandals. They applauded as if they meant it, and crowded round to give their approval to the writer, who received it loftily.

This then was the man to whom Michiko Toshio was losing her heart. Not an unworthy man. But what could come of it? In two more weeks the Festival would be over and Michiko would be gone, their love affair dying after the farewell performance. The Kamikura Quartet had engagements in Ontario; whereas Duntyre – Crowne would have taken a bet – would stay rooted in Scotland, wedded to the cause he had embraced.

Well, it wasn't a new situation. Musicians on the concert circuit tended to make these temporary relationships and little harm came of it.

Yet Michiko, he kept remembering, took things to heart. She had been in a passion when Shige accused her. She had given up precious hours of music practice to her campaign against the vandalism of Japanese industrialists. When she played, her music was like a lover to her. But now she had a lover of the flesh.

Speaking of love affairs, he must ring Liz Blair. 'Come to Edinburgh,' he said. 'The city's looking great.'

'I don't know. I'm having a lot of arguments with the window dressers . . . They say all the clothes look as if they're made from dishcloths this year.'

'You mean they aren't?'

'Tut-tut. You stick to music and I'll stick to fashion. I know these clothes are right for next winter.'

'Then leave it all in your assistant's hands, if you're so confident, and come to Edinburgh.'

'*You* come to London.'

'Not till after the Bachianas Brasileiras. I've got a recording man laid on; there's a lot riding on it, Liz. So you see I can't come south. You come north.'

'What'll you give me if I do?'

'Not on the phone, my love. I'll tell you when I see you.'

'We'll see,' she said, very businesslike. 'I'll just turn up if I'm coming.'

He guessed she wouldn't show up. He was taking second

place to a vanload of dresses. So much for the Royal Highness McVay admired so much and enjoyed boasting of to others.

Sighing, he turned his mind to business. There was after all life after the Festival. His Geneva office confirmed that the celebration of Caribbean music seemed likely to take place, and he was invited to organise a set of guitar recitals. Rosa Lyall was having a baby and couldn't accept any engagements after January. Where were the scores for 'The Beatitudes' by César Franck, which were needed in Montreux? 'Buy a set and fax them,' the prince said crossly, then had to apologise to his part-time secretary.

The weekend came. Sunday was spent in preliminary rehearsals for the Bachiana No. 5. Crowne went round all his eight cellists, at either their hotels or their places of performance, to remind them that they were expected at the Usher Hall on Sunday morning for the first run-through.

When they arrived he was struck by the sight of it – eight cellos being taken out of eight cases, end-pins being screwed in, eight bows being tightened, the players ranging themselves in an arc behind the place left on the platform for the singer.

There was something exotic in it – as if the cellos were eight giant insects coming out of their cocoons, attracted by the bright orchid colours of Anne Gleghorn's dress.

There was no conductor: Talik Edder was to act as leader of the octet. If Anne thought this was wrong, she said nothing about it and accepted his suggestions and corrections without comment. A certain tightening of her lips occurred when he said he thought her tone needed more sensuality, but instead of the outburst that Crowne had feared, she went to chat to Mr Shige.

Most of the performers had brought a friend to listen to the rehearsal. Crowne would have brought Liz if she'd arrived; Michiko had brought David Duntyre. Talik had either brought Angeliza Kelly or allowed her to come, but she disappeared mysteriously for part of the rehearsal.

'Where did you get to?' Talik asked her in vexation as she reappeared, clutching a package in a plastic carrier-bag.

'I just slipped out to the shops to buy something—'

'Good heavens, couldn't it wait until Monday?'

'I needed some . . . er . . . I needed tissues. I feel a cold coming on . . .'

'Stay away from me, then!' growled her beloved. 'The last thing I need is the cold in the head before a first night.'

Crowne smiled to himself. Edder might say he found her boring, he might say he didn't need a woman hanging around, yet if she was less than completely at his beck and call he got annoyed.

Everything seemed good. All the players were pleased at the chance to take part in the Bachiana, which is rather infrequently performed because of the business of getting eight good cellists. A pity, thought the crown prince, for it was full of lovely tunes, easy to remember and sing in the bath, liltingly reminiscent of South American dances like the rumba and the samba.

On Monday there was another rehearsal, which Crowne didn't attend. He always tried to steer clear when recording engineers were around because they were so frenetic and so demanding. He heard from Talik that they had behaved with their usual idiocy.

'What is the use of having every single note perfectly recorded,' he wailed, 'if by their interference they make the interpretation wooden?'

There had also been what he called 'lack of seriousness' in Anne. 'If you wish to flirt with Mr Shige, do it in your own time,' he rebuked her.

'Oh you!' She pouted at him. 'You take yourself so seriously now you've got a Strad!'

It was true, thought Crowne. She sounded almost frivolous. Could it be love? For Takamasa Shige? Perhaps that relationship was bringing out hidden shallows.

In the afternoon, those who could, rested in preparation

for that evening's performance. Some of the cellists had orchestral rehearsals or performances, but Talik retired to bed, as did Anne Gleghorn. Separately, of course.

Michiko went for a stroll hand in hand with David Duntyre. 'You'll be back by five o'clock, won't you?' fussed the prince.

'Dinna fash yoursel',' said David, 'I'll no lead her so far astray she canna get back by five o'clock.'

'She's got to have a meal and rest before the performance.'

'All right, Gregory, I promise,' said Michiko in demure agreement.

Duty done in that respect, the prince went to the hall to hear the rehearsal of other numbers in that night's concert. They were really no concern of his, for they were for full orchestra under the baton of Emile Durachin, but he felt he owed it to goodwill to turn up and look pleased.

Once again, everything seemed to be running smoothly. M. Durachin got tetchy about the 'native instruments' in the Choros No. 10, but it's unreasonable to expect a plump Provençal timpanist to play the maracas like a Brazilian peasant. On the whole it sounded fine – rich, throbbing, exciting. Crowne was happy with the whole affair: glad he'd thought of a Villa-Lobos tribute, sure the audience would love it, delighted that a recording contract had ensued so that he could unite money-making with music-making.

That evening was a triumph. Talik looked superbly handsome and played like an angel on the Emilio. Of the other seven cellists, three were women – and, luckily, good-looking women. Michiko wore a loose gown of dark green with magenta flowers across the front; Claire Enjou was in a red trouser suit; Magda Kussov was in the traditional black dress, but her blond hair above it looked like gold.

Anne sang well, and took centre-stage like the figure on the prow of a ship. Her strong body was clothed in grey-blue silk, her handsome, bony face framed by her dark hair held back in a silver band.

If there was a certain lack of attention in some of her entrances, no one but perhaps Gregory Crowne could have noted it. Perhaps she was resisting Talik's leadership. That minor flaw apart, the total ensemble was magnificent.

Listening intently to the audience around him, the prince heard remarks like: 'Why haven't I ever heard that before?' and 'I must get tickets for the other one.'

The Bachianas Brasileiras finished the concert. The nine performers smiled and bowed, came back and bowed, put Anne forward to bow, came together and bowed, and went away. At last, as encore, Talik Edder came forward alone to play, unaccompanied, the 'Melodia' from the Peguena Suite. Wily devil, thought Crowne, he must have had that up his sleeve just in case . . .

He went backstage while the audience was still applauding that final offering. The other players were in the green room, reacting in their separate ways to the excitement of the evening. Some became talkative, some grew reticent and weary. They put away their instruments. They waited. They had been asked to be ready to come to the manager's office, where drinks and sandwiches were laid on, so that the Brazilian Consul could say a few words of appreciation.

When Talik Edder arrived, the rest were wandering towards the door of the green room. Sensing that he was holding them back, Edder quickly put his cello in its case, washed his hands and smoothed his moustache. 'Ready,' he said. He held the door open for Anne.

'Oh, you first, sir,' she said, looking up teasingly. 'The leader always goes first.'

'Hurry up,' hissed the assistant manager, aware that the Consul was patiently sitting in the manager's office.

Everyone hastened after Talik. Crowne found himself with two of the women, Claire and Magda. He noticed Michiko had not been able to inveigle David Duntyre into the gathering.

All in all, a successful event. Crowne had brought his hired car along, and helped Michiko and Talik to load their instruments in the back as they set off for the Hill Hotel. Anne Gleghorn sat in front with her coat up about her throat as if she were protecting her voice from the chill night air.

'Anything wrong?' asked the prince as he drove off.

'No, why should there be?'

'You seem quiet.'

'I'm thinking of the voice. I've got to do it all again tomorrow, and I don't achieve the result by drawing a bow across four strings – I have to be my own instrument.'

'You're not having throat trouble, are you?'

'No.' She bristled. 'Did you get that impression from my singing?'

'No, I thought you sang well.'

'Not your best,' put in Talik, 'but well.'

'Oh, thank you so much.'

It was only a short drive to Hill Crescent; David Duntyre was on the steps to welcome them. He helped Michiko out and carried her cello in for her, the long case tucked effortlessly under his arm. Talik watched him walk ahead. 'No one comes to carry *my* cello,' he observed.

'You wouldn't let anyone touch it,' Anne pointed out, her tone still full of pique.

'Quite true,' he said, hugging the case against him like a baby.

They went to their rooms to deposit their instruments and then assembled for the midnight buffet. Tonight they didn't seem to break up into quite the same groups as before but there seemed no reason for this except that Shige appeared disinclined to talk, even to Anne.

He had been in the audience tonight, and he had just heard Talik Edder play superbly on the instrument he had wanted for his daughter. Perhaps for the first time he really understood what it meant to own the Emilio.

About twelve thirty they broke up and headed for bed.

After all, there was another concert tomorrow evening and though there would be no rehearsal tomorrow each player would want to spend a long session in practice.

Talik invited the prince into his room to look over the pieces he had brought as encores. Perhaps tomorrow night, as an extra, he should play unaccompanied Bach? After all, Bach was implied by the title Villa-Lobos had given his pieces – Bachianas Brasileiras, Brazilian melodies in the style of Bach.

Crowne turned over the scores, muttering that a lot of people didn't like unaccompanied Bach on the cello.

'Nonsense, nonsense, my friend,' Talik scoffed. 'It can sound wonderful.' He picked up his cello case, laid it on the bed and opened it. 'I won't play, just pick out—' He broke off.

He made a stifled sound.

'What's the matter?' asked Crowne in alarm, looking round from the music manuscript.

Talik straightened. He was staring at the instrument in the case. He pointed a trembling finger.

'That is not my cello!' he gasped.

Six

The crown prince stepped to his side and looked down. The instrument lying in the case was certainly not the Emilio.

His first reaction was one of stupid practicality. 'Perhaps you picked up the wrong case.'

'Don't be a fool,' Talik groaned. 'That's the case of the Emilio. Do you think I don't know my own instrument case?'

'Perhaps . . . Perhaps the Emilio got transferred to one of the other cases,' Crowne said. He knew he was being idiotic, but looked about the room.

Talik Edder had come to Edinburgh with two cellos, a Guarneri and one by Abraham Prescott. Having bought the Stradivari, he intended to sell the Guarneri but, as every cello needs to be played, he had been in the habit of practising on it for part of each day. So there was just an outside chance that in mistake Talik had put the Emilio in the case belonging to the Guarneri or the Prescott.

Although he knew it was not so, Talik opened the Guarneri case. Crowne opened the Prescott. Each cello was in its proper home.

They turned, in silent consternation, to the one lying in the case belonging to the Emilio. 'What make is it?' Crowne asked.

Talik picked it out, tilted it and held it to the light. Inside, a handwritten label could be seen. Talik Edder read out in a trembling voice: 'George Duncan, Glasgow, 1889.'

'My God,' said Crowne.

'Whose is it?' the cellist asked, looking about him as if he expected the owner to appear from his bathroom. 'Who does it belong to, this nothing of a cello?'

'And where's the Emilio?'

'Oh God. My Emilio.'

They stared at each other in total stupefaction.

'It can't have gone,' Crowne said.

They searched the room. It was absurd, Chaplinesque. They looked in the bathroom, in the wardrobe, under the bed, which was too low to admit a cello with its bridge erect. They looked behind the dressing-table.

'It's been stolen,' Talik said, breathing out the word as if it burned his throat.

'But it's impossible! Your door was locked?'

'Of course! It locks itself as you come out.'

'But if you put up the catch—'

'No.'

'Then how—? Wait a minute, Talik. Perhaps it's just a mix-up. After all, damn it, there were eight cellos there tonight, not to mention those in the orchestra—'

'You mean one of them put my Emilio in his cello case?'

'Perhaps,' said Crowne, leaping for the door, 'perhaps Michiko . . . ?'

They raced up to the next floor and ran along the corridor. They banged on the door, calling, 'Michiko! Michiko!' She came to answer, already in a little kimono which served as dressing-gown and sleepwear. Her hair hung down around her shoulders. She looked even more fragile and childlike than ever.

'What's the matter?' she said in a frightened voice as they burst in upon her.

'Michiko – your cello—'

'What about my cello?'

'Have you got it?'

'Of course I've got it,' she said, looking from one to the

64

other with her short-sighted gaze. She went to the dressing-table, found her glasses and put them on. 'What's the matter?'

Her cello case was on the luggage rest by the bureau. She pressed her glasses against her temples and said, 'There's my cello – why?'

'Have you looked at it?'

'Looked at it?' She glanced from one to the other as if she thought they were drunk.

'Since you got back from the concert,' Crowne prompted.

'No, why should I?'

'Look at it now, I beg you,' Edder urged.

'But why? Why on earth—'

'You may have his Stradivarius,' Crowne said.

'Don't be silly.' But she walked to the luggage rest, picked up the case and laid it on the bed as Edder had done. She snapped open the fastenings.

Her back was towards them. They saw it stiffen.

'That's not my cello,' she said in an unsteady voice.

Edder and Crowne came either side of her. They both stared at the cello. It was a recent instrument – certainly not the Emilio.

'That's not yours,' Edder said, for a cellist recognises a friend's instrument after short acquaintance.

'Of course it isn't. This looks like a Pressenda. Whose is it?' she asked, her small hands touching the belly of the instrument.

'I've no idea.'

'But it's *absurd*!' cried the prince in angry bewilderment. 'Talik hasn't got his cello and you haven't got yours. Where on earth have they all got to?'

'Never mind about "all",' breathed Edder. 'Where is the Emilio?'

His face was ashen. No doubt it was a shock to Michiko to lose her own instrument, but hers was a Vuillaume, a good cello but with nothing like the tone of the Stradivarius. She could go out tomorrow and buy herself a cello as good as the Vuillaume – but where would Edder find the equal of the Emilio?

All these thoughts rushed through Crowne's head and he knew that there was no use talking of a simple mix-up. Whatever else had happened – and he simply didn't understand it – the Emilio was missing. Insured for an astronomical sum, but absolutely irreplaceable.

It had to be recovered. And it could not have gone far because only two hours or so ago Talik had actually been playing it.

'May I?' He picked up the phone by Michiko's bed and asked the switchboard operator to put him through to the police.

'The police?' said the night porter on duty. 'What way do you want the police, sir?'

'There's been a theft.'

'In the hotel?'

'We don't know. Please put me through to the emergency service.'

There must have been a patrol car in the vicinity – perhaps a car asked to ensure all was quiet at the hotel where the Crown Prince of Hirtenstein was staying – for within five minutes a uniformed constable was shown by the hall porter into Michiko's bedroom. By this time Michiko had gone into the bathroom and put on slacks and a sweater. She, Edder and Crowne were all standing looking down at her cello.

'Now, sir, you reported a robbery?' the constable said, looking into the air between the two men.

'I reported it, officer. My name is Gregory Crowne, I'm a concert agent here for the Festival. This is Mr Talik Edder, the cellist—'

'Talik Edder,' said the policeman, writing in his notebook.

'And this is Miss Toshio, also a cellist.'

'Indeed? And which one of you is it that's had his cello stolen?'

'I have,' said Michiko and Talik together.

'Beg pardon?' said the constable, with a glance at his colleague, who had come up to join him.

The glance suggested that they were mad, or perhaps drunk. 'Whose cello is this, then?' he went on in a humouring tone, waving his notebook at the one in its case on the bed.

'We've no idea,' said Crowne.

'No idea? Would you explain that, sir?'

'When we saw that the other one was not mine we came to Michiko to see if she had it and she opened the case and that is not hers.'

'It's not hers. Not her cello. And what other one was this you just mentioned? Was that the one that was stolen, the one this lady—'

'No, the first one was the Emilio—'

'Mine is stolen too,' Michiko put in. 'It's a Vuillaume.'

'A what?'

'It's a make of cello, officer,' Crowne explained. 'Can I try to set out what happened? We were in Mr Edder's room. He opened the case which should have contained the Stradivarius but it contained another cello—'

'Another cello. How many cellos are we talking about, sir?'

'Two. No, four – the two that should be in their cases and the two we found in their places.'

'Six,' Edder interjected. 'Don't forget the Guarneri and the Prescott.'

'Six?' said the constable faintly.

'Six cellos?' said his partner.

'No, no, there's no problem over the Guarneri and the Prescott. They're where they should be, in their cases in Mr Edder's room—'

'Mr Edder has *two* cellos?'

'Three – or at least I had until a few hours ago—'

'Look here,' said the constable, closing his notebook with a stern look, 'this kind of joke—'

'It's not a joke!' shouted Talik. 'They have stolen my sweetheart – my beloved!'

'Eh? There's a lady missing?'

'No, no, he's talking about his cello—'

'His cello?'

'Good God in heaven!' Talik roared. 'What else have we been telling to you? My cello is gone, my Emilio—'

'Who is Emilio?'

'That's the name of the cello.'

The constable turned towards the door. 'We've got more important things to do . . .'

'Wait! Wait a moment.' The prince caught at the navy-blue sleeve. 'Wait, one of the missing cellos is worth a fortune—'

'What's that you say?'

'It was in the papers the other day. Talik Edder bought a Stradivarius cello in Gower's in George Street—'

'Aye, aye, Dave, there was a traffic hold-up – do ye no recall?'

'Oh, *that* cello.'

'Constable,' said Crowne, '*that* cello is missing. So is the less valuable cello belonging to Miss Toshio. In their place are two different cellos, one being of much less value.'

'Less value . . .' said the police constable, following closely. 'How much less?'

'The one in Mr Edder's cello case is worth approximately two hundred pounds, I'd guess—'

'Two hundred pounds? They're no cheap, are they?'

'This one . . .' He looked at Michiko, who said, 'I think it's a Pressenda; you could buy it for about ten thousand.'

'Pounds?' asked the constable, looking up from note-taking.

'Yes. And the Vuillaume that's missing, about the same. The Emilio, however, is worth about two hundred times as much.'

'Eh?'

'The point is, constable, the missing cellos can't be far away. They were both being played in the Usher Hall up until ten thirty.'

'Is that a fact?' said the policeman in a scared voice. 'I think I'd better flash a report and get someone along from CID. It's not a thing I can get the hang of myself.'

He removed himself to the corridor and spoke into his personal radio. Hector McVay shoved past him. He had clearly put his clothes on in a hurry.

'Your Highness – sir – the porter called me. What's been happening?'

'A disaster,' Talik Edder said, and sank down on the only chair in the room with his great head in his hands.

The two constables now looked more cheerful, having been in touch with high command.

'Chief Inspector Fairmil will be here in a minute,' said the senior of the two.

'Chief Inspector Fairmil?' cried McVay. 'What for?'

'And who are you, sir?'

'I'm the manager of the hotel. What . . . what was that about Mr Fairmil?'

'Well, sir, in the case of a very valuable object going missing—'

'*What's* missing?'

'My cello,' groaned Edder.

'So you see it's a case for CID—'

'Oh, my God,' cried McVay, with something that looked like terror, and turned to plunge away.

'Just a minute, bide a wee, sir,' said Constable Johnson, grabbing his jacket, 'where are you off to?'

'To – to see if the pass-key is missing.'

'Oh aye. A good thought. Right you are.'

McVay dashed off. Constable Weir, the senior of the two, said, 'Could I see the other case with the other cello, please?' He paused. 'You did say there was another case with another cello?'

'In my room,' groaned Edder. 'This way.'

The younger officer was left on guard with Michiko and her replacement cello. The senior stared at the cello in the case on Edder's bed. 'You're sure that's no your cello, sir?' he asked.

Talik uttered a horrendous word and lifted his fist. Crowne stepped between them. 'We're sure,' he told the innocent policeman, and then in German to Edder: 'Don't be angry with him. He thinks you're a mad foreigner.'

'I *am* a foreigner and I am being *driven* mad,' Talik replied.

'It won't help matters to assault a policeman.'

'I want to assault someone. Dear God, I want to *hit* someone, or run out and scream at the top of my voice!'

'If you please, sir,' said the constable, 'would you speak English? I can't carry on an investigation if you speak French.'

'All the while this imbecile is asking me idiotic questions,' Talk said in English, 'my Emilio is getting farther and farther away.'

'We don't know that, Talik. It's probably still here in Edinburgh.'

'I don't know what makes you think so! Somebody probably took it on a plane to Moscow or Paris by now.'

'Easy, easy. There are no planes to Moscow from Edinburgh. Almost every flight goes via London. The police will have sent out messages. Oh yes, they will,' he insisted as the Finn shook his head in despair.

'That's right, sir,' said Constable Weir with unexpected sympathy. 'I can see you're fair cut up about it. We've got the wheels turning, don't you fret.'

'But I do fret! Some jealous fiend has taken my darling away—' He broke off.

He and the crown prince stared at one another.

'Shige!' said the cellist.

'No, no, Talik—'

'I tell you, it's Shige! He's taken my cello!'

'How could he possibly have taken your cello? Don't be silly, man! He couldn't get into your room—'

'If he bribed a maid . . .'

'No, look here, Talik—'

'Shige has my cello!' cried Edder, catching hold of the constable's arm. 'Come and get it back!'

'Just a minute, just a minute – who is Sheegay?'

'A Japanese businessman staying in the hotel.'

'A Japanese. Like the wee lady upstairs?' said Constable Weir, scenting conspiracy.

'Yes, but that's got nothing to do—'

'She and him thegither, is that it?'

'The last thing Michiko Toshio would do is help Takamasa Shige,' said Crowne. 'You know that, Talik. Besides, *Michiko's* cello is missing.'

'Oh, crivens, aye,' said the constable, and took a great relieved breath when a tall man in a raincoat shouldered his way in.

'Chief Inspector Fairmil,' said the newcomer. He jerked his head at a younger man at his elbow. 'Sergeant Haggerston. Now, which is Mr Talik Edder?'

'I am Edder.'

'So you must be Mr . . . er . . . Crowne,' said Fairmil, with something like a bow in the direction of the prince. He had been quickly briefed at police headquarters in the High Street before he came out. 'Good-evening, sir – or rather good-morning. A terrible thing, this. A very valuable piece, I hear.'

'The value is not something that can be measured in money,' Talik mourned. 'It has just come back into circulation, the Emilio – after being silent many years, she has spoken again.'

'This one on the bed,' said Fairmil, 'have you ever seen it before?'

Edder shook his head.

71

'It's odd. Why should the thief bother to put another cello in the place of this Emilio?'

'Perhaps he wanted me to play the Bachianas Brasileiras on a Scottish instrument,' the cellist said bitterly. 'This broomstick was made in Glasgow.'

'We'll get yours back, never fear,' Chief Inspector Fairmil replied. 'After all, a cello's a big thing, a noticeable thing. The thief must have been seen. We'll get it back.'

'Will you also get back Miss Toshio's cello?' Edder asked.

'Miss Toshio's cello?'

'Hers has gone too,' Crowne explained.

'What?'

'Didn't you get the message?'

'Well, I got a message – I thought it had got garbled . . . You mean there are *two* cellos missing?'

'Oh, not again,' said Edder, near to tears.

Crowne took the detective into the corridor to explain the situation. He had to go over it twice before even the chief inspector got it right. 'In each case a less valuable instrument has been left?'

'Well . . . I don't know that that is necessarily true in the case of Miss Toshio. She's lost a Vuillaume, she's got what she says is a Pressenda. I think they're about equal, give or take. But that's not the point. It's not *her* cello.'

They turned back into the room. The constable said to his superior officer, 'Sir, this gentleman says a Mr Shige has got his cello.'

'Mr Shige,' said Fairmil. 'Who is Mr Shige?'

'He wanted to buy the Emilio but I wouldn't sell to him. I thought he had stolen it from my room. But,' said Edder in a lacklustre voice, 'now I realise . . . Michiko's Vuillaume is gone too. Shige would have no use for a Vuillaume. I withdraw the accusation.'

'All the same, sir . . . We'd best look into it.' Fairmil

looked at his sergeant. 'Ring the manager – it's Mr McVay, isn't it? I want to know which is Mr Shige's room.'

The sergeant obeyed. The phone rang and rang in McVay's office but there was no reply. 'Where the hell is he?' growled Fairmil.

'He went to see if the pass-key had been taken, sir.'

'Then he ought to be in his office.'

'I dare say people may have been roused by the upset; perhaps he's soothing them,' Crowne suggested.

Hector McVay reappeared at that moment. 'The pass-key is in my office,' he reported.

'Where have you been, Mr McVay?'

'I beg your pardon?'

'You went to see about the pass-key but you didn't answer your office phone.'

'I . . . er . . . I . . . I went to tidy myself up, I didn't look presentable.'

As far as Crowne could tell, there was no alteration or improvement in McVay's appearance. He looked like a ruffled little rooster.

Fairmil nodded, accepting the excuse. 'Which is Mr Shige's room?'

'Mr Shige? What about him? You're not suggesting we wake him up?'

'There's some suggestion he might have stolen Mr Edder's cello.'

'I knew I should never have let that man into the Hill Hotel,' McVay sighed, with a glance of reproach at the prince.

'If you'd all please stay here. Mr McVay, which is Mr Shige's room?'

'This way.' He led off along the corridor and round a corner. The prince and Talik Edder sat down to wait with Sergeant Haggerston. After a considerable time the detective returned, bringing with him McVay and Michiko Toshio.

'Mr Shige's room has been searched and he doesn't have

the Emilio or any other cello.' Something in Fairmil's tone suggested that the wealthy Japanese had not taken kindly to being woken for such a strange reason. 'Now we'll all go to Mr McVay's office, if you don't mind. Miss Toshio's room and this room are sealed for the moment and I'm leaving men on guard.'

As soon as they reached the office McVay asked permission to have refreshments brought. He telephoned for sandwiches and coffee. The time was now three thirty in the morning. Crowne felt as if his eyelids had splinters of the Castle rock under them. Talik looked ghastly. Michiko was white and rather trembly, clearly scared by the big-boned Scots detectives.

While they waited for the food, Fairmil went on with his questions. 'When was the last time you had your own cello, sir?' he asked Edder.

'In my room. Before I came downstairs for the midnight buffet.'

'You saw it then. Actually saw it?'

'Well . . . no . . . but I brought it back from the hall.'

'How do you know you did?'

'It was in the case. I could feel it.'

'What you mean is, you knew the case had a cello in it. When did you last actually *see* the Emilio?'

'When . . . When I put her in her case after the performance. In the green room at the Usher Hall.'

'You then came straight home to the hotel?'

'No, we had to go to a little drinks party with the Brazilian Consul in the manager's office.'

'This was known beforehand?'

'Yes, of course,' Crowne put in. 'I was asked to let everyone know, and I did so.'

'So everyone went to the manager's office.'

'Yes.'

'Leaving the cellos in the green room.'

'Yes.'

'And after the drinks you came back and took your cello cases and went home.'

'Yes.'

'And each case had a cello in it.'

'Ah . . .' said Crowne.

'What do you mean, "ah"?' shouted Edder. 'This fool is stating the obvious.'

'No, Talik, no. That's why another, less valuable cello was put in your case. So that you would take it up and bring it back to the hotel without noticing. If it had been empty, you would have known at once.'

'Oh, Mother of God,' blurted the cellist, hitting his head with his fists. 'I brought back that floorsweeper of a cello instead of the Emilio?'

'Yes.'

'And Michiko—'

'I must have brought back a strange cello,' she said, huddling down into her sweater.

'When did you last actually see your own cello, Miss Toshio?'

She hesitated. 'At the hall. Same as Talik.'

'The green room wasn't locked?'

'Of course not,' the prince, Edder and Michiko said all together.

'Even with an instrument as valuable as the Emilio – you don't lock up?'

'But there's always someone around.'

'Not if you all go off to have drinks in the manager's office after the show is over, surely.'

'Well . . . no . . .'

Talik said suddenly, 'If Shige hasn't got it – and I agree he has not – who has it? What good is it to anyone? No other player can use it. The moment he put his bow on it it would be recognised.'

'Is that a fact, sir?' said Fairmil, his eyebrows going up. He thought for a moment. 'But you'd pay to get it back?'

75

'Anything!' cried Edder.

'Ransom?' asked Crowne.

'Looks like it.'

'But the Vuillaume? Surely no one is going to ask a ransom for the Vuillaume?'

'If he does, Gregory, he'll be wasting his time, for I have no money for a ransom.' Michiko's voice was quavering with weariness.

'All the same, sir,' Fairmil said, doggedly addressing the prince, 'we're beginning to get a picture of what happened. Somebody came to the hall with two cellos to exchange for the two valuable ones while you were off having drinks with the Consul. Now that's hopeful. A man carrying two cellos would be noticeable.'

'What makes you think so?' said Crowne, and, 'Of course he wouldn't!' said Edder, simultaneously.

'Pardon?' said the detective.

'Anybody carrying a cello or even two cellos wouldn't have been a bit noticeable last night,' sighed Crowne. 'There were eight cellos playing the Bachiana Brasiliera No. 5 by Villa-Lobos.'

'Eight?'

'To say nothing of the cellos in the Orchestre Savoie – eight of them,' added Talik.

'No, only seven more – one of their cellists was in the ensemble for the Bachiana, don't forget.'

'Wait a minute—' Fairmil began.

'So in actual fact there were fifteen cellos in the Usher Hall tonight – last night, I mean.'

'Fifteen?'

'Although only eight of them were in the green room.'

'Let me get this right,' said the Chief Inspector, making a snatching movement as if to keep hold of his sanity. 'Fifteen cellos were assembled at the Usher Hall for last night's performance?'

'Yes.'

'All of them valuable.'

'Valuable to their owners,' said Michiko.

'It's like this, Chief Inspector. None of them would be as valuable as the Emilio. A cellist buys the best instrument he can afford but, unless he's got private means or a grant from a performing-arts fund, he has to finance himself out of his earnings. That usually means a younger player has a relatively inexpensive instrument and an older man has something better. Let's say they average out at about eight thousand pounds apiece—'

'Good heavens,' gasped Fairmil.

'So fourteen at eight thousand comes to something over a hundred and ten thousand pounds. Plus the Emilio, which is worth more than twice that on its own.'

'That's four hundred thousand pounds' worth of cellos,' Fairmil said like a man in a dream.

'But the thief wouldn't have stolen them all,' Edder objected. 'He just took the Stradivarius and the Vuillaume—'

'He knows what he's doing, doesn't he?'

'But look here . . . He could have stolen Talik's Guarneri from the hotel – it's worth nearly as much as the Strad – so why waste time taking a Vuillaume when he could have got a Guarneri?'

'I don't understand this,' said Fairmil, rubbing his forehead. 'I don't understand this at all.'

'Wait. Wait. He didn't try for the Guarneri because it's here in the hotel. He took the Stradivarius because it was at the Usher Hall. He could only take instruments that were being used at the Usher Hall . . . ?'

Fairmil took a moment to think. 'The other cellists – have they got their instruments?'

'Oh come,' grunted Edder in derision. 'No thief walks out of a concert hall carrying fifteen cellos!'

'Remember, Talik – there was a symphony orchestra that got its entire truckload of instruments stolen!'

'You mean this man loaded eight cellos – or fifteen

cellos – into a truck?' Fairmil looked horror-stricken. 'I'd better check. Who would have the names and the Edinburgh addresses of these people?'

'Well, as a matter of fact,' said Crowne, 'I have the names, addresses and telephone numbers of those whose cellos were in the green room. I arranged for them to take part in the Bachiana, you see.'

Fairmil wanted to laugh or frown. It sounded as if the prince had said 'take part in the Bacchanalia'. But this was serious. Instruments worth about £400,000 . . .

With the help of the list supplied by the crown prince, his sergeant sent a request over the car radio: all the players were to be contacted and asked to check their cellos.

While that was being done, Crowne ate roast-beef sandwiches and drank coffee. Talik Edder stared at the wall. Michiko stood at the window, looking out between the curtains to watch the sky turning dove-grey with the approach of dawn.

Twenty minutes later the phone in the manager's office rang. Chief Inspector Fairmil picked it up. 'Yes? Fairmil speaking.' He listened with an impassive face.

Then he turned. 'Mr Crowne,' he said, 'not one of the cellists we've just contacted has got his or her own cello.'

Seven

What was left of the night became sheer chaos.

Chief Inspector Fairmil caused it by wondering whether the cellists of the Orchestre Savoie had their own instruments. Crowne, nearly dead with sleep, was aghast but rose to it like a man.

'One of the cellists you already contacted, Marcel Augustin, is a member of the Savoie. He'll know how to get in touch with the others.'

Fairmil rang M. Augustin, who was sitting in his room with a wet towel to his brow, bewailing the loss of his own cello and wondering what to do with a modern German one.

'*Comment?*' he shrieked when he heard Fairmil's question. '*Qu'est-ce que c'est que ça? Les écossais sont-ils fétichistes de cello?*'

He rang Charles Lefubure, the lead cellist of the Savoie. Lefubure, in great consternation, rang the conductor, M. Durachin, and also rang the orchestral manager Hutin, first horn player. They, not unnaturally, flew into a panic. They too remembered the famous occasion when the entire instrumental equipment of a great symphony orchestra had been driven away at midnight.

Durachin checked all his players. Those who had instruments that were portable flew to their instrument cases and opened them. All found they had their own. The double basses and the timpani had been left at the hall, for it's no fun carting round a double bass or a set of drums. Their owners became extremely anxious, the manager of the hall was roused from his bed, and after cross-checking with Chief Inspector Fairmil appeared bleary-eyed with the keys.

Chief Inspector Fairmil had a talent for organisation. He recognised this as an opportunity to gather together under one roof all the players who had been at the hall the previous night, and he dispatched police cars to bring them.

In the mean time his sergeant, two detective constables and two uniformed men were carrying out a search of the Hill Hotel. Hector McVay stood by in shock while his early-morning cleaning staff were told to stop work as policemen ferreted in linen cupboards, pantries and ornamental niches. Guests appeared at their bedroom doors, heads tousled, eyes fogged because of a night disturbed by the sound of people tramping about in the corridors.

He took careful note, did Mr McVay, concerning who appeared at which door. Some of the appearances surprised him. The residential staff were also roused, and he was not only surprised but definitely annoyed at which rooms they emerged out of.

Talik Edder, Michiko Toshio and the crown prince kept at the heels of the searchers, anxious to see if the two cellos missing at the Hill Hotel would turn up, and perhaps equally anxious to make sure they weren't damaged if found. When the detective sergeant went through the kitchens, Edder began to look anxious; when he opened the deep-freeze chest, he looked as if he might faint. But the chest contained only meat, fish and ice-cream.

'Thanks be to heaven,' Edder whispered. 'Gregory, who-ever took the Emilio, please God he knows it must be looked after like a baby.'

On the bedroom floors it was necessary not to be too close behind the searchers for fear of stumbling on something embarrassing. Most of the guests were on nodding terms with Gregory Crowne and Edder, but they weren't likely to wish to nod at that hour of the morning.

Takamasa Shige came to his door looking grim. 'Is it a

plot to prevent me from sleeping?' he demanded, glaring out at the detectives.

'I'm sorry, sir, we're conducting a search.'

'My room has been searched once. Do you want to do it again?'

'No, thank you, sir.'

Anne Gleghorn took a long time to open her door. When she did so, the reason was clear. A damp towelling robe was clinging to her, and she smelled of soap. 'Sorry,' she said, 'I was in the tub.'

'At four o'clock in the morning, madam?' said Sergeant Haggerston in surprise.

'Ach, she takes baths both hot and cold, at all hours of the day and night,' muttered Edder. 'She is a health fiend.'

'If you must know,' Anne said with an angry darting glance at him, 'I've scarcely had a wink of sleep all night. I was taking a warm bath in hopes of getting relaxed enough to drop off. What's this all about?' She stared at the group in the corridor.

Sergeant Haggerston made his explanations. Anne's eyes opened wide. 'The Emilio? Gone?'

'My cello too,' Michiko put in.

'How awful! Why, that must have been what I heard, about two o'clock – some sort of activity – it must have been the burglar—'

Said Crowne, 'That was me and Talik, dashing up to Michiko's room to ask her—'

Anne was frowning a little now. 'Why are you here, sergeant?' she said to Haggerston. 'What's it got to do with me?'

'We have to search every room, madam.'

Anne whirled on Edder. 'This is your idea,' she exclaimed. 'Of course if your precious Strad went missing you'd take it for granted I stole it!'

'It never entered my head—'

'What on earth would I want with your cello? It's absurd!'

'May we look, madam?'

Assuming a pose that derived from her performance of Tosca scorning Scarpia, she allowed the detectives in. In a few minutes they reappeared, shaking their heads. Anne banged the door shut after them.

At Senhora Kelly's room, a strange sight met their eyes when she opened to them. Though it was a few minutes after four o'clock of a cool Edinburgh morning, Angeliza, who came from the sun-kissed pampas of Brazil, had the window wide open. As if to protect herself against the cold, she was wearing one of the blankets from the bed draped round her shoulders.

'Angeliza!' exclaimed Edder in consternation. 'Why are you up and awake at this hour? Are you unwell?'

'No, I'm quite well, thank you, Talik dear. No, I've been awake a long time. I . . . heard strange noises—'

'Oh God,' said Hector McVay, 'this will be the ruin of my hotel's reputation. I'm sorry, madam, you probably heard the uproar when it was learned that Mr Edder's cello has gone missing.'

'Your cello is gone?' Angeliza said, holding out a hand to Talik. 'Oh, how dreadful.'

Oddly enough, to Mr Crowne, who had a very acute ear, it sounded as if it had been rehearsed.

He watched as the detectives recited their requirements – might they search the room, they were looking for at least one cello and possibly two. Senhora Kelly listened and nodded, casting little shivering glances over her shoulder at the window.

'Senhora Kelly, why don't you let me close the window?' McVay said, walking into her room.

'Oh . . . yes . . . Why don't you?' She watched the detectives opening doors, looking in trunks. She seemed perturbed, and yet there were very few places big enough to hold a cello and those were soon examined.

'Sorry to have troubled you, madam,' said the detectives, widthdrawing.

'Go to bed, Angeliza,' ordered Talik.

'Try to get some rest,' McVay said in a much kinder voice. 'I'll have some hot chocolate sent up.'

'Thank you, Mr McVay. You are . . . you are *so* kind.'

To the surprise of the crown prince, McVay blushed.

At about a quarter to five Fairmil announced that the cellos were not hidden in any part of the hotel that could be reached without taking up floorboards or pushing out wall panels. The place had once been three Georgian houses, knocked into one before Edinburgh awoke to its responsibility as curator of the New Town's architecture and slapped a preservation order on it. The early alterations had been skilfully done but of necessity there were nooks and crannies – visible and, perhaps, invisible.

But then, reasoned Fairmil, how could a burglar know there was some hidden cupboard large enough to take two cellos?

'Besides,' said Crowne, 'it seems clear the cellos were stolen from the green room of the concert hall.'

'Aye, but you have to stick to the routine. It's the time you don't do it that you come a cropper. But now I'm satisfied that the cellos aren't hidden here and I can move on to the hall.'

By now the press had got wind of it. The local give-away was first on the scene, followed by the *Scotsman* and then the Glasgow papers. The reporters from Glasgow thought the whole thing hilarious; they had been waiting for years for the Edinburgh Festival to get a custard pie in its face.

Eight cellos stolen! And one of them belonging to the great Talik Edder, who was getting more and more demoniac as the minutes went by and nothing useful was achieved. From Edder they got marvellous quotes: 'Morons . . . inefficient oafs . . . half-educated baboons . . .'

Then along came the stringers from the nationals, to whom the price of the missing Emilio was the star attraction. They badgered Edder with questions about insurance, compensation, the cost of a replacement. 'It is irreplaceable! I have lost the love of my life!' wailed Edder. The *Express* man at once went to the phone to ask for a woman reporter, to get all the pathos out of the situation.

The press corps piled into their transport when the police cars set off for the Usher Hall, bearing the two anxious cellists with the cellos that had been left in their cases, the crown prince, the chief inspector and his team. By a little speed-track driving on the empty roads, they managed to arrive at the hall first. The reporters from the Glasgow papers raised an ironic cheer as Fairmil led his men in.

'What's so funny?' Edder asked, perplexed.

'*Schadenfreude*,' said the prince.

'What?' asked Fairmil.

'Enjoyment of other people's troubles.'

'Oh, aye,' sighed Fairmil; 'trust a Glaswegian for that.'

The bass violists gave a shout of relief when they saw their big instruments lying on the raised dais in front of the organ. The timpanist mounted the stage to give a triumphant drum-roll. Here at least were a few happy musicians.

All the cellists who had performed at the hall had been asked to come and bring their instrument cases with whatever cello now reposed in it. Fairmil had his men take the cases one by one and lay them on the platform.

'Now, ladies and gentlemen,' he said, 'would you please go up and see if you recognise any of the cellos?'

The fifteen instrumentalists went up on the platform and each snapped open the case that belonged to him. Edder looked down in glum recognition at the George Duncan he had somehow inherited. Michiko, next to him, took out the Pressenda that had been left in place of her Vuillaume.

Then all at once there was the most extraordinary scene. Little cries of loving recognition broke out. Men and women began to cross and recross the stage as if they were dancing some sort of eightsome reel. Players embraced cellos.

'What are they *doing*?' roared Fairmil. 'Stand still, every-body! How can I check if you mill about—'

'Wait,' Crowne said, pulling him back as he was about to clamber on stage. 'Wait a minute, chief inspector.'

Ten minutes later all the cellists were standing more or less still, most of them beaming at each other and with a cello held close.

Michiko had her Vuillaume. Augustin had his Pressenda, the Mittenwald cello was in the arms of its owner. Only Talik Edder was still staring down at the changeling in his carrying-case.

If anything, the photographers from the Glasgow papers were even more delighted than before. The scene they had just witnessed was unlikely ever to be repeated but they had it on film – eight distinguished, if not famous, performers caught in the act of running about the stage in rapture, with the enraged features of Chief Inspector Fairmil in the background.

To crown it all, the most famous of them, Talik Edder, was left with a cello by a Glasgow instrument maker. It was perfect. One of them might even win the Press Photographer of the Year Award.

Chief Inspector Fairmil, on the other hand, was almost in despair. There might just possibly have been fingerprints on the cellos that would have helped find the culprit. But not now, not when eight of them had passed the instruments from one to the other. Some had even cuddled them to their bosoms, and one happy owner was at this moment engaged on polishing his darling with a silk handkerchief.

He couldn't even find out who had had which cello. The moment the first player spotted his own instrument, there had been a mêlée. The only ascertainable thing was that the Emilio had not come back.

After an hour of discussion about who had taken which cello – 'You picked up my Mayer'; 'No, that was Raoul, I picked up Claire's Mittenwald' – Fairmil gave it up.

The glowering eye of Emile Durachin was upon him: his musicians had been brought out on a wild-goose chase and given a quite unnecessary fright; how was his orchestra to play that evening if the members didn't get some sleep?

Fairmil gave them all permission to go, apologised to the manager of the hall, thanked him for his co-operation, and withdrew.

'He asks about how his orchestra is to play tonight,' groaned Edder, 'but how am *I* to play?'

'You've still got the Guarneri, Talik.'

'I am speaking of my spiritual condition,' he said in despair. 'I am broken. Broken!'

Crowne knew Edder of old. He would recover, especially as the moment drew near for him to play. But nevertheless it was important that he get some rest. He asked Fairmil to let them go back to the hotel and they were duly taken, the unassuming Victorian cello lying on the back seat of a police car as 'evidence'.

McVay had by now accepted that the Hill Hotel was in the middle of a scandal and he would have to make the best of it. He had food ready for all those who had been to the hall to witness the reunion of cellos and cellists, and had already heard from the Kamikura players that Michiko had retrieved her Vuillaume.

Experienced in the handling of musicians, he took over the care of Edder from the crown prince. He even had a doctor unobtrusively ready to prescribe a sedative if necessary – but one glance at the tall, angry musician was enough to warn him not to suggest it.

In the end it was Angeliza who persuaded Talik to go to bed. 'Dearest Talik,' she coaxed in her little-girl voice, 'you owe it to the rest of us to take some rest. We suffer with you, we cannot rest unless you do. And besides, you have a duty to your audience tonight.'

He frowned and hesitated. But clearly there was no news

for the moment. Staying awake would not produce any. He gave in.

Gregory Crowne went to bed too. First he drew the curtains, and as he stood at the window about to do so he was intrigued to see that Angeliza Kelly had opened hers again.

A fresh-air fiend? he wondered. But he was too tired to care.

He bathed, crawled between the sheets, and seemed to have been sleeping only a few minutes when his phone rang. A voice he would have loved to hear at any other time said: 'Greg, what on earth have you been up to?'

'Liz . . .' He dragged his mind away from the gigantic chess game he'd been playing in his dreams, with cellos and bass fiddles for pieces. 'I've only just gone to bed.'

'And I've only just got up. Do you realise you're a "funny" on morning TV?'

'*Santo cielo!* Not me personally?'

'No, eight cellos in a muddle and your friend Edder in a still picture looking tragic. Is it a publicity stunt?'

'It is not a publicity stunt,' he grunted, irritation thoroughly waking him. 'Talik's Strad is really missing.'

'Honestly?'

'It's been stolen.'

'Oh dear. I *am* sorry. How is Talik?'

'Suicidal.'

'But it all seemed so comic on TV—'

'BBC or ITV?'

'BBC, actually. And by the way, they've got you taped.'

'Taped? I never said a word!'

'No, I mean they know who you are. "His Serene Highness Prince Gregory of Hirtenstein, well known in musical circles for his work . . ." and so on and so on.'

'Oh, hell.' Sleep had gone for ever. All the trouble he took to sink into the background, and now he was found out, like some poor scene shifter discovered centre-stage when the curtain goes up unexpectedly.

'A shame, isn't it? The *Express* has gone to town on it. Apparently they got one of their women reporters to do a thing about the romantic Mr Edder, and she'd seen you around at some charity concert. If there's a pretty girl at the hotel, watch out – she's probably got a tape-recorder tucked in her bra.'

'Liz, you've spoiled my day. Not that it was great to begin with, what with poor Talik's Emilio. I wish you could have seen him last night, Liz – I mean this morning. Standing there quite desolate while everybody else got their own cello back.'

'Never mind Talik, think of yourself. You know how they always want to have you in the middle of some hot romance. There aren't any suitable royals up there in Edinburgh, are there?'

Liz was always acutely aware that his family didn't approve of her. Gregory was of course supposed to marry some suitable young woman from among the minor royalties of Europe, and had in fact been more or less matched off to Princess Almeda of Aquitaine. But she had run off with a Canadian millionaire.

Since then there had been a lull in his grandmother's matchmaking activities, Princess Almeda's disloyalty having shaken her. But Liz Blair knew very well that at any moment the old lady might start up again and, although Greg wasn't going to marry just to please ex-Queen Nicoletta, life would be made difficult for him.

Liz herself had no intention of marrying him. She didn't fancy the idea of being an ex-crown princess or a crown-princess-in-waiting. What worried her was that someone else might snare him.

Sensing her anxiety, he said, 'I really think you ought to come to Edinburgh to give me moral support.'

'I can't, darling. I really am too busy.'

'Wouldn't you like the gossip columnists to link your name with mine?'

'We-ell . . . it might be good for business.'

'Ouch. That's me put in my place. You really won't come?'

'*Can't* come.'

'I'll just have to console myself with the reporter with a tape-recorder in her bosom. Now go away and let me get back to sleep.'

'But it's eight o'clock, Greg.'

'Damn it, I went to bed at six! I've been up all night, running after the Emilio.'

'You lead the wrong kind of life,' she told him. 'You should settle down with some good woman.'

'Good-*night*,' he said, and put the receiver down.

He had a premonition that the phone would go on ringing now that his identity had been discovered. For some reason that he could never quite appreciate, newspaper gossip columns were fascinated by the lifestyle of dethroned royals.

He himself was a disappointment to them – he had no yacht, didn't play roulette or go skiing, at least not at St Moritz or Klosters. All the same, they liked to include his name when they could, with a phrase of description: 'tall, rangy, music-loving Prince Gregory' or 'the handsome crown prince of Hirtenstein, an unofficial but popular ambassador for his country'.

Hector McVay, with the intuition that made him good at his job, had told the switchboard girl not to put through any newspapermen, but the moment came when one of them was wily enough to outwit her. Crowne assured the caller that the taking of the Emilio was not a publicity manoeuvre, that he had no idea who had taken the cello, and that he was not in love with Michiko Toshio. When he had got rid of him he decided he might as well go down to breakfast and meet the rest of the world.

A gang of journalists was waiting to pounce. He saw them watching the lift as he came down the staircase; he turned and went back again. By dint of going down the back stairs he made his way unmolested to the dining-room.

Eight

T he press he could avoid, but not the police. Chief Inspector Fairmil came back to the hotel shortly after nine and once again there was a search. From the detective's point of view the situation was changed. He was no longer looking for a busload of cellos but for one, a valuable antique, capable of being taken away in the boot of a car.

Police were everywhere – asking to have the keys of every car in the car park, crawling in the space under the roof, creeping about in the bushes in the crescent's central garden. By mid-morning they had still found nothing.

The owner of the lost Emilio stayed in his room, watching the activity from his window. 'I am praying,' he told Gregory, 'praying that they do not put their great feet through my cello in their search.'

'Why skulk up here watching them and worrying? Come downstairs.'

'And be mobbed by those wolves from the press?'

'Well,' said Crowne, clearing his throat, 'since the Emilio *has* been stolen you might as well get something out of it, even if it's only publicity.'

Edder lifted his head like an old warhorse scenting battle. But he felt it would be beneath his dignity to go downstairs. Instead, with the agreement of Chief Inspector Fairmil, the press were invited up to his bedroom. Crowne, who understood what pressmen were like, ordered liquid refreshments. Hector McVay brought them himself, and stayed to monitor the interview. He wanted to make sure that his hotel got favourable mention.

90

The reporters were primarily interested in the money side. How could a cello be worth so much? Once they had it explained to them that it was a masterpiece by a master craftsman whose work had never been equalled, they turned to the personal side. Edder had said last night that he felt as if he had lost a lover. Was he wedded to his art? Was there no woman in his life?

'There is always a woman in my life,' Talik replied with a tug at the Zapata moustache. 'But it is not always the same woman.'

'Is there someone special at the moment?'

He considered the question. 'Well,' he said, 'I am almost tempted . . . But you know, my friends, there is always some flaw that spoils a love affair. It is wrong of me, but I expect perfection in a woman, just as I expect it in a cello.'

'Male chauvinist pig,' wrote the woman from the *Express*, while smiling sweetly at him.

'The Frank Sinatra of the classical world,' whispered one of the men to his neighbour, a pop fan.

'What kind of flaws put you off, Mr Edder? Bitten finger-nails? Snoring in bed?'

'Muscular women are tiresome,' said Talik. 'The kind who do boring exercises in the morning when you want to admire them in their flimsy négligee.'

'Oh, do go on, Mr Edder.'

'And women who are devoted to pets. I don't wish to be in competition with a cat or a dog.'

The pencils scribbled, the tape-recorders whirred. They were still putting silly questions when Crowne decided that enough was enough and herded them out.

As he returned McVay was pottering about collecting glasses. 'They're not very civilised,' he mourned, indicating the cigarette ends dropped on the carpet, the rings on his impeccably polished furniture.

'But your hotel will be named. Some of them took your publicity brochure.'

'What was that about women who are devoted to pets, Mr Edder?'

'Mm? Oh, Angeliza, you know—'

'Senhora Kelly?' said McVay, stiffening.

'She stops to say baby-talk to every dog being walked in the gardens. She pets every cat on a doorstep. Boring.'

'Oh, I see . . .'

'In Venice, you know—'

'Venice?'

'She followed me about in Venice, in the spring. Poor little darling – so lovesick . . . One day I shall give in. I nearly did, in Venice, after my big row with Gleghorn. Angeliza was so sweet, so unmuscular. It almost happened! But I couldn't stand the cat.'

'What cat?' said the prince.

'Oh, some cat she adopted. You know, Italy is full of stray cats.'

'Is that a fact?' murmured McVay without interest, picking up a tray of glasses and heading for the door.

'You were in fine fettle, Talik,' Crowne acknowledged.

'Fettle? What is fettle? Good or bad?'

'Good. You'll be in all the gossip columns tomorrow.'

'Before that, I must ring Bornhem in Vienna.' Bornhem was his business manager, a little bird-like creature of whom the tall, vigorous Finn was in mortal fear.

'Shall I have the call put through for you, Mr Edder?' McVay suggested, hovering in the doorway.

'Oh, for heaven's sake let's get out of this room and let it recover from the onslaught of the press-men,' the prince urged. 'Come on, Talik; you can't sulk in your tent for ever. Let's go out and get some fresh air.'

'But we shall be caught again by the reporters.'

'Not if we go out the back way, through the area.'

'This way, gentlemen.'

Led by the manager, they went down the back stairs and out of the tradesmen's entrance into the mews, which had once housed the carriages of the crescent's inhabitants. The two men set off at a fast, long-legged stride, Edder hiding behind sunglasses that were quite noticeable in the quiet gleam of an Edinburgh September.

They headed away from the town centre, where they might encounter Festival visitors who could recognise Edder. They went instead to a strange, quiet valley that Crowne had found on previous visits, a place called the Dean Village although it was close to the very heart of the city.

An hour wandering along the banks of the stream called the Water of Leith was pleasant, but enough. Edder began to feel the need to put in some practice. It had been part of his life for so long: four hours every day. Besides, when he got back to the hotel there might be news of the Emilio.

As they came into the foyer it was clear something had happened. The reporters were on the alert again. They descended on Edder. 'Mr Edder, what do you think? Are you going to go? Is it a hoax? Who do you think is behind it, Mr Edder?'

Talik fended them off, staring over their heads at Chief Inspector Fairmil. 'What are they talking about?' he shouted.

'Clear the way, clear the way there,' intoned the uniformed policemen. They moved forward like a blue battering-ram, to make a path for Edder to come in.

Fairmil whisked him into the writing-room, closing the door on the importunate reporters. He reopened it at Edder's request, to summon Gregory Crowne to join them.

'There's been a message for you,' he said to Edder.

'For me? Then how is it that everyone seems to know it except me?'

'We couldn't find you! Where the hell have you been?'

'Out for a walk, chief inspector,' soothed the crown prince. 'What's the message?'

'It was telephoned to all the papers, so of course all the reporters knew of it before we did. It's about the Emilio.'

93

'My angel is coming back to me!'

'We hope so, sir. The message goes . . .' He read from a piece of paper: '"If Mr Talik Edder will be at the speakers' ground by the National Gallery when the gun goes off, he will get his Stradivarius back."'

There was a shocked silence. 'I am being threatened with guns?' Edder said after a moment.

'Threatened? How d'you make that out?' said Fairmil, taken aback.

'No, Talik, it's the one o'clock gun. It's fired from the Half-Moon Battery on the Castle – Edinburgh people set their watches by it.' Crowne thought it an endearing custom, typically British – military hardware used for purely ceremonial purposes.

'Good,' Talik said with relief. 'I would have braved guns for my Emilio, but of course I would rather not. Where is this ground I must go to?'

'It's a bit like Speaker's Corner in London, if you've ever been there, sir?'

Talik shook his head.

'Well, it's a spot on the side of Princes Street in front of the National Gallery where anybody with a cause can spout about it. Mostly it's either Communists or cranks.'

'That's it!' cried Crowne. 'The Emilio was taken by someone who wanted to draw attention to a cause!'

Fairmil looked cautious. 'It may be just a hoax.'

'Do you think it is?'

'I've no way of knowing. Shall you go, Mr Edder?'

'To the speakers' arena? For my Emilio I would go to the arena of Rome, facing wild bears.'

'The caller has contacted all the national dailies, the TV networks and the radio stations. So whatever he's up to, he understands the media. Not like the others.'

'What others?'

'Och, we've been inundated with crank phone calls ever since this story broke – a lot of 'em from people who say

94

it's sinful that a fiddle should sell for so much money when there are people in want all over the world. The usual thing,' grunted Fairmil.

'Shall I go, Gregory?'

'I thought you just said you would?'

'But shall I look without dignity if it is a hoax?'

Crowne raised a warning finger. 'Was anything said about what would happen if Talik doesn't go? Any threat to the cello?'

'Dear heaven!' breathed Edder. 'I will go – I will go at once, it is nearly the time. Nothing must happen to my Emilio.'

'There's no guarantee one way or the other, sir,' warned Fairmil.

'I will go. How far to this place?'

'Two minutes in the car, sir.'

'We have time for a brandy,' said Talik. 'I am not afraid, you understand. But I should like a brandy to settle the stomach.'

Once again McVay officiated, and when he returned with the drink some of Talik's colleagues from the hotel came with him.

'Are you going, Talik?' asked Anne Gleghorn, with a sharp glance at his anxious face.

'It's a hoax,' Takamasa Shige declared in a very positive voice. 'Someone's cashing in on the publicity.'

'Talik's doing all right with publicity,' Anne said. She was frowning. 'Maybe he set this up himself.'

'That is cruel,' sighed the cellist. 'Just because we are no longer lovers, there's no need for us to be enemies, Anne.'

Michiko Toshio was clasping and unclasping her hands. 'I can see you're suffering, Talik,' she said in a breathless rush of words. 'It's strange to see you suffering – I always thought you were so strong.'

'The strong suffer,' intoned Edder, enjoying himself despite his anxiety. 'The strong suffer more than the weak because their soul can bear it longer.'

Michiko began to cry.

'Oh, dry up, Michiko,' Anne said in undisguised anger. 'He's nothing but a great big fraud – he doesn't *deserve* to get his cello back.'

Michiko looked shocked.

'Ladies, gentlemen,' Fairmil interposed, 'I must ask you not to upset Mr Edder. There's no way of knowing what's waiting for him on this jaunt.'

'If you are suggesting he is in danger, you are on the wrong track,' said Shige. 'It is a hoax.'

'What makes you so sure?' Crowne asked him as they made their way out to the crescent amid a mob of following reporters.

Shige grimaced. 'I have been in business thirty years. I can tell a trick when I meet one.'

Crowne thought his attitude strange. But then he thought they were all behaving strangely. Michiko ought by now to be a lot happier because she'd got her own cello back, but she seemed in a muddled emotional state. Anne Gleghorn's manner was scornful, totally without sympathy, yet envious.

Angeliza Kelly's attitude was strangest of all, in the prince's opinion. She'd been nowhere near Edder since the theft, except for that brief encounter in her draughty bedroom in the early hours of the morning. Yet now, if any time, was the opportunity to be useful to the great performer – to give him sympathy and devotion when he might actually need it.

The journey took longer than the two minutes promised by Fairmil. Traffic is as bad at either end of Princes Street as in any other modern city. TV cameras were already set up at the flat area in front of the National Gallery of Scotland, directors were examining angles to see if they could get the Castle or the Scott Monument in the background, reporters had already taken up their posts, and others came hurrying up as the police escorted Talik Edder into position.

Talik's friends attached themselves to the crowd. Flash bulbs popped. TV lights came on.

'I'm going to get angry if nothing happens,' Edder growled to the prince.

'If you do, please don't swear in English or they'll have to cut it out of the recording,' he replied.

The minutes ticked past. Traffic rushed by in Princes Street. Buses manoeuvred round the difficult corner and trundled up the Mound to the dreaming spires of the City Chambers. The Castle gleamed on its green hill beyond the Gardens.

A puff of smoke blossomed from the battlement. A second later came the dull boom of the gun. A hush fell on the little crowd by the gallery. Everyone looked at everyone else.

Nothing happened.

'A hoax,' groaned Edder.

Then a tall figure stepped forward. 'Since you all happen to be here,' said David Duntyre, 'I should like to say a few words about the disgraceful wastage of Scotland's resources by the governments who have ruled in Westminster since oil was—'

'Shut up!' called a voice. 'Where's the cello?'

'Ladies and gentlemen,' went on Duntyre, louder, 'Mr Edder has come here in hopes of seeing his Stradivarius. I have come here to demand that the Scottish Parliament ask for reparations. Quid pro quo—'

'Just a minute, sir,' Chief Inspector Fairmil intervened, walking close up to Duntyre. 'Am I to understand you are asking to address this crowd on the subject of politics in return for Mr Edder's cello?'

'I didn't say that, Mr Fairmil,' Duntyre replied. 'And I'd think shame to it if the only way to get people to listen to the views of the Scottish Progressive Party was to hold a masterpiece up to ransom.'

'You deny you have Mr Edder's cello?'

'Look at me,' said Duntyre, holding his arms away from his tweed jacket. 'Do I look as if I had a cello concealed about my person?'

A laugh went up. Edder shouted, 'This is not funny!'

Duntyre nodded with emphatic agreement. 'You're right, it isn't funny. My country has been bled of the resources that should have flowed into it from Scottish oil. The landscape was ruined. People were manipulated from Westminster and still are despite so-called "devolution". Coalmines are closed, shipyards sold off, fisheries left dying due to EEC regulations, farms sold to absentee landlords—'

'Mr Duntyre, I must ask you to accompany me to the police station,' Chief Inspector Fairmil interrupted.

'On what charge?'

'I'm not charging you. I'd like you to come and discuss the missing Stradivarius cello.'

'I will if you insist, chief inspector. But I'd rather stop here and discuss politics, having at last managed to get an audience of ordinary people to listen to me.'

'Wait, chief inspector,' Edder cried. He seized Duntyre by the sleeve. 'Have you got my Emilio? If you have, I bring no charge – only give her back!'

'I haven't got the Emilio,' David Duntyre said, almost gently. 'I never had. On my word of honour, I never touched your Emilio.'

'Then you got me here under false pretence? You send a hoax message?' He threw himself on Duntyre, who staggered and fell. In a moment they were scrabbling on the ground, Edder on top, aiming punches at Duntyre, who defended himself by folding his arms over his face but made no attempt to retaliate.

'Talik!' cried Crowne. 'Don't damage your hands!'

At the same time, the police dragged the cellist off. The TV cameras were filming it all. Duntyre arose, relatively unaffected, to grin in their direction. 'Temper, temper,' he said with great good cheer.

'My God, if I get at you I'll strangle you—'

'Now, now, sir,' appealed Fairmil, 'mind what you're saying. Mr Duntyre, I must repeat my invitation to you to come to the police station and help with our enquiries.'

'I'm afraid I must decline. I have no information to offer.'

'You sent out those messages inviting the press to the speakers' ground.'

'Who says I did?'

'I could charge you with causing a breach of the peace.'

'I didn't cause it, *he* did. I was exercising my right as a citizen to address—'

Seeing he was not going to cow the unquenchable Duntyre, Fairmil decided discretion was the better part of television. 'I must ask you all to disperse,' he said to the crowd, both spectators and press. 'The show's over.'

'Not quite,' protested Duntyre. 'I must use my right to speak here as dozens do every week. Ladies and gentlemen, I appeal to you on behalf of the Scottish Progressive Party to write to your MP demanding—'

But the TV cameras had been turned off, the crowd was melting away.

Crowne had been looking about him. The reactions of those who knew Duntyre were interesting. Michiko Toshio was looking at him with tearful affection. Takamasa Shige seemed baffled by the whole episode. Gleghorn was grinning almost in triumph at Edder's disappointment. The three other members of the Kamikura Quartet had joined Michiko and were arguing among themselves, Henry Holt trying to explain the politics involved to Shemnitzi.

From much further off, plump little Angeliza Kelly was gazing at Edder with compassion, as if she understood his suffering.

It had been a truly terrible humiliation for Edder to come here and be made a fool of in public, and in fact Angeliza knew exactly what he was going through. In her own land she had suffered something very similar.

She was the widow of a rich landowner, whose father had come from Ireland to seek his fortune. Soon after her husband's death there had been a rumour that she, with her tender heart, would do something for the landless peasants who clamoured for the means to raise food for their families. The rumour was false, raised perhaps by other landowners who wanted to cause exactly what happened.

She was cornered by a group of protesters in the fashionable shopping area of Rio. Her arms had been full of packages in pretty paper. These had been taken from her and torn open, the contents strewn about. Her fur wrap had been seized and draped over a beggar-woman. Her gold chain and crucifix were snatched from around her throat. In the end, with her clothes torn and her hair pulled about her ears, she was rescued by the police. 'Political undesirables,' they told her. 'You ought not to go unaccompanied.'

Frightened, she sold her property to the neighbouring landowners and left her homeland. Ever since, she had been nervy, particularly where anything to do with politics was concerned.

And now here was her beloved, used as a political puppet by that great mad Scotsman whom Michiko seemed to admire so much. Perhaps, Angeliza was thinking, perhaps even Michiko was not to be trusted, even though she played the cello well.

Duntyre gave up his speech when he saw his audience vanishing into the shops across Princes Street. Edder was conducted back to the police car with Crowne at his elbow. His broad shoulders were drooping.

The press corps stuck with them. They swept out of Princes Street and down Shandwick Place in a body. A turn to the right brought them into the splendid squares and terraces of the New Town, past the Georgian House Museum. Within minutes they were entering Hill Crescent.

There were parking meters in the crescent, but the police

had seen to it that a space was kept for official cars. A uniformed man on guard at the porch stepped forward as they came up the shallow steps to the foyer.

'Excuse me, sir, this was left by hand a few minutes ago for Mr Edder.'

Chief Inspector Fairmil's colour rose. 'By whom? Where is he?'

'I'm sorry, sir, it was given to the receptionist and the messenger was gone before she caught on. All she can say is, it was a wee lad.'

'Did you see him?'

'No, sir.'

'What is it?' cried Edder. 'Let me see – what has been left for me?'

'Hold on!' Fairmil said, holding the envelope out of the cellist's reach. 'There may be fingerprints.'

He went up to the reception desk, carefully holding the envelope by the corner. Everybody surged around him. He told his men to keep the reporters back then laid the envelope on the counter. With a delicacy of touch Crowne wouldn't have suspected of so burly a man, he took the contents out of the unsealed envelope.

It was a greeting card with a picture of Edinburgh Castle on its front. With a glance of annoyance at the others, Fairmil flipped it open. Inside were the usual printed words: *Greetings from* . . .

Below that, stuck on with scotch tape, was a piece of poetry, cut from a miniature book to judge by the typeface. The lines were:

> I'll aye ca' in by yon town,
> And by yon garden green again . . .

Bewilderment.

'What does it mean?' Edder wailed.

'It's a piece from a song by Rabbie Burns,' said the Chief

inspector. 'It . . . well, it just goes on about meeting his lady-love when he goes to the town.'

'In a garden green?' prompted. Crowne.

'"In yon garden green again" – the crescent garden?'

Like many of the streets and squares of north Edinburgh, Hill Crescent had a garden with railings around it, guarded by a gate to which only the residents had a key. It was a tranquil place – no flowers, only a half-moon-shaped lawn inside a gravel path edged with shrubs and trees where one could sit in the shade in the event of its ever becoming too hot in Edinburgh.

Fairmil rapped on the reception desk. McVay, who had been in attendance, jumped to attention.

'The key to the garden?'

'Of course.' He disappeared into the office, and emerged a moment later with a large key.

Fairmil hesitated, then he said, 'We may as well get it over with.'

He led the way out. The reporters, unsure what was happening, tailed along. A tide of questions lapped about him. He didn't reply.

They all crossed the roadway to the gate in the railings. Fairmil unlocked it, and went in with Edder at his heels and the crown prince at his elbow.

The reporters were still begging for information, the photographers holding their cameras aloft in hopes of getting a picture of whatever-it-was over the heads of the crowd.

Fairmil walked round the path. On the far side of the grounds a bench came into view.

On it stood a cello case with a tartan scarf tied round its waist.

Nine

From that moment on the police were on a losing side in the Cello Case, as the newspapers dubbed it that evening.

Euphoric at getting the Stradivarius back, Talik Edder announced that he forgave everybody involved in the hoax. He publicly shook hands with David Duntyre when he came back from the police station, whither he had been dragged after the tartan-clad cello was found.

He further invited Duntyre to have lunch with him. Hector McVay, delighted that the matter had been settled so amicably, had tables put together so that Edder, Duntyre, the prince, Anne Gleghorn, Michiko and two others of the Kamikura Quartet sat either side of a long row.

Takamasa Shige, who had been a witness to the morning's events, was urged by Edder to make up the fourth place on the side of the table opposite him. To the prince's surprise, he did so.

'Champagne!' cried Edder. 'We must have champagne in celebration!'

'Be reasonable, Talik, we've got a recital this afternoon,' said Henry Holt.

'Oh, true, and I must practise – God, I have not had the bow in my hands all day so far! Well, we shall have champagne at the midnight buffet! I insist! But now, you are all my guests. Waiter, what is the chef offering today?'

The waiter said that the chef had a special dish of pork noisettes in a cider and cream sauce.

'Not for me,' Anne interrupted. 'You know I'm careful about what I eat – good, simple food, no rich sauces.'

'The other special dish is poached salmon with hollandaise . . .'

'I'll have that,' said Shemnitzi.

'Are you into organic food?' asked Henry Holt of Anne.

'Sure am. You may not think it to look at me—' she tilted her head coquettishly – 'but I had all kinds of health problems as a child. It was only when I went to study with Maranaga that I learned it was the diet I'd been eating. He put me on wholefoods only—'

'Vegetarian?'

'Not at all. In fact, waiter, I'll have a small steak, rare, and a salad.'

The others gave their orders. Michiko said to Edder, 'I never saw you look so happy.'

'I never was so happy!' He spread his arms along behind his two neighbours at table – the prince and Anne. 'Having been parted from my darling for twelve hours, I realise how much she meant to me.' He looked across at Shige, and gave a gentle little shake of the head. 'I know, Mr Shige, that you have stayed on in Edinburgh hoping I would change my mind and sell the Emilio to you. But this episode has made me only more attached to her.'

Shige compressed his lips and said nothing.

'Did you ask Suso about taking the Guarneri instead?' Michiko said in a quiet voice. Over the past few days, Shige's attitude to her had changed from ferocious disapproval to distant politeness. It was the first time she had ever addressed him directly.

'We discussed it. She still wants the Emilio. But I suppose now . . .' He fell silent.

On the whole, despite the strangely mixed company, it was an enjoyable meal. David Duntyre would make sly remarks that almost admitted that he had arranged the disappearance of the Strad, yet when they tried to pin him down he eluded them.

Chief Inspector Fairmil heard this with gloom when the prince passed it onto him. 'So he flirts around with admitting it, and Mr Edder forgives him. But what's the Fiscal going to say?'

The Procurator Fiscal was thinking the matter over, he said. So far as Crowne could see, it was difficult to know what to charge Duntyre with, or even whether he could be charged.

His version of the affair was that he had gone to the speakers' ground along with everyone else to see what would happen. When there was a pause after the one o'clock gun it seemed to him, as he said, an excellent opportunity to get some publicity for the Scottish Progressive Party.

There had been a fracas. But Talik Edder had caused that. And the Procurator Fiscal was certainly not going to charge Talik Edder.

All Duntyre had done was make a few remarks to an open-air gathering. If the Strad was found in the case belonging to the 'cheapie cello', perched on a park bench and with a tartan scarf round its middle, what had that to do with him?

There had been no theft; the Emilio was back with its rightful owner. The most that could be charged was that, like a car, it had been taken away without its owner's consent. Anyway, the Strad had been taken from the hall, so how could David have got at it? The man on the door of the artistes' entrance would never have let him pass.

Chief Inspector Fairmil had been painstakingly checking the events of the previous evening. Duntyre had attended the concert as a member of the audience but had definitely not gone backstage. He had returned to the hotel with Shige and Angeliza.

As to the George Duncan cello, Fairmil had just learned that the owner of an antique shop in Stockbridge remembered selling the Duncan in a case on the previous Saturday.

'Why should he have remembered it?' Crowne enquired.

'Well, two things. First of all, he's not a seller of musical instruments, he's in the nostalgia game. He got the cello when he bought the contents of a house after the owner died – it was just part of the contents. So that cello was the only one he's ever handled. It was part of a window display showing a Victorian parlour – you know the kind of thing. The shop's called Yesteryear.'

'You said two things . . . ?'

'The other thing is, it was bought by an Englishman.'

'An Englishman. Is that a thing to note?'

'Well, Scots notice English accents. I'd take a bet they put the price up for an Englishman! The shopkeeper says he had a very English voice.'

'We-ell . . . He doesn't sound like a supporter of the Scottish Progressive Party, does he?'

'I'll ask him when I find him.'

'But if you find him, what charge could you bring? It isn't a crime to buy a cello.'

'Ach,' sighed Fairmil. 'It's downright damnable. I'll charge him with wasting police time if it's the only charge I can bring!'

Edder was on his way to practise in one of the basement rooms. 'I need to find out if my sweetheart has missed me,' he said for the benefit of the reporters who were still hanging around. What he really wanted was to find out if the Emilio had suffered some invisible damage from having been in strange hands overnight.

'Are you going to have a run-through later? Just to make sure everybody's settled down?' asked the prince.

'I think that would be best. Shall we say six o'clock at the hall?'

'I'll have to get in touch with the other cellists, but I'm sure it'll be OK. And of course Anne is here.'

'Have you noticed how that Japanese watches her? I think he fancies her, Gregory.'

'Fancies Anne? You're joking!'

'No, why shouldn't he? She's different from the Japanese women he's accustomed to – twice the size of little Michiko, bursting with life and self-importance.'

'What a pair they would make,' said the crown prince, half laughing at the idea. 'Both of them full of their own importance, both strong-willed and aggressive. It would be like something out of the *"Walküre"*!'

'However, I don't like it that he should be too friendly with Anne.'

'Don't be such a dog in the manager, Talik! It's over between you and Anne – let her have some fun with some-one else.'

'He's not a bad fellow, I suppose,' Edder said out of the mellowness induced by the recovery of the Emilio. 'He's asked to be allowed to give us a celebration tonight after the concert. You know I spoke of having champagne—'

'He's hoping to get you drunk so you'll sell him the cello.'

'I hope he doesn't raise it, Gregory. I'm beginning to think even the Guarneri should go to a performing artiste.'

'I agree. But you needn't tell him that tonight if he's going to pay for your champagne.'

'Oh, champagne, and a special buffet – having regard for Gleghorn's food fads, and so forth. I said to him, "Gleghorn may have these foolish ideas but *I* like large eatings." So he promises me fish in the Scandinavian style, which is very good, Gregory – it makes me sorry I can't help him over a cello for his silly daughter.'

Crowne betook himself to his room to telephone everyone involved in the proposed run-through at six o'clock. Michiko wasn't in her room but after a moment's thought he asked to be put through to David Duntyre.

'Forgive me for asking, but is Michiko with you?'

'Och, well now . . . How did you guess that, Mr Crowne?'

'I'm psychic.' He explained about the rehearsal at six.

'It's going to be a rush for me,' said Michiko. 'The

quartet's playing at the City Chambers. But the recital ends at five – I'll manage, Gregory.'

'Fine. I'm just going to get in touch with the other cellists and Anne.'

'Anne's gone out for a walk with Mr Shige.'

'Ah.'

'Yes, "ah". But she said they wouldn't be long. She said she needs a rest and then some vocal exercises after what we've been through since last night.'

'I'll try her again when I've rung round the others.'

He also had business calls to make to Geneva and Amsterdam. By then Anne Gleghorn had come back. She agreed to the run-through without demur.

That accomplished, Crowne went downstairs to seek out Senhora Kelly. She'd been frozen out at lunch. Sitting at the far side of the hotel's restaurant, she'd looked sad, neglected. He felt someone ought to show some kindness to her and proposed to ask her to have afternoon tea with him – in Scotland, a ceremonious affair with fresh-baked scones, home-made jam, shortbread, Dundee cake and all kinds of starchy goodies: just the kind of thing Angeliza would enjoy.

He found her in the lounge, in conversation with Hector McVay.

'They can say what they like about no proof that he took the Emilio,' he was saying in indignant tones, 'but it would be completely in character. The man's a philistine!'

'Not the kind to care about a sensitive artiste like Talik,' ventured Angeliza, pulling at her lace handkerchief. 'The hours of torment he endured while the cello was missing . . . !'

'I don't think you need worry about Talik's torment,' Crowne put in, trying to suppress his amusement. 'He's on top of the world at the moment.'

'Do you know Mr Duntyre well, Hector?' Angeliza asked McVay.

'He's stayed at the hotel one or twice before, when he's

had a play on. But let me tell you, it's the last time I'll accept a booking from him! I'd ask him to leave now, but Mr Edder wants the whole thing forgiven and forgotten.'

'So like him,' breathed Angeliza.

'I wish you'd speak to Miss Toshio,' the manager said unexpectedly, turning to Crowne. 'No good can come of the way she and that man are getting friendly.'

'Miss Toshio is a radical also, is she not?' Angeliza enquired, shivering a little. 'The two of them, revolutionaries?'

'Oh, not really, Angeliza,' McVay said in reassurance. 'It's different here – nobody shoots anybody over politics here, and Miss Toshio I'm sure is too devoted to her music.'

'But Hector, I heard she tried to kill Mr Shige—'

'No, no, it was a student caper, and you saw yourself at lunch, she sat at the same table; all that's been banished to the past. Don't worry about it, Angeliza.'

Seeing that she was in good hands, Crowne withdrew. Angeliza, Hector . . . first-name terms . . . Well, she needed someone to be kind to her if Talik was going to ignore her while he tried to resume his affair with Anne.

At the rehearsal, Crowne could have foretold that tonight's performance was going to be outstanding. A spirit of what the Americans call 'togetherness' had infused the players, brought on by the overnight episode they had all shared. The concert, already a sell-out because of earlier publicity about the buying of the Emilio, was now attracting tremendous attention. Television companies were vying with each other to film it for future transmission, and Crowne's contract with the record company now seemed to have been signed at much too low a figure.

While he changed for dinner he turned on the television set in his room. Scottish TV had a whale of a time with footage of the turmoil at the speakers' ground, but on the whole Talik looked not too foolish in the punch-up and came out well over the handshake with David Duntyre. 'All in all,'

109

the commentator remarked, 'this has been a programme of events that the Festival organisers didn't intend but which has given a good deal of entertainment to the public. And, what's more important in Scottish eyes' – roguishly – 'it was *free!*'

As for himself, Crowne was only mentioned in passing: 'The agent responsible for staging the performances of the works of Villa-Lobos is a friend of Mr Edder, Gregory Crowne, otherwise known as His Serene Highness Prince Gregory of Hirtenstein.'

A still photograph of him accompanied the voice-over – he was standing back from the crowd at the crescent gardens, staring towards Takamasa Shige, who for his part was scowling like a Japanese warrior mask.

It was only natural that everyone at the Hill Hotel who owned or could beg a ticket should be at the concert. The Orchestre Savoie received perhaps less attention than it deserved during Debussy's 'La Mer', but Durachin had no reason to be displeased with its performance. After the interval came the item everyone was waiting for, the Bachiana Brasileira No. 5 with eight cellos and soprano.

A superb rendering. The sound-man from the record company congratulated himself on getting it on tape. In days to come it would a collector's piece for the archives. The audience clapped and cheered and demanded encores, Anne Gleghorn obliged with unaccompanied folksongs from the Appalachian Mountains, and then came what the audience really wanted: Talik Edder alone with the Emilio.

Crowne reflected that it was the first concert he'd ever attended where the audience seemed as aware of the instrument as they were of the player. And Edder didn't disappoint them. He played solo arrangements: Bach to show off his nimbleness of finger, Saint-Saëns to allow the instrument to sing, Poulenc to let it laugh, Elgar to reveal its soul.

At last the crowd was persuaded to let him go. He bowed

and blew kisses, bowed again, and walked off stage. It had
been a triumph.

The gathering in the writing-room that night was larger
than usual, but McVay had expected that. He had set aside a
special corner for Edder and his friends, where the champagne
was already waiting in the ice buckets and the special buffet
was laid out. Looking it over, Crowne felt the food wasn't
exactly what he would have ordered – a vast display of
Japanese and Scandinavian dishes featuring a great deal of
raw fish – but Edder was delighted.

The spirit of celebration overflowed from the concert to
the party. Quite possibly everyone ate and drank too much,
but it seemed allowable: none of the musicians had heavy
schedules the next day.

Michiko didn't drink much, though she exchanged mock-
toasts with Duntyre. He let himself become more than a little
merry, but with good reason – he had scored a bull's-eye
for publicity that day. 'I think McVay should have supplied
haggis!' he declared. 'This has been a great day for the
Scottish Progressive Party!' Lacking haggis, he tucked in
to the national dishes, though he said he preferred herring
cooked in oatmeal rather than raw.

Shige explained the Japanese dishes to those who found
them strange. 'They're very simple, plain dishes,' he said.
'I thought Anne would appreciate them after what she said
at lunch.'

'Ah, dearest Anne,' cried Talik, raising his glass in toast
to her. 'How well you sang tonight!'

To her own surprise, Anne blushed. 'Do you really think
so, Talik?'

'You were superb. Last night, no – you were edgy last
night. But tonight the voice was all tropical sunlight and blue
skies. I drink to Anne, my friends!'

He went on being nice to her all through the party. Poor
Angeliza Kelly grew more and more depressed. She found
comfort, as many plump people do, in eating. 'Are you sure

you like raw fish?' Crowne whispered to her. 'There are some Swedish meatballs across the table – shall I fetch you some?'

'Fish is very good for you,' Talik said. 'Full of vitamins and minerals – isn't that so, Shige? Your country and mine – we understand how to use fish.'

'That's so. Try the sashimi, Anne – you just pick it up with your fingers.'

By and by Crowne noticed Angeliza popping food into her handbag. A moment later she crept away, having lost hope of getting a kind word from her hero. Presumably she was going to her room to have a little midnight feast.

Michiko and David Duntyre were openly holding hands. Henry Holt had fallen asleep with a piece of *Othellokage* spilling down his shirt-front. Anne, more than a little tiddly, was singing 'The Man That Got Away' in a good imitation of Judy Garland.

As Gregory Crowne went up to bed, he had no idea he had just heard Anne Gleghorn's farewell performance.

Ten

The bedside phone rang. Gregory Crowne didn't wake. The phone rang again, and again.

At last the sleeper roused. He stretched out a hand from under the sheets and with difficulty picked up the instrument.

'Your morning call!' the switchboard girl chirped with terrible brightness. 'Seven thirty, Mr Crowne.'

His tongue refused to make words. He grunted. Somehow he managed to get the receiver back on the handset on the bedside table. He collapsed back against his pillow, made a grumbling noise, and went back to sleep.

Forty-five minutes later he came back to consciousness. After some seconds of staring at the ceiling he thought to himself: The phone rang. He heaved up on an elbow, picked it up. Nothing. He waited, perplexed. The click of the connection struck him as odd.

'Can I help you?' the telephonist enquired.

'Did . . . you . . . just . . . ring?'

'Ring? No, Mr Crowne. You rang me.'

'To wake me?' he persisted.

'Oh. That was three-quarters of an hour ago, sir.'

'What?' He struggled up to a sitting posture. 'What time is it?' he asked, getting the words out against a strange resistance in his mouth.

'Eight fifteen, Mr Crowne.'

'My God. I must have gone back to sleep again.'

That was most unlike him. He hated getting up in the morning so he did it with heroic efficiency every day.

113

'Are you all right, sir?' asked the girl.

'Oh . . . I think so . . . Thank you.' He knew she was supposing he had a king-size hangover.

Well, a *prince*-size hangover. If he hadn't felt too terrible for amusement, he might have had a slight smile at that.

'Would you ask . . . the floor waiter . . . to bring a pot of . . . coffee?'

'Right away, sir.' The bright Scottish voice ceased. He hooked the instrument in place, pushed back the bedclothes and swung his legs out of bed.

Or rather, he tried to swing his legs out of bed. There seemed to be a braking device on his movements. His legs eventually came over the edge and his feet touched the floor, but the floor seemed made of marshmallow. There was no sense of hardness under the dark brown carpet.

Nevertheless he pushed his feet into the marshmallow and stood up. That worked quite well – no sense of giddiness, no throbbing headache. He picked up his Derek Rose dressing-gown from the end of the bed. Strange, he couldn't feel its nubbly cloth under his fingers. He pulled it on, missing the sleeve-hole on the second side through several attempts.

He walked to the dressing-table and stared at himself in the mirror. As far as he could tell, he looked much as usual. He sat down on the stool, leaned his elbow on the table. Strange, the table felt like marshmallow too.

He was still sitting there when the coffee arrived. The waiter, an old man who had seen many visitors suffering from an excess of Festival hospitality, set the tray in front of him. 'Shall I pour, sir?'

'Please.'

When he picked up the cup, it dipped away from him. Hot coffee poured on to his robe.

'Look out, sir, you'll burn yourself.'

But he couldn't feel the hot coffee soaking through on to his thigh.

'Shall I get you an Alka Seltzer, Mr Crowne?'

114

'Would you? Thank you.'

After Jock had gone he picked up the coffee pot with two hands on the handle, refilled the cup, set down the pot, and with infinite care got the drink to his lips. He sipped. He couldn't feel the coffee going past his lips but when it reached his tongue he could taste it, strong and hot and reviving.

'This is a damned funny hangover,' he said to himself, prodding his lips. There was the same sensation as when the dentist has filled your gums with Novocaine.

Why did he have it? As he remembered it, he had drunk only two glasses of Mumm.

His mind seemed to be working fairly clearly, he noted. He might feel like a physical zombie, but he could still think.

And what he was thinking was that it might be some form of exhaustion. He had been working very hard, getting his concert artistes to the Festival and looking after them. Against the odds, too, what with the temperament of Anne Gleghorn and the theft of the Emilio.

Jock came back with the Alka Seltzer. He drank it. Once again, no sensation of its frothing in his mouth.

'Better, sir?' Jock enquired with sympathy.

'I think I'll live.'

'Shall I run a bath for you, eh? Soak it out of you.'

'No, thanks, I'll shower in a minute.'

By dint of turning the shower from hot to cold and back again half a dozen times, he restored the sense of feeling to his body. It seemed as if the nerve ends at his skin needed to be schooled back into obedience.

By now he ought to be downstairs having breakfast, checking on his musicians. He had to get the Kamikura to Leith Town Hall this morning for a run-through of the Schubert at about eleven thirty, so they could have a rest and a bite to eat before the recital at three. At various points between those times he had to ring Geneva and London, get the tank of his Hertz car refilled, and look at the bank foyer where Gleghorn was going to sing Haydn this evening.

When he went downstairs at nine o'clock he took the lift. Though he felt almost normal again, the idea of walking down the staircase was unattractive – suppose he missed his footing and went toppling into the hotel lobby? Any reporters still hanging about in hopes of more drama over the Emilio would simply love that.

The lobby was quite busy. Tourists who had already breakfasted were consulting brochures about visiting a factory where Edinburgh Crystal was made, a pretty young florist was arranging flowers on the Georgian side table, two reporters were chatting to Joseph Klein of the Kamikura. Crowne collected his morning mail – a letter from Liz, bless her, a folder with the programme for the Montreux Festival, and an ominous air letter from New York which probably meant one of his bookings had gone wrong.

The elegant dining-room was almost empty. Crowne sat down. Without bidding, a waitress hurried up with those excellent rolls called baps, butter and marmalade. Another pot of coffee arrived with the food.

He waved to the other occupants. Two of the quartet players were there but not Michiko. Talik Edder was probably having breakfast in his room as he usually did, but it was odd not to see Anne Gleghorn. She liked to go out in Nike jogging shoes and a tracksuit at an early hour, then come back to eat muesli and drink grapefruit juice in an ostentatious way – look at me, how diet-conscious I am.

But outside it wasn't a very encouraging morning. The Edinburgh sky was misty with coming rain and the trees drooped a little in the unexpected warmth of a muggy September day.

Gleghorn ought to be cosseting her throat, not jogging round the squares and crescents in that. But you never could tell with her – sometimes she was playing one part, sometimes another.

The two string players were deep in an argument. Those who didn't know them would probably imagine they were discussing the harmonies of the 'Death and the Maiden', or the probable conclusion Schubert had in mind for the C minor. But Crowne guessed they were probably talking about the proposed visit of the Flying Scotsman to Waverley Station.

Senhora Kelly wasn't here either. Every morning she came downstairs to eat breakfast early and keep watch for Talik Edder going by. Not this morning, however – at least not so far. Perhaps she too was suffering some kind of hangover?

Shrugging to himself, Crowne unfolded his copy of the *Scotsman* and bent his light grey eyes upon the latest disasters in the alarming world beyond the civilised round of the Festival. China was once more worrying that it had gone too far with its move towards capitalistic Marxism; a group of terrorists had hijacked a millionaire's yacht in Indonesia, but no one was aboard her; the euro was in trouble again.

As he always did, he turned the page quickly to the foreign news to see if Hirtenstein was mentioned but, as usual, not a word. He then turned to the arts page. Last night's concert got a justified eulogy. 'Tone of voluptuous warmth . . . velvety passages . . . Miss Gleghorn's easy artistry . . . a triumph . . .'

'That's the stuff,' muttered Crowne to himself, and put marmalade on his bap.

It was just as he was conveying a tricky segment to his mouth that the door of the dining-room was thrust open and Angeliza Kelly came rushing in. She was dressed, but in a way that suggested she'd stopped halfway – her blouse was only partly buttoned and she had no shoes. From her lips emerged a spate of Portuguese, very loud and fast and broken by distress.

'Ajuda! Ajuda! Chame un medico! Esta gravemente doente!'

Everybody looked up. Crowne dropped his piece of bap on his tie. Brushing at it with his napkin, he rose to meet her.

'Who is ill, *senhora*?' he asked.

She was too upset to heed him, casting wild glances about

117

the dining-room. '*O gerente!*' she gasped. '*Onde e o gerente? Onde e Hector?*'

Crowne gathered her into the shelter of his arm, where she wept on in voluble Portuguese that she had tried to call the hotel manager on the phone but the stupid, stupid girl didn't understand and she *must* speak to Hector!

No doubt the lass on the switchboard had been baffled by this flood of foreign sobbing. Crowne murmured soothingly, '*Desculpe, Angeliza, faca favor de falar mais devagar . . .*' but at that moment Hector came hurrying in.

'I heard you were—' He took the weeping woman from the prince's shoulder and turned her towards him. 'Angeliza, Angeliza, what's the matter?'

'Cha-cha!' she sobbed. 'Oh, Cha-cha!'

Over her head Hector caught Crowne's eye, with a glint that said, 'Too much champagne last night, eh?' To Angeliza he said gently, 'Come with me, my dear. You're ill. Come with me.' If it was the champagne, it had affected her differently. She'd gone emotional whereas Crowne had gone numb.

He sat down again, and had picked up his coffee cup when her words came back to him. She'd been sobbing, 'Fetch a doctor, he's terribly ill.'

Who was ill? Who else but her adored Talik?

Abandoning his breakfast, Crowne went out to the lobby. He picked up a house phone, dialled Talik's room number. The ringing seemed to go on for ages. At last the deep northern voice said, rather muffled: 'Room one-fifteen.'

'Talik? Are you all right?'

'Gregory . . . How strange you should ask me . . . This morning, not so right. I should not mix champagne and whisky, no . . . Oh . . .' The negative ran on into a groan of discomfort.

'What are your symptoms, Talik?' the prince asked with concern.

'Symptoms? Ah – what am I suffering, you mean? Pins

118

and noodles of the arms and legs. And I cannot feel in my mouth.'

'I'm coming up,' said Crowne, and banged the phone down.

When the cellist opened the door to him he noticed he had trouble turning the knob. 'How long have you been awake, Talik?' he demanded.

'Not so long. I slept too well.'

'So did I. I felt very drowsy, couldn't wake up. But once I was up and about the numbness began to wear off.'

'You have had it too?' said Talik. He made a pass at his droopy moustache, as if to tug it in thought, but missed it. 'I feel strange,' he said.

'It must be some illness that's going round. Senhora Kelly was just in the dining-room crying about you being ill.'

'What is it you say? How could she know? Don't tell me she looks through the keyhole!'

Crowne laughed. 'I don't know; I took it for granted she meant you.'

Talik was opening and closing his left hand, then ran his fingers down an imaginary fingerboard. 'I could not play even the Emilio at the moment,' he said in alarm. 'My fingers feel like sausages!'

'But it passes off, Talik, if it's the same as I had. An hour or so ago, I couldn't hold a coffee cup. But now I'm back to normal.'

'Normal for you. But you don't have to play Bachiana Number 1 tonight.'

'Have you had breakfast?'

'No, I was about to order when you rang.' He had on a handsome blue silk dressing-gown given to him by one of his lady admirers. He put his hands in its pockets and sat down on the edge of his bed. 'Why did I let you talk me into Edinburgh?' he said with a dark look at the crown prince. 'First the jealousy of Gleghorn, then the thing of the Emilio, and now *this*!'

119

'Anne,' said Crowne with a little grimace. 'Anne wasn't down to breakfast. I wonder if she's had this hangover effect?'

'I would be happy if she suffered,' said Edder, but in a tone of gruff joviality.

'Don't say a thing like that. May I use your phone?'

'To order my breakfast? Please do. I always have lemon tea.'

'I meant, to ring Anne and see if she is all right. But we'll order your breakfast first.' He did so, then asked to be put through to Miss Gleghorn's room.

This was the second time in ten minutes he'd listened to a telephone ringing and ringing, on tenterhooks for a reply. This time there was none. The ringing tone went on but no one picked up the receiver.

'She doesn't answer.'

'Out galloping around in her grey sweatshirt and clumsy shoes,' said Edder, waving it aside as unimportant.

'I'll just check she's gone out. I shouldn't like to think of her lying in her room, feeling as odd as I did this morning – or maybe even worse.' He got the switchboard, asked for reception, and enquired if Miss Gleghorn had gone out.

'I don't think so, sir. Her key's not with the desk.' That didn't necessarily mean she was in her room. Crowne himself had been guilty of going out with his hotel card-key in his pocket or his briefcase.

'Would you find out if she's in the hotel? In one of the music rooms downstairs, perhaps. I'm in Mr Edder's room – ring me back.'

'I invite you to stay and watch me eat breakfast,' Edder said, with heavy irony.

'You don't mind, do you? I should really like to make sure she—'

'Did you say Angeliza told you she was ill?'

'I thought Angeliza was weeping over a man, but maybe

she meant Anne. No, she cried on my shoulder and I'm sure it was all masculine adjectives. Could she have meant Duntyre?'

'Why the devil should she cry over Duntyre?'

'I suppose not. Then who else . . . Who drank champagne with us last night?'

'Shemnitzi? Klein?'

'They're downstairs, so is Holt. Michiko?'

'Shige?' said Edder.

Now that it was mentioned to him, Crowne thought it strange that Shige hadn't been at breakfast. Michiko and David Duntyre – well, he could imagine how it could come about that those two didn't appear. But Shige had grown to like the Scottish breakfast served at the Hill Hotel. It was odd that he should miss it.

'Should I ring him?'

'Why not, my friend? The guardian angel of the Hill Hotel.'

'Very well, I will.' Once again he listened with growing alarm to the lack of response on the other end of the line. He almost gave an audible groan of relief when the instrument was picked up.

Shige said something in grunting, interrogative Japanese.

'Takamasa? Are you all right?'

'That is a good question. I will tell you in an hour or so. I feel very strange.'

'You do? Talik isn't well, and I felt rotten first thing . . . We suddenly wondered if it was a virus or perhaps something to do with the drink last night, and we rang Anne Gleghorn—'

'You did? How is *she*?'

'I don't know.' Real apprehension gripped Crowne. 'She didn't answer.'

The waiter tapped with Edder's breakfast. Beyond the open door Crowne could see the manager guiding a weeping Angeliza along the corridor. Against the quiet beige walls

121

her bright orange blouse and dark, disarranged hair looked like something blown in from a storm.

'McVay!' called Crowne.

'Yes?' The manager looked back, unwilling to be stopped, one arm still urging Angeliza on.

'Have you seen Miss Gleghorn this morning?'

'Miss Gleghorn, no, I can't say I have, Mr Crowne. But that's not unusual.'

'I've asked reception to find out if she's in the hotel. Could you go and knock on her door? I'm worried about her.'

Hector looked harassed, torn between his duty to a hysterical lady and the need to be polite to a crown prince, even if exiled. 'I'll go in just a minute, Mr Crowne. Just let me see Mrs Kelly safely back to bed.'

'Back to bed? Is she ill?'

'Not she herself, sir . . . She . . . well . . . I'll see to it, never you fear,' McVay said, moving on.

Crowne went back to the phone, where Shige was still on the line, comparing symptoms with Edder. 'But it seems to be wearing off,' Edder was saying. 'Wait, here is Gregory back.'

Crowne took the receiver. 'How long have you been awake, Shige?' he asked the industrialist.

'About an hour and a half. I feel better than I did when I first woke up.'

'Me too.'

'What is the news about Anne?'

'Nothing so far. McVay is going to check.'

'Shall I come along and—'

'No, no, thank you – keep quiet and get over the symptoms. I'll go up to Anne's room.'

Leaving Talik to his breakfast tray, he hurried out and up to the next floor. He rapped sharply on the door of Anne Gleghorn's room, but there was no reply. He stayed there, knocking from time to time, until Hector appeared.

'There's no reply, McVay.'

'She may be out.'

'But all the same . . . Three people who were at that post-concert party last night have been feeling ill this morning.'

'What?' said the hotel manager, going pale.

'Mr Edder, Mr Shige and myself.' He took a mental survey. 'I haven't seen Duntyre, Anne Gleghorn or Michiko Toshio this morning. The others of the quartet are up and about, but not Michiko. I think you should make sure they're all right, McVay – and since we're here, we may as well begin with Anne.'

'You mean – open her room door?'

'I think it's justified. She may be lying there ill.'

Very shaken, McVay went to a wall phone to ask for the pass-key to be brought up. When it came, he put it in the lock and opened the door with a wary hand.

'Miss Gleghorn?'

No response.

'Go on,' Crowne said.

They stood together in the doorway, Crowne tall, angular and anxious, McVay small, round and terrified. At a little push from Crowne, Hector McVay stepped into the room. 'Hello?'

As in all the rooms at the Hill Hotel, the bathroom was just inside the outer door so that the bed or beds were behind it, in the alcove formed by the further wall. The bathroom door stood open and the light was not on. There was no way to see the bed without going right into the room.

The curtains were still closed, but the light of the rather misty morning filtered in around the sides. Quiet lay over all. The crown prince, whose hearing was acute, could make out none of the usual sounds of occupancy – no rustle of bedclothes, no rise and fall of a sleeper's breath.

'Miss Gleghorn!' said Hector, almost in appeal. He threw out a hand to Crowne. 'I think . . . I think . . .'

Gregory Crowne walked across the room to draw open the curtains. Light grew in the silent room. It revealed the bed.

Anne Gleghorn lay there, eyes closed, one hand against her cheek. She might have been sleeping except that it was strange that she hadn't heard the voices calling, the knocking on her door.

'Oh, Mr Crowne,' said Hector in a voice of despair.

The prince went forward. He laid the back of his hand against her forehead. It was utterly cold. Even if his nerve endings had still been as numb as when he first awoke, he would have felt the chill of that brow.

Anne Gleghorn was dead.

Eleven

Impossible. No one so full of life and energy could be dead. She was too young and strong to have given her farewell performance.

Crowne's second thought, of which he was afterwards very ashamed, was: Thank God we've finished the Bachiana No. 5! This was typical impresario-thinking: there were problems enough in putting on events without sudden death throwing the programme out of gear.

Later, when Chief Inspector Fairmil sent for Crowne and sought his view on the death of Miss Gleghorn, he didn't confess that feeling of relief. He didn't know what to tell him. What had relevance or importance? Anne was dead, and the rest of them had been attacked by some virus or infection or whatever it was.

Talik had recovered, so had Takamasa Shige. David Duntyre, that big strong man, was still in bed, unable to get up as yet. It occurred to Crowne that David had knocked back more whisky than anyone else, on the grounds that it was the Scottish national drink.

Of the string quartet, only Michiko was the same as usual, strange to say. Joseph Klein confessed that he had felt unwell when he woke very early on but had recovered by seven. Henry Holt had thought he had a migraine coming on when he first opened his eyes but was so accustomed to them he simply got on with getting up. Shemnitzi had gone back up to his room after his interview in the lobby, and when Crowne came to look for him was trying to cure with aspirin what he thought of as a case of the morning after the night before.

Angeliza Kelly was quite well except for a strange hysteria. She wavered between helpless tears and a tottering firmness.

Crowne felt well enough. Anxiety over first Talik and then the others seemed to have sent adrenalin pumping through his blood so as to hasten his recovery. But this germ or virus seemed to affect different people in different ways.

Physique and normal good health didn't seem to enter into it. For instance, though Crowne was a normally healthy specimen, he didn't take anything like so much care of himself as Anne Gleghorn. Early-morning exercise, jogging, careful diet – none of these seemed to have been any defence in Anne's case.

Duntyre, too. David was a big man, taller by some three inches than Crowne and by a good deal more than Shige. Yet Crowne and Shige had recovered relatively quickly whereas Duntyre was still laid low, with Michiko sitting by his bedside holding his hand.

Something to do with the drink . . . ? Duntyre had put away plenty, both whisky and champagne. But then so had Talik, and he was up and about. Yet Anne, who had had little alcohol, was dead.

The doctor brought in by the police declared himself puzzled. It was reasonable to suppose they had all suffered in a lesser degree from the same factor that had caused Anne's death. But the symptoms they described didn't fit anything he expected. He muttered that the effects were perhaps masked by the consumption of alcohol. He took specimens, advised them all to eat nothing, drink milk and soda water, and to wait twenty-four hours to see how they fared.

It was decided not to admit any of them to hospital unless their condition worsened again. The less attention drawn to the event, the better.

As for Anne, only the post-mortem could establish the cause of death.

'You were all at this so-called midnight buffet,' said Fairmil. 'This was food laid out on the table?'

'Yes.'

'Did you all eat and drink the same things?'

'I've no idea. I should think perhaps not. McVay might know. He was hovering round.'

'His reply is the same as yours, Mr Crowne. He didn't pay attention to what people were choosing to put on their plates. But he thinks everyone had champagne.'

'But that's no help. It was first-class champagne and in any case Miss Toshio had a glass and she is perfectly well.' He thought for a moment. 'Couldn't you get some idea of what was eaten and drunk from the leftovers and empty bottles?'

'The bottles have been impounded. As for food . . .' The chief inspector sighed. 'Unfortunately for us in this case, McVay has strict views on kitchen hygiene. He feels that, having stood on display for a couple of hours on a buffet, any food left over must be covered with germs. So it's a rule in his kitchen that anything gathered up from the midnight buffet must go straight into the waste disposal unit. A great American invention plugged into a big stainless-steel sink in the kitchen. You tip the rubbish in, switch on, and it all gets ground down very fine and washed away down the drain.'

'Oh!'

'My first thought was food poisoning, of course. We're very conscious of that risk in Scotland, Mr Crowne. We had one of the worst cases of botulism on record in the twenties. Eight people died. But Dr Simpson says the symptoms are nothing like it – usually there's vomiting and stomach pains . . .'

'No, no one's had anything in the least like that.'

'McVay was indignant when I put the idea of food poisoning to him. He's apparently a leader in the field of hotel-keeping, he's lectured on kitchen procedures and he's very strict. It's true, too – I talked to the staff in the kitchen; they really do carry out his instructions.'

'This is a blow for him,' Crowne said with a sympathetic sigh.

'It's not much fun for anyone,' Fairmil said, 'especially after all the stramash over your friend Mr Edder and his fiddle. Press-men everywhere and TV cameras . . . My chief takes a poor view of it all.'

'Miss Gleghorn hasn't enjoyed it either,' Crowne said in sudden anger.

'Yes, of course. I'm sorry. I'm not heartless, believe me. But the last thing the environmental officer wants is a food-poisoning scare during the Festival. So we're playing that very close to our chests, especially as it seems clear it *isn't* food poisoning.'

'Chief inspector . . .'

'Aye?'

'If anyone wanted to cause trouble and get publicity – you know, in the style of hijacking the cello – this would be a good way, wouldn't it?'

'Och, we've thought of that. But Mr Crowne, to put something in the food – who would do it? Only McVay's chef and his minions touched the food—'

'But it was sitting there, Fairmil – laid out on a buffet table in a corner set aside for us. Anyone could have—'

'But members of the public aren't allowed in for the midnight buffet, only hotel guests.'

'You're saying it was one of the guests? For publicity?'

'The first name that springs to mind is Duntyre – because in my heart's heart I'm sure he took the Strad – but he's upstairs very poorly, so the doctor tells me. He may be devoted to the cause of the Scottish Progressive Party, Mr Crowne, but not enough to lay himself low. Nor do I think the man would endanger anybody else's life, especially not the wee Japanese lass.'

'Yes, you're right.'

The medical team left with their samples, the doctor shook hands with Fairmil and went away to look up textbooks, and Anne's body was quietly taken from the hotel by the back way.

Crowne went to speak to McVay. He had a lot of sympathy for the hotel-keeper, who had taken such pride – and justifiably – in his cuisine. To have seven guests taken ill and one dead due to anything he had put before them seemed incredible.

Crowne had stayed in the Hill Hotel during previous Festivals, and though he wasn't a food fetishist he had listened to Hector on the subject. 'The meat's the best Angus, and home-fed lamb and pork, the fish comes straight from Musselburgh. The bread and cakes are made specially for us to my orders by a small baker, who knows he'll lose my custom if he doesn't keep his standards high. Everything is under my direct control.' These statements could be called forth from Hector any time he was given the chance.

Crowne remembered, when they were searching the Hill Hotel for the Emilio and Fairmil had opened the big deep-freeze, how little there had been in it: mainly ice-cream and a few of the more exotic meats and fishes. Nor was Hector the kind of man to allow anything to be quick-thawed in his kitchen, with the possible danger of bacterial growth.

Yet *something* had gone wrong. Anne Gleghorn was dead.

'I don't understand it, sir,' Hector said in a weary voice. 'It's the kind of thing I felt I had taken every possible safeguard against.'

'The Chief Inspector was wondering if someone had added something to the dishes while they were waiting on the buffet . . .'

'Yes, he tried out that one on me. But who? And what? It wasn't anything you could get hold of easily – I mean, not crushed-up tranquilliser tablets or laxatives, nothing that a crank could find or buy; the symptoms don't match anything like that.' Hector hesitated. 'Sir, Miss Gleghorn passed

129

on, but have you thought . . . it might have been meant for you?'

'Me? Who'd want to kill me?'

'Well, you know, Your High— I mean, sir, you are who you are.'

'Exactly. Nothing useful could be achieved by killing me off, Hector. I don't think I was the target.' He paused. 'All the same . . .'

'What, sir?'

Crowne decided not to utter the thought that had just come to him. Takamasa Shige had been a target – a target for protesting students in Tokyo. He and his driver might have been killed. Now he had been made ill by something or other to do with the food he'd eaten last night – and Michiko Toshio, who had been with that group of protesting students, had also been present. And Michiko was the only one of them who had suffered no ill-effects at all.

About five hours had gone by since Anne's body was found, enough time for New York to be awake and doing business. Crowne now had to ring Anne's agent to tell him what had happened.

It was a depressing conversation. Verendorf's chief interest, after the first surprise of hearing the news, seemed to be whether the attending publicity would help sell Anne's recording of the Bachiana Brasileira No. 5.

'That's up to you,' Crowne said in a very terse manner; 'you're her personal agent. What I need to know is, who is going to get in touch with her parents?'

'I suppose I should. I got a note of the mother's address somewhere. They're divorced, of course.'

Of course. Everybody seemed to be divorced. Crowne sighed. 'Will Mrs Gleghorn want to come over for the funeral or what?'

'I'll ask. What kind of date would that be?'

'When the police release the body. There has to be a post-mortem.'

'Oh yeah . . . You found her dead in bed, you said? What do you reckon, heart?'

'No, think about it – she was a very healthy woman, Mr Verendorf. The authorities here are very puzzled.'

'If that isn't just like Anne! Nothing was ever plain sailing with her. Her own worst enemy, in many ways. And of course the way she made a fool of herself over Talik Edder in Venice . . . Bad publicity is better than none, but pics of her having a public row with Edder, that was a no-no. Say, he's there, isn't he? He didn't by any chance strangle her?'

It was meant to be a joke but Crowne couldn't laugh. After a few more exchanges he rang off.

Talik? Could Talik have put something in the food to harm Anne? Anne herself had said at some time yesterday that she had had all kinds of ailments in her childhood and had had to learn to be careful what she ate. Talik must know that, if anyone did, having lived with her for several weeks.

And over the last few hours before her death he'd been taking pains to flatter her, to seek her company. Crowne had thought he did it just because he didn't want her to make a relationship with Takamasa Shige but suppose . . . Just suppose Talik had wanted to harm Anne? Suppose he had learned how Anne spoiled his chances of the directorship of the Conservatoire . . . Angeliza might have let it slip.

But, if so, Talik would have confronted her. Not for him the slyness of slipping something into her food.

And what, in any case? What 'something'?

Crowne reviewed the buffet as he remembered it. Salads, fish in various versions including raw, a veal fricassee sprinkled with herbs . . . Sprinkled with herbs? What did marijuana look like? If crumbled up, could the dried leaves of marijuana look like herbs?

Edinburgh had a drugs problem. Probably it would be easy enough to get hold of marijuana. Or even cocaine or heroin. What would be the result if you added cocaine or heroin to a veal fricassee?

131

Heroin was a narcotic, that much he knew. And all of those affected after the buffet had felt unable to rouse themselves in the morning. Yet to affect seven people and kill one, there must have been an enormous amount of the stuff in the food, and besides . . . He called to mind his own reflection in the mirror this morning. No pinpoint pupils, no sweat on his brow. No, he would be very surprised if the forensic tests revealed heroin.

As to cocaine, that was stimulant. Surely enough to kill would have caused convulsions, whereas Anne had been lying quite peacefully.

The more he tried to think of something that could have been added to what they ate, the more he felt it impossible. And that left aside the matter of who.

Who would want to do such a thing? Talik, to punish Anne; Michiko, to harm Shige; Duntyre, to create publicity; Angeliza, to get rid of Anne, of whom she was jealous? Or to punish Anne for harming Talik? Was that why she was so upset, because her plan had gone awry and her beloved Talik had suffered too?

What about McVay? McVay himself, claiming to be so distressed and stricken over the damage to his reputation. Suppose he'd wanted to harm Talik, so as to get Angeliza for himself. There was no doubt Hector was very fond of Angeliza. Yet to act in such a wild and dramatic fashion – was that in Hector's character?

Besides, there were ways of gaining Angeliza's affection without going to such extremes as ruining his own hotel.

The Kamikura players. None of them had been greatly affected, Michiko not at all. Could they, in conspiracy or singly, have done it?

But why, why? Henry Holt and his schoolboyish passion for steam trains, Klein and his phlegmatic common sense, Shemnitzi and his rather cynical cosmopolitanism . . . Who would have been the target? What could they have wanted to achieve?

Takamasa Shige. Now . . . Takamasa Shige wanted the Emilio. Could it be that? Kill off Talik Edder and buy the Emilio? But Shige had been ill too – it was illogical to think the man might kill himself as well. Dead men can't buy Stradivari cellos. Besides, you don't commit murder to get hold of a cello for your wayward daughter.

And in fact, Anne Gleghorn had died, not Talik Edder.

Fairmil returned to the hotel at about two. His blue eyes were grim under sandy eyebrows. 'Mr Crowne,' he said, 'I'm afraid there's a flap on. The Foreign Office have been on to us, and they've asked us to give you special protection.'

'*Quelle sottise!* McVay started that hare, did he?'

'No, sir, I understand it was your grandmother ringing up from Geneva.'

'Grossmutti? How the hell did she get hold of it?'

'I'm not sure, sir. But you won't mind having one of my men attached to you?'

'Must you?'

'I'm afraid I must, sir.'

'Oh, well . . . I was thinking of going out for a walk to clear my head. I suppose he has to come too?'

'Yes, sir. Dempsey, here!'

A tall young man in jeans and a worn leather jacket came across the hall. 'Sir.'

'Mr Crowne is going out for a walk.'

'Yes, sir.'

'Are the reporters still outside?'

'Yes, sir.'

'Then we'll go out the back,' said the prince. 'Come on, shadow.'

They emerged into the mews, two tall men with their coat collars turned up against the drizzle. Crowne's light brown hair was glinting with the damp in a moment. From the corner they could see the group of press-men hanging about the porch of the hotel, and among them, a tall girl in a clingy dress and with artfully tangled blond hair.

Liz!

Could it really be that she had dropped what she was doing to come to Edinburgh? He was about to call out to her but then, mindful of the reporters, thought better of it.

'Mr Dempsey,' he said, 'I wonder if you'd be so good as to go up to that tall young lady in the grey and blue dress and ask her to come here?'

The constable frowned at him. 'Now then, Mr Crowne—'

'It's not a trick. Her name's Elizabeth Blair. If I go up and speak to her, the press will be all over us.'

'Oh. Oh, I see. Oh, aye, then. I'll go, but mind you stay right here.'

Crowne needed no urging.

A moment later she was hurrying up at Dempsey's side. As she reached the corner she ran to throw herself upon the prince.

'Greg! Are you all right? Oh, Greg!'

'Here, hold on – what's the matter? Liz! Liz, what's wrong?'

'You beast! You've had your mobile switched off again!'

'Yes, but why does that—'

'When I saw the headline in the *Evening Standard*—'

'What headline?'

She thrust at him the folded newspaper that had accompanied her on the plane from London.

He opened it. 'Assassination Attempt,' he read.

Now he knew why Grandmama Nicoletta had rung up the Foreign Office.

Twelve

He shook his head at her. 'I assure you, the reports of my assassination are greatly exaggerated.'

'Now he tells me,' she said, recovering her sangfroid. 'So what's been happening?'

'If we hadn't had all the brouhaha about the Emilio, this would have been accepted as death by natural causes—'

'What would? Who's died?' She knocked the paper with her fist. 'It doesn't say what's been happening. All it says is that the Edinburgh police are taking precautions because of—' She stopped. 'Somebody's died, Greg?'

'Anne Gleghorn.'

'Anne? But she – I can't believe it! How?'

'It may be some virulent infection – not Legionnaire's, but you know these summer ailments that go around—'

'So why are the police alarmed?'

He sighed. 'Grandmama has been ringing up some former lover at the Foreign Office, I gather. And they've set a watchdog on me.'

'Then it *is* serious. They wouldn't waste a man—'

'Oh, Liz, you know what they're like. They get their ambassadorial knickers in a twist if there's any threat to anybody who's even a cousin twenty times removed to HM. I wish Grandmama had shown a bit more sense.' After a moment he said, 'I'd better ring her. She'll order me back to Geneva.'

'But you won't go,' Liz said, taking hold of his arm.

'I can't go. I've got those damned recitals and concerts to

135

rearrange. Michiko Toshio is in such a state over Duntyre's health that, even if the others are able to gather themselves together, they couldn't play this evening. So I'll have to cancel today's recital in Leith Town Hall, and Anne was supposed to sing in a place in St Andrew's Square . . . Talik too – he was supposed to be playing . . .'

'Who's Duntyre? Why is Michiko upset about him? What are you talking about?' Liz demanded.

'You may well ask. If I'm to explain, we need to go somewhere we can talk.' As she moved towards the back entrance of the hotel he said, 'Not there. Somebody's sure to came waltzing up. Or if we go to my room, the phone will ring.'

'We'll go somewhere for a drink—'

'I'm not allowed to drink, I'm on milk and soda water. And what about the guard dog?' he said with a glance at Constable Dempsey. He, with unexpected tact, had taken himself a few yards off.

Liz was a girl who believed in the direct approach. She walked up to the constable.

'You have to go where Mr Crowne goes, is that it?'

'Yes, miss.'

'We want to go somewhere quiet where we can talk. Can you recommend anywhere?'

'Liz, you're embarrassing Constable Dempsey,' said the prince, seeing the man's colour rise.

'I don't see why. He's got to go where we go, so we may as well be in agreement, Mr . . . Dempsey, is it? I'm Liz Blair.'

'Most folk call me Jack,' said Dempsey. But as Liz had never heard of a boxer called Jack Dempsey this little joke went right past her.

'Right, Jack, Gregory and I want to have a cup of tea – at least I want tea and he wants milk. You're a native Edinburghian – where's a good place?'

'Well, as a matter of fact, the crypt of the Tron Church – that's like our cathedral, you know.'

'Do I look like the sort of girl who goes to church crypts?'

'No, honest, miss, you get the best scones in Edinburgh there, and it's the last place the press boys would look for His Highness.'

The prince gave him a grin. 'Marble halls yes, church halls no. Lead on, McDuff.'

'As a matter of fact, sir, that's incorrect. It should be "Lay on, McDuff."'

'Thank you, Jack, I'll remember that. Come on.'

'Er . . . I'm supposed to follow you, not walk along with you.'

'Get on with you,' said Liz, and took his arm.

The three of them, unremarked because they looked like a trio of tourists, made the walk to the ancient High Street. The crypt of the great old church was a handsome home for a café. There Jack had the tact to sit at another table after they had fetched their refreshments from the sales counter. He hid himself behind a large piece of home-made cake and a copy of the *Scottish Church* magazine.

'They're taking a lot of care of you,' Liz said, staring past Crowne's shoulder at the constable. 'There must be a good reason.'

'I honestly don't think so. It would make as much sense for them to put a man to watch over Mr Shige.'

'Who's Mr Shige?'

He brought her up to date with what had been happening. Then he said, trying not to sound wistful, 'How long are you staying, Liz?'

She made a ferocious grimace. 'I oughtn't to be here at all! But when I saw that terrible headline . . . Well, I loaded all the responsibility on to Godfrey for the moment and I'll try to stay a couple of days – at least until I'm sure nobody's trying to put you six feet under.'

'Have you got somewhere to stay?' he asked, ignoring the last remark. 'Edinburgh's crammed full at the moment. You could share my room at the hotel – I wish! – but we'd have reporters in our lap all the time.'

She looked gloomy. 'Anyone who thinks it's fun being in love with a handsome prince has never tried it,' she muttered. 'Couldn't you turn into a frog?'

'If you know the spell, say it and see what happens.'

'It's OK about a room. I've got a friend in the rag trade here, she's got a little boutique out near that rugby ground—'

'Murrayfield?'

'Yes, and she lives over the store so she can put me up on her sofa for a couple of days—'

'It doesn't sound very comfortable, darling.'

'Beggars can't be choosers. If I get a slipped disc I'll come and beg a room from your Mr McVay and damn the reporters.'

'Poor Hector. Normally he'd be pleased as Punch to have his hotel mentioned in the papers, but not in this connection. If he turns out to be in any way responsible, he'll be ruined.'

'I know how he feels. If those dresses don't sell, *I'll* be ruined.'

'Yes, but nobody will have died in the process. Hector is such a funny little man, takes everything so much to heart. He was genuinely angry with David Duntyre over the theft of the cello. He said some very rude things about leftists—'

'Could it possibly be that this thing with the food is someone taking revenge on him? Red revolutionaries?'

'Damned if I know,' Crowne said, thinking of Michiko, and determined not to talk about it any more.

Some half an hour later he reluctantly announced that he really would have to go back to the Hill Hotel to make his phone calls. He wrote down Liz's Edinburgh address and phone number, arranged to be in touch as soon as he knew how the evening was going to turn out and, with the help of the obliging Jack Dempsey, found a taxi for her.

The constable fell into step with him as they headed back

to the hotel. 'That's a very good-looking young lady, sir,' he ventured.

The prince smiled. 'I agree with you.'

He was still buoyed up by the pleasure of her company when he settled down with the telephone in the conference room of the hotel. He rang Geneva. The phone was picked up almost on the first ring.

'*Grossmutti?*'

'*Ach, du!*' A torrent of Hirtenstein German ensued, to the effect that he was an undutiful grandson, careless of her feelings, wilful and obstinate, always doing things to make her nervous, and he was to come home at once.

'No, I can't.'

'Can't? Can't? What sort of word is that for a prince of the Hirtensteins? You will come home at once. I command you.'

'Now, now, you know very well you'd think me weak-kneed if I came. And anyhow, I've got Talik to think of, and the Kamikura – and then there's a sort of inquiry, with the equivalent of a *juge d'instruction* – I don't think I'd be allowed to leave.'

'My child, let me speak to this *juge*! I've dealt with many like him—'

'The Procurator Fiscal won't be browbeaten by an old lady speaking from Geneva. Be reasonable, *chère madame* – I have responsibilities to fulfil here.'

He knew she was always accessible if you talked about duty. She began to relent. 'But you won't take unnecessary risks?'

'I haven't taken any risks, necessary or unnecessary, and don't intend to. Besides, thanks to you I've got a nanny looking after me.'

'Good.' She gave him other instructions as to his safety, told him Papa sent his love, and they parted on good terms.

He had scarcely put the receiver down when the phone rang again under his hand. He picked it up.

139

'Speak to Michiko Toshio, please?'

'I'm sorry,' Crowne said. 'You've come straight through to an inside line. Just a moment and I'll try to get the switchboard.'

He tried and failed. He lost the call but at last the bright little girl replied. 'There was a call coming in for Miss Toshio,' he said. 'Have you got it? It came straight through to the conference room.'

'Oh, I'm sorry, Mr Crowne. I'll see if it's still there.'

He hung up and left the room, wondering who it was on the other end of the line. That had been a Japanese speaking, or someone who spoke the Japanese language. He had pronounced Michiko's name in the proper manner. Crowne, in common with every other European he knew, called her *Mitch*iko *Tosh*io. The man asking for her had uttered it in the same way as Takamasa Shige – more like Mishko To-sho. Well, there were probably quite a few Japanese besides Shige and Michiko in Edinburgh for the Festival. And there would be Japanese students at the university.

At that he paused. Shige had said that Michiko would have friends wherever there were students of her own political persuasion. Could that have been one of them? And who is better placed to obtain germ cultures and other harmful things than a student in a medical faculty?

Now now, he told himself, don't let's get fanciful. All that's happened is that a young woman has died in a hotel where one or two exceptional events have happened to one or two well-known people.

He had an impulse to go in search of Michiko. She wasn't downstairs and she wasn't in her room when he tapped on her door. He went to Duntyre's room and knocked. It was Michiko who came to answer.

'Oh . . . Mr Crowne . . . How nice to see you. Are you all right now?'

'Quite recovered, thank you. You haven't been affected?'

'No, not at all. But I'm very upset about David.'

'How is he?'

She turned back into the room. 'David, it's Mr Crowne. Can he come in?'

Was there some unwillingness in the acquiescence? And if there was, did it spring from a desire to preserve the tête-à-tête with Michiko, or from some other reason?

Duntyre was up and dressed, but he certainly looked as if he had been under the weather. His long-chinned face was pale, his eyes seemed duller than usual. There was an air of carefulness about the way he was holding his tall body in the small armchair, as if he weren't quite sure it would obey him.

'How are you feeling?'

'All right. At least I'm able to talk properly again. I couldn't seem to get any words out earlier on.'

'You seem to have been worse affected than the rest of us—'

'Except Anne,' Duntyre said.

'It's a bad business.'

'I hear you found her?'

'This morning – yes, Hector and I.'

'It seems so impossible,' Duntyre whispered. 'She was so alive. Just when she had so much to look forward to.'

'In what way?'

'Well, she and Talik . . . I got the impression they were going to get together again from the way he spoke to her last night.' He shook his head. 'Ironic, when you think of it.'

'Ironic?'

'He means, after the awful things they said to each other,' Michiko put in quickly.

'Not so much ironic as unlikely. I don't think Talik would ever have got involved with her again. She could be very difficult.'

'I didn't find her so,' Duntyre declared.

'But then you hardly knew her, darling.'

141

'That's quite right, you only met about a week ago,' said the prince.

'Is it so short a time as that? It seems longer. That must be because we found so much in common.'

'You and Anne?' Crowne said, taken aback. 'What did you have in common?'

'He was thinking about writing the libretto for an opera. Weren't you, David?'

'Oh, yes.'

'Really?' said Crowne, frowning. It all sounded odd to him. 'With a part for Anne, you mean?'

'Yes.'

'But I thought you only wrote in Scots dialect?'

'It isn't a dialect, it's a language!' David Duntyre roused to something like himself at the blunder. 'And I choose to write in it because it's the rightful language of Scotland.'

'But Anne would hardly suit a part in—'

'Oh, it was just in the very first stages,' Michiko intervened.

'She never mentioned it to me.'

'Anne had a life and convictions outside the concert platform, you know.'

'I don't think you should talk, darling,' said Michiko with anxiety. She gave Crowne a glance. 'He's really been quite sick.'

'I can see that. I mustn't tire you.'

'As a matter of fact,' said Duntyre, with a gleam of something like his usual humour, 'I think most of the ailment is a common or garden hangover. I knocked back the whisky, didn't I?'

'But I didn't, and I got whatever it is. Michiko, how is it that you seem to have escaped it?'

She met the question with perfect innocence in her face. 'I don't know. I was so strung up after the concert – didn't it go *wonderfully*? – I just didn't want to eat or drink, really.'

A handy explanation, if she'd wanted to avoid taking something harmful.

'By the way, did you get that phone call?' he asked as he moved towards the door. 'A Japanese, asking for you.'

She seemed genuinely surprised. 'No, I didn't get it.'

'I expect they'll ring back. There was a muddle at the switchboard. Have you any Japanese friends here?'

'Not that I know of. But of course, people who know my family sometimes ring me when I'm in the same town.'

'I see. Well, I hope they catch up with you.' He nodded goodbye and went out.

As he walked down the corridor he told himself that there was something between those two, something more than the love affair. Michiko had been checking Duntyre as he spoke, steering him away from saying the wrong thing.

Yet no man in his senses would have made himself so genuinely ill as David Duntyre just so as to bring ill-repute on a minor enemy like Hector McVay. And if the motive had been political, the target Shige, and the instigator Michiko, would she have endangered Duntyre?

Stop it, he said to himself. It may still be established that there is nothing other than accident involved.

He was walking down the staircase to the ground floor, his footfall lost in the thick and expensive Axminster. As he reached the first floor, Hector McVay rounded a corner and stepped just in front of him.

'Hello, Hector,' he said.

Hector leapt about six inches in the air, half turned, lost his footing, and staggered backward down two or three stairs in a state of unbalance. Crowne grabbed him and steadied him.

'Are you all right?'

'Yes, yes . . . Dearie me . . . What a fright you gave me, sir.'

'I'm sorry, Hector. I didn't think you were so nervy.'

'I'm not, not a bit, in the general way. I'm . . . The thing is, I'm upset. This whole thing has upset me, Mr Crowne.'

143

Crowne could see that. The man looked almost hunted. Was it because he felt he was a target of some kind?

'It's bad for business, I imagine,' he agreed, keeping his hand under the other man's elbow as they continued on downstairs.

'Not entirely, that's the awful part. We've picked up quite a lot of casual trade – for dinner tonight, for instance. Yes,' Hector said as Crowne looked surprised, 'it's dreadful, isn't it? Sensation-mongers, that's all. But it's money, after all. I can't turn them away. Mind you, if it turns out that I'm to blame for Miss Gleghorn's death, it will be the end of me.'

'Don't say that, Hector. I'm sure your kitchens aren't to blame.'

'Oh, I hope not, I do with all my heart. But you see, I sometimes buy in made dishes – during busy times it's unavoidable. Just suppose I've had contaminated food brought into my hotel! I could never live with myself again!'

'I'm sure you'll be exonerated,' soothed Crowne.

'Even so, I think I'll sell out. Half of the shares in this hotel are owned by a company, you know. I could easily sell my half to them and retire. I don't know why I don't! The *problems* in running a hotel! You just don't know, Mr Crowne! People rely on you, just because you're the manager, they drop their problems in your lap – it really isn't fair!'

This was certainly a *crise de nerfs*. 'What you need is a good stiff whisky,' Crowne said. 'Come on, let me buy you one. I'm dying for something myself—'

'But the doctor said none of the patients were to have anything stronger than milk and water for twenty-four hours. You really better obey him.' A touching smile wreathed his round face. 'But I'm honoured that you should have invited me, Mr Crowne. Thank you.' He went into his office.

Crowne looked at the clock. It was now ten to eight in the evening. He crossed to Jack Dempsey, who was sitting pretending to read the *Scottish Field*.

144

'Listen, Jack, I'd like to ring Miss Blair and go out somewhere. What's the situation outside?'

'The reporters have called it a day, sir.'

'Well, that's something. Have you got transport?'

'No, sir, but I can acquire it.'

'No need. You can come with us. Where's a nice romantic place to go in a car?'

'To eat, you mean? I understood you weren't to—'

'Don't you start,' Crowne said. 'I ate breakfast before we discovered what had happened to Miss Gleghorn, and it did me no harm. That's now almost twelve hours ago, and I'm starving.'

'But the doctor said—'

'I promise to eat plain food – I'll even eat tapioca pudding if you know where I can order it.'

Dempsey chuckled. 'There's a very romantic wee place at Cramond, sir.'

'Would it come within your instructions to go with me to collect Miss Blair and drive to Cramond? You can eat at the next table if you promise not to eavesdrop.'

The detective blew out his lips. 'I wish everybody was as cooperative as you, sir.'

Liz said she would be ready in half an hour. She came down from her friend's flat looking fabulous in black silk trousers and a plain white blouse. Crowne's heart gave a little skip at sight of her.

Cramond was all Dempsey had said. Crowne kept his promise to eat only bland food – pasta with a light cream sauce, crème caramel. Liz on the other hand had a large helping of *boeuf bourgignon* followed by hazelnut gateau. Liqueur brandy completed the meal.

Liz raised her snifter towards Dempsey, who grinned and raised his mineral water in response.

'If we were married, would you have a bodyguard around all the time, Greg?'

'If there was some kind of flap on, yes. I'm afraid so.'

145

'It's so . . . inhibiting.'

'Well, let's stroll out to look at the sea. I dare say the constable can find something to look at in the opposite direction.'

The view was very pleasant, especially after the northern sun had gone down and the sea to the east became a grey silk mist. Like a lone, pale firefly, the planet Venus hovered in the blue sky of evening.

'"Venus now wakes, and wakens love,"' quoted Crowne, and kissed Liz.

'Is that a real quotation,' she murmured against his cheek, 'or did you just make it up so you could get romantic?'

'It's a real quotation, from Milton's *Comus*, and I don't need Milton to get romantic.'

'Greg, I'm glad I left Godfrey in charge of the dresses.'

'So am I.'

'If we went down this flight of steps to the river-mouth, and strolled into the shadow of those trees further up the bank, do you think Mr Dempsey would feel impelled to follow?'

'Let's try it and find out.'

Constable Dempsey followed like a wolfhound about twenty yards off. When they reached the foot of the steps, he stayed at the top. When they walked up the bank of the River Almond, he came down the steps. When they went into the wood, he hovered on the verge of the copse.

It was very late indeed when Crowne returned to the hotel. There was another man waiting to relieve Constable Dempsey, a uniformed officer who muttered something about how long he'd been standing about. Crowne left them arguing and went upstairs.

He wasn't sleepy, and stood at the window for a long time, picking out the patrol car a little further along the terrace where his watchdog for the night was on duty. A waste of time. Nothing was going to happen.

Without putting on the light, he dialled his Surrey flat and called up the messages on his answering machine. He made notes on a hotel pad in the dark, a skill he had acquired through writing notes for future reference during a performance in a concert hall or opera house.

The luminous hands on the bedside clock told him it was nearly one thirty. He ought to ring for a hot drink to help him get to sleep. His hand was on the telephone to make the call when he heard a sound outside in the corridor. He stood silent, wondering if after all the police were right, and someone was about to attack him.

But though he watched the handle of the door in the dim light from the window, it didn't turn. A moment later he heard another sound, from further along the corridor. Someone was moving very quietly from the front to the back of the house.

Was it just some hotel guest seeking out his lady-love? Was it some late reveller coming in from the Festival Club? Was it any of his business?

For reasons he couldn't explain, he felt it was. He quietly opened his door and put his head out. Nothing. The night-light of the corridor, a light bulb of very dim wattage, was burning. There was enough illumination to tell him no one was about.

He came back into his room and proceeded very gently to close his door. But before he had it closed, he heard another sound, this time from the back staircase. This was less splendidly carpeted than the staircase and corridors used by the guests, and it was possibe to make out the faint hollow sound of someone ascending slowly and stealthily.

Crowne slipped his shoes off and left them in his doorway so that the door would not swing entirely shut behind him. He didn't have time to fetch his room-key from the dressing-table, but he wanted to be able to slip quietly back into his room if it proved that he was sticking his nose into someone's love affair.

He went soundlessly along the corridor eased open the fire door. The footsteps were still going up. Crowne went up too, taking three steps at a time with his long legs. He reached the third-floor fire door as it swung behind his quarry.

Even in the low-wattage dimness he had no difficulty in recognising Hector McVay.

He opened the fire door very gradually. Hector was at the other side of the landing, opening the door that led to a flight of iron stairs which gave access to the roof of the hotel.

And he had something hugged against his chest.

Whatever it was, it was neither heavy nor bulky. For a moment Crowne hesitated. What Hector did in his own hotel was his own affair.

Yet why was he moving so stealthily? And, now he came to think of it, why had he been so shocked and startled when Crowne had come across him earlier that evening? Almost as if he'd been up to something he shouldn't.

Intrigued, Crowne waited, standing quite still with the third-floor fire door a little open. Hector had now unlocked the upper door, pocketed the key, and was mounting the iron steps. His legs disappeared; only the faint clang of his foot hitting the ironwork told that he was still moving.

When that sound ceased, Crowne went to the upper door, climbed the wrought-iron staircase and stepped out on to the flat roof of the Hill Hotel.

This was a Georgian building. Under the roof there were attics lit by small mansard windows, below which was a decorative parapet of curved balustrading. Inside this parapet there was sufficient space for some long troughs of earth in which Hector had planted various creepers so that from the crescent below the passer-by could see green leaves reaching down between the balustrade stones.

Hector had stepped out on the roof, and then down two steps to the balustrading. He was out of sight. Crowne moved to the downward steps, leaned over and gazed about.

He saw Hector kneel down, deposit his burden then take something out of his pocket. It proved to be a trowel, with which he proceeded to dig in one of the long wooden troughs of soil.

Good God, he can't be going to cultivate his garden in the middle of the night? thought Crowne.

But that was exactly what he was doing. Yet there was something frenzied about his actions, and he seemed to be gasping to himself, with either anxiety or exertion.

As he watched, the prince realised it wasn't gardening he was witnessing. It was excavation. Hector McVay was digging a hole.

He heard the little man make a sound that was almost a sob as his trowel hit the thick root of one of the plants. It shifted under his attack and for a moment there seemed a danger that a sturdy ivy plant would go helter-skelter down the front of the building, to the amazement no doubt of the policemen in the patrol car.

But after a moment's hesitation McVay took the plant out bodily and threw it on to the roof. This left a suitable hole, it seemed, for he sat back on his heels as if satisfied. Then he turned in the dimness to the burden beside which he had been kneeling. He lifted it. It seemed to be a bag or holdall. From it he extracted something, something rounded and about the size of a small cushion.

He cradled it in his arms a moment, then began to lower it into the hole he had made in the trough.

'McVay,' said the crown prince in a low voice, 'what in God's name are you doing?'

With a yelp of terror McVay huddled forward, shielding his handiwork with his plump body.

Thirteen

Crowne had expected a reaction of alarm or guilt, but not the utter panic that seemed to radiate from McVay.

He said, in an instinctively soothing tone: 'I'm sorry, Hector, I didn't mean to frighten you.'

Slowly McVay lifted his body until he was kneeling upright by the plant trough. 'Mr Crowne . . . ! That's the second time today you've given me heart failure!'

'But what are you doing?'

'Aye . . . well . . . the plants . . .'

'Come off it. What's that behind you?'

'Mr Crowne, it's just a household chore. Nothing for you to concern yourself with.'

'A household chore, on the roof in the middle of the night? Come on, Hector. Let's go back into the light and see what you're up to.'

He took the other man by the arm and helped him up. After a moment's futile resistance McVay obeyed the pull of his hand.

'Bring the bundle with you,' Crowne said.

'Oh, sir – I'd rather not. You shouldn't involve yourself in this, really you shouldn't.'

Involve myself in what? wondered Crowne. Nothing would have made him give up the pursuit of knowledge. He had to know what McVay had intended to bury.

Using his princely voice, he ordered: 'Do as I say!'

It worked like a charm. Submissively the manager stooped, gathered up the bundle he had taken from the holdall, and the holdall itself. He allowed himself to be escorted back to the narrow landing at the foot of the iron staircase.

'Now,' said Crowne, 'let's see.'

McVay knelt. He laid the bundle on the landing. It was wrapped in an expensive silk square from Christian Dior and fastened with a brooch that looked as if it might be real diamonds.

McVay unfastened the brooch. The corners of the silk square fell apart.

What Crowne had expected he couldn't have said: money, jewellery, 'the plans of the secret weapon', an antique vase, even a hoard of marijuana.

What he saw was a small grey cat.

Dead, of course. It was curled loosely into itself as if in sleep, but there was no movement or breathing.

'What the hell is *that*?' he exclaimed in astonishment.

'It's a cat.'

'I can see that. Why are you burying a cat at dead of night?'

'Well . . . you see . . . it upsets the hotel guests to think of an animal dying. So I thought I'd bury him while everybody was asleep.'

Crowne stooped beside McVay and looked at the little cat. It was thin yet well kept, with a silky coat. It had a narrow, elegant head and upstanding ears. He picked it up gently and turned it in his hands. He had never seen the cat anywhere around the hotel.

'Where does it come from?'

'It's the kitchen cat.'

Lie Number One. Hector McVay would never have allowed any cat in his kitchen; he had too high a regard for culinary hygiene.

'What's its name?'

'Eh . . . Tam o' Shanter.'

'I've never seen it around the premises.'

'No, sir. It's kept in the basement.'

'You mean you've got mice in the basement?'

'Of course not!' For the first time lies were displaced by truth, dismay by indignation.

'I thought not. Then why keep a cat?'

'I . . . eh . . . I like animals.'

'You do?'

'Devoted to them.'

'Had many cats?'

'Och aye. Tam o' Shanter is the last of a long line of kittens I've reared.'

Crowne turned and sat on one of the treads of the iron staircase. He set the little cat down on the ground in front of McVay on its rich winding-sheet of Christian Dior silk. It seemed to him he recognised the silk square.

He gave himself up to moments of recollection: Angeliza Kelly running off to do 'shopping' on a Sunday in the middle of Talik's rehearsal, and coming back with a squarish packet in a carrier bag. Angeliza Kelly with her window open to the raw morning air when clearly she felt very cold. Angeliza Kelly folding scraps of food into a napkin last night and going up to bed. Angeliza Kelly in the breakfast room that morning, in a state of hysterical tears over the unexpected illness of someone she loved.

'Well now,' he murmured, 'I'll tell you something, my devoted animal lover of long experience. This cat should more aptly be called after a female character from your Scottish poet. It's a she.'

Hector drew in his breath. 'She called it her "little boy",' he burst out.

'Senhora Kelly?'

Hector closed his lips firmly and turned away.

'This is – what did she call it? – Cha-cha! It was Cha-cha she was crying over this morning. This is Angeliza's cat.'

'Nothing of the kind, Mr Crowne. It's mine.'

'Then how come you don't know it's a female cat?'

Hector was silent.

'The fact is, you know nothing about cats. And neither does Angeliza, I imagine. She's the silliest creature I ever met – God knows how she's going to survive in this cruel world unless she finds someone to look after her.'

'Mr Crowne, that's not a nice thing to say.'

'But it's the truth, isn't it? And you feel you've been elected to the role.' He paused to collect his thoughts. 'I see now what she did. She brought this cat with her from Venice. Talik mentioned it.'

'She did nothing of the kind,' Hector insisted. 'That cat is a kitten from the baker's shop—'

'I don't believe you. Cats around here have small square heads and short ears. This is a southern type – you see them roaming all over Italian cities at dawn.'

'I assure you Tam o' Shanter—'

'And of course that's why you were trying to bury it like that bit in *Hamlet* – how does it go? – hugger-mugger . . . But why the roof? Why not out in the crescent garden?'

'Because there's a policeman on guard outside, looking after you!' McVay wailed. 'I promised Senhora Kelly I'd bury Cha-cha among the plants and trees, but I can't get *at* them. And I dare not keep the poor wee thing around any longer with the police making searches, and in and out of the hotel all the time.'

Crowne laid a hand on the other man's bowed shoulder. 'Poor Hector! I see what you meant about guests putting their troubles upon you. So Angeliza asked you to bury Cha-cha among the plants, did she? And you're doing your best to keep your promise. Poor little cat. It's a long way from home.'

'Oh, if you knew how worried I've been! She was in such a state this morning when she found him – her – dead! Then the next thing I knew, you'd called the police – in fact, before that, you had me on tenterhooks over the Emilio. When I heard you'd telephoned out that night—'

'You mean you knew the cat was in the hotel before it died?'

'Naturally,' Hector said in a tone that had a faint tinge of scorn. It implied, 'Anything to do with my hotel, I know it.' 'She was taking food to it from the hotel meals – in a table napkin – I ask you! Well, you know, Mr Crowne, I'm not daft. When I had it reported to me that once or twice a napkin was found in Senhora Kelly's room with remains of food clinging to it, I got suspicious.'

'So what did you do?'

'I kept an eye on her. I noticed, for instance, that she would order afternoon tea in her room. But she doesn't like tea with milk, she likes that South American stuff, *maté* – so why was she having tea with milk sent up?'

'To give it to Cha-cha in a saucer.'

'Right. And then I saw her letting it out of the window. You know that ornamental ironwork on the first floor? The cat walked along there, jumped down and went into the crescent gardens. So in a way it was no trouble. Quite well trained, I'd say.'

'But you realised there was something wrong because she was doing all this in secret.'

'Exactly. There's no rule against guests bringing pets – why, Lady Haddingford brings her Siamese for a week every winter when she comes to do her Christmas shopping. A destructive wee brute, far more destructive than poor Cha-cha. So I asked myself, Why is she not letting on about this cat? And then I guessed . . .'

'That she'd smuggled it in illegally, from Venice.'

'You *are* quick, Mr Crowne. Aye, it had to be that. She'd avoided quarantine regulations.'

'Oh, hell,' said the prince.

'You can understand why, sir,' Hector said quickly. 'She's lonely and forlorn, hanging about after Mr Edder and him not taking too much notice. And she'd got fond of this cat in Venice; it came to her when she stopped to feed a group of them in a square behind Santa Teresa, she tells me. It was young, hadn't yet grown up wild the way they do, I hear – you've seen them, have you, sir?'

'Oh yes, basking in the sun among the ruins of Pompeii, stalking birds in the Tivoli Gardens . . . Kind-hearted people try to help them, bring food and leave it . . . On the whole they manage to get by, but of course a kitten that comes up and purrs . . . I can understand she might feel a special interest.'

McVay was nodding at the prince's words. 'That's how she describes it, sir. And of course, once she'd taken Cha-cha in, she couldn't bear to part with him – her. She fed her some sedatives in her food before bringing her to London in her holdall. She couldn't bear to be separated over the long six months' quarantine required by law – that would have been unbearable to her, and besides, if she was following Mr Edder, she'd have moved on before Cha-cha was free to come to her again.'

'So you felt you couldn't report her.'

'Och, she's so helpless and timid . . . And anyhow,' Hector said with a sudden access of frankness, 'it wouldn't go down very well with my clients if I clyped on my guests.'

'Did what?'

'Told tales. I get a lot of foreign visitors, sir, particularly during the Festival, and I'd take a bet that nine out of ten of them don't agree with our quarantine laws.'

The prince himself, as a much-travelled man, had had to come to terms with them. He had a devoted setter at home in Geneva, trotting around his father's stables and looking up in hopes of seeing his master every time a car drove in.

But he had seen rabies, which happily Hector McVay had not. Crowne was prepared to abide by any law that could keep it out of England's green and pleasant land. (Or Scotland's, of course.)

The existence of Cha-cha explained the guilty look he had noticed in Hector over the last few days. No wonder the poor man had been nervy and anxious. First there had been the live Cha-cha snoozing in Senhora Kelly's room – in the wardrobe, no doubt – during daylight, and being let out in the crescent gardens at night. A few scraps from the dinner table, dry catfood bought in a packet when she'd gone 'shopping', an occasional bird caught in the gardens – and Edinburgh's gardens were full of blackbirds. No problem in feeding the animal while it was alive.

But then there had been the dead Cha-cha, and that was a different story. Senhora Kelly in fits of hysterics, sobbing out the news that her cat was dead – but luckily in Portuguese, which no one except the crown prince understood, and even he, as it happened, had only heard that 'he' was gravely ill, nothing about smuggling.

A dead cat. You can't keep a dead cat in a hotel. So Hector had undertaken to perform the funeral rites.

Poor Angeliza, thought Crowne, looking at the fine silk square she had supplied as a shroud, and the costly brooch as a last tribute in place of flowers. She would probably have loved to bury the little foreign cat in a pet cemetery, with a headstone, where she could weep buckets of tears and leave sheaves of lilies.

Instead, Cha-cha had been destined for a nameless grave in the plant trough.

Hector said, looking beseechingly at him: 'What are you going to do, sir?'

'I don't know. The authorities ought to be informed, Hector.'

'But why? After all, the wee beastie's dead. It can't do any harm to anybody now.'

'But how did it die? That's the point.'

'Certainly not from rabies! Look how peaceful it is.'

A long silence.

'We may as well bury her,' said the prince, getting up. 'They can always come for her if they want her.'

Hector picked up the cat and climbed the iron stairs to the

roof. There he placed the cat in the hollow he had made. Then, after a moment's thought, he settled the ivy plant in place again, and spread the soil on top.

'That's it, I think, sir.'

'Right then, let's go down. And I think this time we *will* have a whisky. I think we deserve it, and you must agree enough time's gone by for the doctors to allow it.'

They made their way down to McVay's suite, a pleasant, finickally tidy place where the whisky lived in a crystal decanter with a Georgian silver label round its neck.

The drink warmed and cheered them both. Crowne wiggled his stockinged feet in the deep carpet and felt comforted. 'I bet you're wishing I'd never come to the Hill Hotel,' he suggested. 'Guards and plots and sudden deaths.'

'Oh, don't say that, Your Highness. It's always a pleasure to have you.'

'But if I hadn't followed you upstairs you could have buried Cha-cha and no one the wiser.'

'Er . . .' Hector rolled his glass between his hands. 'You're going to tell the police?'

'I think I must.'

'Well, could you delay it a bit? I've got to prepare Angeliza for the shock.'

'You have to report back on the burial, I suppose?'

'Yes, at breakfast tomorrow.'

'I shan't be seeing the police before that, naturally.' They sipped. Pursuing his own course of thought, the prince said, 'You've never married, Hector?'

'Oh, yes, aye, there was a Mrs McVay. We divorced some years ago. She said I gave more attention to the guests than to her.'

'It could be she was right.' Crowne laughed. 'Look at what you've done for Angeliza.'

'That's different.' The round face crumpled in thought. 'She's so *rich*,' he sighed. 'It's a problem.'

'To whom? To you?'

'Me? Mercy, no!' He recovered himself. 'I meant to herself. Her money has cut her off from ordinary people – reinforced her widowhood.'

'No children, I take it.'

Hector shook his head. 'There's a nephew that she seemed to dote on but he quarrelled with her over her husband's will, I gather. He expected to inherit almost everything but he offended her husband somehow and got nothing.'

'Oh?' said Crowne with sudden interest. 'And where would the money go if Angeliza had died, instead of Anne Gleghorn?'

'Mr Crowne!'

The prince nodded his head. Why not? It was a motive, one of the greatest – money.

'If Angeliza had eaten what she took from the buffet last night – the night before last, I mean – who knows? But instead she gave it to Cha-cha.'

'Yes, of course she did.'

'I saw her myself, putting something into her napkin. I thought she was taking a piece of cake upstairs, for comfort – plump people often eat at times of unhappiness, or so I read. But she was taking food upstairs for Cha-Cha.'

'You're taking it for granted something was put in the food, sir! I assure you—'

'If Angeliza's nephew wanted it done, he could find a way, Hector.'

'But there's no proof as yet that there was anything toxic in the dishes on the buffet!'

Hector was fighting a rearguard action for his hotel. But Crowne was too sleepy now to want to argue. The whisky was having its effect; it had been a long, long day.

He prised himself out of his armchair, said good-night to McVay, and went to bed with the resolve to tell Mr Fairmil first thing to investigate the nephew.

The police made no early effort to be in touch next day. Crowne surfaced at ten o'clock, feeling quite well and extremely hungry. It was too late for breakfast in the dining-room, but room service brought him coffee, baps and wholemeal toast. He ate in bed, which would have scandalised his grandmother. He telephoned his answering machine, rang his office in Geneva, read the morning paper and then devoted ten minutes to conversation with Liz.

'Oh, so you're still in the land of the living,' she observed.

'"*Il faut que je vive*," as the Abbé Desfontaines said.'

'That means "I must live," if I remember correctly. And the answer was, "I don't see the necessity."'

'Did you get out of bed the wrong side this morning?'

'I should like to know where you were last night, *mon ami*! I rang you to tell you I couldn't sleep for thinking of you, and the night porter said there was no reply from your room.'

'Liz! You're jealous!'

'Not in the least; I'm just curious. Where were you?'

'I was at a funeral.'

'Oh, well, if you're going to talk nonsense—'

'I really was, Liz—'

'In the middle of the night?'

'I'll tell you about it at lunch. We are lunching together, aren't we?'

'All right, but only because I want to know about this funeral.'

'Meet you in the Sheraton Bar at one thirty.'

'We're lunching in public in the Sheraton?' she asked in amazement.

'No, we're meeting there.'

'Oh God,' sighed Liz, 'why can't I have an ordinary man-friend?'

'Because you're not an ordinary girl, my darling. *Arrivederci!*'

He had letters to dictate, for which Hector McVay supplied a secretary. Then he had to go down to the basement in search of the Kamikura, who were practising.

'All set for this afternoon?'

'Yes, thank you.'

'I just want to remind you that Herr Tarnhold will be in the audience with his wife.' This was a Festival visitor, a German electronics tycoon. 'He'll want to come backstage to chat afterwards – OK?'

'Gregory, have they found out yet what killed Anne?' Michiko asked, looking up from tightening her bow.

'Not that I've heard. Why?'

'What do you mean, why?' grunted Shemnitzi. 'Something gives us all a sickness and you wonder why we want to know?'

'Sorry, that was a stupid question. No, I haven't heard, but if and when I do I'll let you know.'

After he got upstairs to his room he was told that Chief Inspector Fairmil wished to speak to him. 'Ask him if he'd like to come up. And send us some coffee, would you?'

'How are you today, Mr Crowne?' Fairmil enquired when the prince let him in.

'Quite fit, thank you. I've ordered coffee; would you like some?'

'Kind of you, sir. I hear in general you're kind to the cops.'

'I beg your pardon? Oh.' Jack Dempsey had been reporting on him. 'Well, why not? "*Dos linajes solos hay en el mundo*," chief inspector, namely the police and the public.'

'Is that a fact?' said the detective with a shrug. 'It's a pity those "two families" seem often to be unfriendly to each other. But the bodyguard we put on you seems justified, for the forensic results are indicating that some quite rare poison was used the other night.'

'Used? Used purposely, you mean.'

'That's the line we have to take, until we get evidence to the contrary.'

'May one ask what kind of poison?'

'The pathologist can't identify it. Between you and me, sir, he's fairly climbing the walls. Professor McHugh isn't the kind of man who likes to be beaten, but he's never met this one before.'

'Don't tell me it's this famous odourless, untraceable poison of legend?'

'Oh, it's left traces. A lot can be deduced from the way Miss Gleghorn died.'

'How did she die?'

'From respiratory failure. Her muscles ceased to be able to keep her breathing going. The professor says this was due to the action of a neurotoxin that paralysed the nerves and thus the muscles.'

'Like curare?'

'Oh, you've heard of that, have you? Yes, sir, *like* curare but *not* curare. Chromatography shows it to be not a vegetable poison, but animal.'

'Animal? What animal? Oh, snake venom, something like that?'

'Again, like that but not that. McHugh has all kinds of data about snake venom because people do get bitten by snakes – the keeper of the snakes at Edinburgh Zoo got bitten by one of his charges a few years ago, and Edinburgh Infirmary had the antidote in half an hour.'

'Has your expert any views on why Anne died when the rest of us survived?'

'The word he used was "idiosyncratic". It just so happens that the rest of you didn't have the same reaction to the poison. I think you told me Miss Gleghorn had to be careful what she ate, that in the past her health had been poor until she learned to avoid certain foods. And then it's just possible that Miss Gleghorn swallowed more than anyone else of whatever contained the poison.'

'She had a hearty appetite,' Crowne recalled.

After a little pause, Fairmil went on in a slightly different tone? 'I'll tell you something else, sir, since you were so much involved in it. It's about Miss Gleghorn and the missing cello.'

'What!' Crowne was startled.

'You remember that it was useless to try to get prints off the cellos after those idiots – sorry, sir, I mean, after the owners reclaimed them. But we had one cello on our hands other than the Stradivarius. We dusted both of them for fingerprints. Both of them had been wiped, or else whoever handled them picked them up the way musicians do, with the crook of the thumb and forefinger round the neck.'

'Yes, that's just what they do. Go on.'

'We also dusted both the cello cases. On the case belonging to the Emilio we found a great many prints one over the other, so they're no help. But on the case for that old Scottish cello—'

'Yes? What?'

At that moment the waiter brought the coffee, so Fairmil had an opportunity to avoid the question. When they were alone he said: 'It may sound gruesome, but Professor McHugh works to a set method. Often the bodies he examines are in need of identification. So he routinely took Miss Gleghorn's fingerprints.'

He paused to accept coffee from the prince, then set it down with slight emphasis to make his listener pay attention to his next point. 'Now, can you tell me, sir: would Miss Gleghorn have had any occasion to handle the George Duncan cello case?'

This was a question that required some thought. Crowne said slowly, 'Let me go through it. I went to Talik's bedroom on the night of the first performance of the Bachiana. He opened the case of the Emilio to try over some chords. That was the Emilio case. Inside was the Duncan cello. Eventually we went to the hall with that cello in that case.'

'Yes.'

'The police gathered up all the cellos in their cases and laid them out on the platform. The cellists rushed about opening cases and claiming their instruments. After each case was opened, I suppose no one touched the *case* – he picked out his or her own cello.'

'That's right.'

'In the end, everybody had their own cello, except Talik. He was left with the case belonging to the Emilio but still containing the George Duncan cello.'

'That's exactly how I remember it. The George Duncan *case* was never there – only the George Duncan cello.'

'Well then . . . After David Duntyre made his speech at the speakers' ground we came back to the hotel and got that clipping from the Robert Burns poem. We all rushed over to the garden, and there was the case belonging to the George Duncan cello.'

'With a tartan scarf tied round it,' Fairmil said grimly.

'Quite so. Talik opened it, and there was the Emilio.' The prince stopped. 'I don't remember what happened to the George Duncan case after that.'

'*I* took charge of it. No one else touched it until we got it to police HQ.'

'Are you sure of that?'

Fairmil didn't deign to reply to that. Instead he heaped sugar into his coffee and drank.

'Now sir,' he said, setting down the cup. 'Miss Gleghorn came to the speakers' ground. She came back to the hotel. She followed Mr Edder out to the crescent garden. That is the first time of our coming across the *case* for the Duncan cello. Did she at any time touch that case?'

'No.'

'She didn't pick it up, lay it flat, and open it?'

'No.'

'Then,' said the Chief Inspector with a kind of puzzled triumph, 'how can we account for her fingerprints, not on the leather body, but on the snap-lock of the case?'

Fourteen

It didn't seem to make any sense.

'You're saying, chief inspector, that Anne Gleghorn opened or closed the George Duncan case. But when?'

'That's the interesting point. When? I took that case away as soon as it was found in the gardens. I went up to the room while Mr Edder put the Emilio back in its own case, and took the George Duncan cello away with me. I put the cheapie cello in its own case when I got it down to the car.'

He sighed. 'It's funny. I nearly didn't bother about fingerprinting. It was so clear the Procurator Fiscal would want the whole thing dropped, I nearly said "Scrub it." And yet now . . . it looks as if . . .'

'As if Anne Gleghorn was involved in that prank with the Emilio.'

'That's about it.'

The prince got up and walked about his room, thinking. He stared out of the window. Over his shoulder he said: 'Are you by any chance suggesting that that is why she died?'

'I have no way of knowing, sir. I wouldn't have thought so, if it was just a hoax. But I wouldn't have said her prints would turn up on the cello case, either. Only they did.'

'Look here, Fairmil. It is possible that Anne took Talik's cello. At the time she was very angry with him.'

'The woman scorned, eh? Hell hath no fury.'

'She and Talik were in a state of great hostility. Oddly enough, it all faded away after he got the Emilio back. In fact, he quite resented her friendship with Mr Shige.'

164

'Resented it, eh? And mebbe resented her taking the cello, if he found that out somehow?'

Crowne gasped. 'He wouldn't, chief inspector. He really wouldn't kill anyone.'

'But he would have wanted to pay her out a little, eh? It could all have been a mistake, that she died. There was a feller killed off a couple of women by way of a joke – used cantharides, supposed to get them very sexy but used too much and killed them off.'

'But you're saying he would have played that trick on *all* of us, just to pay Anne back for her hoax. No, no, Fairmil. He wouldn't do it. I know him. He's a big, powerful-looking man – but he's just what the Americans call a pussycat.'

'But suppose he was pushed off balance a little. It was a shock to him, wasn't it, losing the Emilio?'

'By God, yes. He was in an awful state.'

'Suppose, after he got the cello back, Miss Gleghorn boasted she'd taken it and deigned to hand it back to him?'

Crowne tried to picture the scene and shied away from it. Instead he went for logic. 'Anne wouldn't have been such a fool. She wanted Talik back. She had a real feeling for him. You can see that in the idiocy of the stolen cello. She wouldn't actually steal it, take it away for ever – that would have been too cruel. Anne was after all a musician. She knew what the Emilio represented to Talik. She made sure he got it back.'

'We don't know that. *Someone* gave it back – it may not have been Anne Gleghorn. She must have had accomplices, you see,' Fairmil said. 'The Emilio appeared in the gardens while we were all at the speakers' ground – someone put it there while we were listening to David Duntyre speechifying.'

'I always imagined Duntyre was the principal mover in the hoax . . .'

'So did I. But it's not his fingerprints we find. It's Miss Gleghorn's.'

'Are there other prints?'

'Oh yes. The shopkeeper's, Mr Edder's – he opened the case in the gardens. Miss Gleghorn's. And one other.'

'Whose?'

Fairmil shrugged. 'You recall "an Englishman" bought the Duncan cello? Well, I imagine those are his prints.'

'"An Englishman" bought it. What's the betting "an Englishman" put the George Duncan case with the Emilio cello in the gardens?'

They sat in silence, trying to make it fit with Anne's death. At length Crowne said, 'Chief Inspector, I have some news for you – on a different topic.'

'Good or bad?'

'Both. First the bad news: Senhora Kelly is guilty of a quite serious crime, I'm afraid.'

'Oh, God,' groaned Chief Inspector Fairmil. 'What now?'

'She brought a cat into this country without informing the health authorities.'

Fairmil said nothing. It seemed to him that his cup was full to overflowing with troubles from the Hill Hotel. First a missing Strad, next a poisoning, now a contravention of quarantine.

'Now the good news: the cat is dead.'

'Dead?' Fairmil started up. 'How the hell is that good news? If it's bitten—'

'It didn't die of rabies. Angeliza's cat died of the food she took up to it from the midnight buffet. She was in the habit of smuggling scraps to it to supplement its diet of dry catfood from a packet.'

'The cat was poisoned?'

'I'd take a wager on it. And, chief inspector, what do you feed a cat on, according to tradition?'

'What?' The detective frowned, then looked enlightened. 'Fish!'

They said together, like a speaking chorus, 'The poison was in the fish!'

The idea had been working to the surface of the prince's

166

mind ever since he heard that the pathologist suspected an animal poison.

'But that makes all the difference in the world!' cried Fairmil, leaping up like a man whose burden has slipped from his shoulders. 'Fish! It's notorious for being dicey, isn't it? Mussels, for instance – they're supposed to be dangerous to eat. Did you have mussels?'

'Yes, among other kinds of shellfish – and there was cuttle-fish and squid and scallops, as well as various kinds of raw fish and crab and lobster. I think there was sturgeon, too.'

'Sturgeon? That's what caviar comes from, isn't it? Surely caviare isn't poisonous.'

'No, but parts of the flesh are poisonous during the spawning season. And the roe of certain common fish – pike, I believe.'

Fairmil raised sandy eyebrows. 'You know a wee bitty about it!'

'As a matter of fact, yes. I'm a keen angler when I get the chance. That's what makes it all the more silly of me not to think of it before. *Of course* it was the fish.'

'That's extremely useful, sir. I'll get this information to McHugh as soon as possible, and with clues like that I dare say he'll be able to wrap the whole thing up as accidental death. And the cat – where's the cat?'

'Buried in a plant trough on the roof.'

Fairmil gaped. 'What on earth?'

'If you're going to disinter it, chief inspector, could you keep the news from Mrs Kelly? It would probably send her back into hysterics.'

'Send her to jail, more likely, when I report this! That was very irresponsible of her, Mr Crowne, to bring in an animal that way.'

'I agree with you; but she hasn't in fact admitted that she brought it in, and perhaps it won't be so easy to prove when it comes to the point. If she says the cat was an Edinburgh cat, and sticks by it, how can you prove she's lying?'

'But she told you she'd brought in into the country—'

'No, she didn't.'

'Then how do you know?'

'I can't remember.'

'I suppose there is a cat in the plant trough?'

'Oh, yes. I saw it there.'

'You saw it? How did you come to be on the roof, if I may ask?'

'I was taking a midnight stroll.'

'Now look here, sir—'

'Mr Fairmil, I told you about the cat because I thought it was important in narrowing down the field about the poison. But I don't think I want to give evidence against Senhora Kelly and if you ask me to I shall have a sad lapse of memory. But the first thing is to have a post-mortem on the cat. In its case there'll be no complicating factor brought about by alcohol intake or human idiosyncrasy.'

'Aye. Aye, well. I suppose you're right.'

Crowne hurried off to meet Liz Blair. For the time being he put Anne Gleghorn and Angeliza Kelly out of his mind.

The news next day was that Professor McHugh had triumphantly identified the poison that had caused respiratory failure in Anne Gleghorn and the Venetian cat. It came from a fish of the Tetraodontiform class, rare in British waters.

Hector McVay looked totally at a loss when this was put to him.

'The fish in the cold buffet that night was a kind of Jenny-a'-things,' he explained. 'There was some lightly salted fresh haddock, thinly sliced – that's a Finnish dish from the district of Savo. Then there was smoked whitefish, what we call buckie, and salmon and trout and herring, and there was crab and lobster and scallops. Are any of those Tetraodontiform?'

'Not one. Go on, Hector.'

'Well, Mr Crowne, don't forget there was the sashimi. I

don't know what was in that. I bought that in, in honour of Mr Shige and Miss Toshio.'

'Bought it from where?'

'From the only restaurant in Edinburgh that sells Japanese food.'

'And which might that be?' Chief Inspector Fairmil, who was no gourmet, enquired.

'It's really a Hawaiian restaurant. Makes most of its money selling gammon steaks with bits of pineapple on it,' McVay said with scorn. 'But it does good roast sucking-pig, and some things with coconut, and I must say their tempura is nice.'

'What's its name?' persisted Fairmil.

'The Lei. Out towards Corstorphine.'

The detective whisked away and nothing more was heard for a time. There was no reason why the crown prince should expect the CID man to confide in him, but all the same, having supplied a piece of information on what the guilty food might be, somehow he felt a proprietary interest.

He was, however, busy. He had to find a soprano to undertake the last of the Schütz recitals in place of Anne Gleghorn; he had to start negotiating for classical guitar-ists to go to Kingston, Jamaica; there was work to do on the imminent Montreux Festival; two of his artistes were scheduled to give recitals in the Wigmore Hall in London; and Grossmutti rang to say he was expected back for the silver-wedding celebrations of a Swiss friend.

Having been told officially that he could eat what he liked, he took Liz out to a handsome restaurant overlooking the classical ruins on Calton Hill for dinner. The only thing to mar their evening was her announcement that she really must get back to London.

'Now that you're not in danger from a dastardly plot but only from some iffy fish, I feel I can leave you to look after yourself.'

'How do you know I'm not in mortal danger?' he pleaded. 'I might have a Japanese Maoist after me.'

'A likely story. I notice your guard dog has disappeared.'

Constable Dempsey had vanished from the scene at the same time that Fairmil left to find the Lei Restaurant. It was undeniable that the police now saw the entire episode at the Hill Hotel as one of those unfortunate affairs where catering had slipped up and the food was harmful.

'If you'll promise to stay on until after Sunday, I'll treat you to a Drambuie.'

'Are you trying to get me drunk and take advantage of me, sir?'

'Not here and now. But a friend of mine has a cottage he can lend us – on the banks of a stream, miles away from anywhere. At night there's no sound but the sigh of the wind and the cry of the curlew.'

'Oh, we're going to be there at night?'

'Naturally. After a long day's trout-fishing, it would be too tiring to drive—'

'Trout-fishing? You think I want to go trout-fishing?'

'No, no. I'll fish for trout; all you have to do is gut them and clean them and cook them for lunch.'

'Thanks a million. One Drambuie isn't enough to make me fall for that.'

'All right then, I'll gut them and clean them and cook them for lunch. And you can have a double Drambuie.'

'Is it a nice cottage?'

'Truly rural.'

'Miles away from anywhere?'

'At the end of the Yellow Brick Road.'

'No reporters?'

'No.'

'No difficult musicians?'

'Not one.'

'No police guard dog?'

'You said yourself, he's gone.'

'All right then, I give in. But I'd rather have Grand Marnier than Drambuie.'

When he got back to the hotel there was a message to ring Fairmil, who said wearily: 'Well, I think we were right. They've got fish in the freezer at the Lei Restaurant which Professor McHugh says he thinks are Tetraodontiform, although he's no itchy – ichny—'

'Ichthyologist?'

'That's it. He's got a pal in the Zoology faculty of the university who'll verify it to him. But we're pretty sure that's what the fish was that you got in the Japanese buffet.'

'That's very careless,' Crowne said in dismay. 'I hope you'll prevent it happening again?'

'Well of course. In any case they won't be serving Japanese food for a while. Know why?'

'Why?'

'The chef who prepared that food for the Hill Hotel order got very anxious when reports appeared in the papers about the death of Anne Glegorn. It seems he spoke very poor English but the kitchen staff could tell something was bothering him. In the end he said he'd ring somebody to sort out his problem.'

'And did he?' Crowne asked, suddenly alert. He was thinking of the phone call that had come through by mistake to the conference room. A voice with a strong Japanese accent.

Asking for Michiko Toshio.

'Yes, he rang somebody. Next thing they knew, he'd scarpered.'

'Scarpered? Run away?' He wasn't sure of the idiom – some aspects of English could still trap him, and Cockney was one.

'Yes, he's run away. So that seems to clinch it, doesn't it? He knew he'd made a terrible mistake somehow over that fish, so he's cleared off.'

After a moment's hesitation, he told Fairmil about the voice asking for Michiko. Fairmil sounded peeved. 'Have you any reason to think it was the chef?'

'I've no idea. Michiko said she never got the call.'

'Why would he ring Miss Toshio?'

'I don't know. Perhaps . . . After all, she'd been mentioned in the newspapers, she's in the Festival programme – if there's a Japanese community in Edinburgh they must chat about her, I suppose. So it could be that the chef realised he was in trouble over something that had happened at the Hill Hotel, but he wasn't quite sure what. So he rang Michiko to ask her about it – have it spelt out in Japanese.'

'But you say she never got the call.'

'That's right. In any case, it may not have been him. She said it could be someone who knows her family and just wanted to make contact. It's understandable.'

'I'll ask her about it.'

Michiko Toshio. She figured frequently in the events at the Hill Hotel. Her cello had been switched, like Talik's. She got it back, like Talik. She partook of the midnight buffet, like Talik and Anne Gleghorn and all the others – but here was a difference: she was not unwell.

No, but very, very concerned about David Duntyre when he was stricken by the poisoned fish. Deeply attracted to Duntyre, physically attracted and politically in sympathy . . .

If *Michiko's* fingerprints had been found on the case of what Fairmil called the cheapie cello, he could have understood it. Michiko might have fallen in willingly and laughingly with a plot to get political publicity out of the hijacking of the Emilio.

Yet it was Anne Gleghorn's fingerprints that turned up. Beyond a doubt, Anne Gleghorn had been mixed up in the taking of the Emilio.

But Anne could not have carried a cello away from the concert-hall green room. Anne was a singer, not an instrumentalist. If she had been seen carrying a cello, it would have been noticeable, remembered.

Therefore someone who *could* carry a cello in its case without being remarked upon had taken part in the theft.

And the natural suspect was Michiko, who admired and

sympathised with David Duntyre. Duntyre had been the instigator of the theft, which he had used for publicity purposes – he had more or less announced the fact by having a tartan scarf tied round the cello case when it was recovered.

It must have gone something like this: David had said to Michiko, 'There's all this fuss and attention being paid to the Emilio. If we could pretend to steal it and hand it back with a lot of public attention, it would draw attention to the cause of the Scottish Progressive Party.'

So Michiko had stolen the Emilio for him. She had carried the George Duncan cello in the case belonging to the Emilio, and walked out with the Emilio in the George Duncan case.

Wrong.

Michiko had walked out of the hall with her own case, containing a Pressenda cello. The prince had *seen* the Pressenda in Michiko's room.

Anne Gleghorn's fingerprints . . .

Start again.

Anne Gleghorn had been the instigator of the plot. She'd wanted to punish Talik Edder for his treatment of her, for his egotism, for his success in buying the Emilio and being so happy about it. She'd said to David Duntyre, 'Wouldn't it be a big newspaper story if we pulled a stunt on the Emilio? Stole it and returned it in a blaze of publicity?'

Very possible. The three of them, David, Michiko and Anne, worked out the scheme. One of the actors in David's play was asked to buy the cheapie cello – how the man would have enjoyed putting on an 'English' accent to hoodwink the shopkeeper.

Then what? That man gave the cello in its case to Michiko. Michiko carried it to the Usher Hall – who would look twice at Michiko Toshio arriving with a cello?

After the performance of the Bachiana Brasileira No. 5, they all trooped off to the manager's office to have drinks and nibbles with the Brazilian Consul. Anne Gleghorn waited behind. She switched all the cellos – easily done: open one case, take out the cello, lay it by, open the next case, take out the cello and put it in the first case, and so on, all round the room.

Merde. Then there would be one extra cello left in the green room when the eight cellists took home their own cases with changeling cellos inside.

There had been no extra cello at the hall. There had been eight cellos at the hall and eight cellos had been taken home.

And then it came to him, in a great blaze of light like the fiery chariot arriving from the heavens for Elijah.

The George Duncan cello had never gone to the Usher Hall. The switching of all the cellos there had been done to concentrate attention on the hall, making everyone think the theft had occurred *there*, and not at the Hill Hotel.

Now wait, Crowne said to himself, wait. Let's get this straight.

In the green room after the performance of the Bachiana Brasileira No. 5, Anne Gleghorn had hung back when the rest of them left. There had been eight cellos, only eight cellos. She had switched them – all except Talik Edder's cello.

Edder had taken the Emilio safely back to the Hill Hotel. He took it up to his room.

They had all gone upstairs more or less together. There had been hugs and friendly calls to one another, promises to see each other downstairs for the midnight buffet. Anne Gleghorn must have lingered at Talik's door, fixed the inside catch in the handle so that the door would close but not lock.

Then, when Talik went downstairs, she'd slipped in with the George Duncan cello in her hands, taken the Emilio out of its case and substituted the cheapie. She had taken the Emilio. *Where* had she taken the Emilio?

Not to her room. Too dangerous. Come to that, where had she kept the cheapie cello while she waited to make the exchange? She was a singer; having a cello in her room would be odd.

Crowne hit himself on the forehead with the palm of his hand. 'You idiot!' he cried aloud. 'Of course. The practice rooms in the basement.'

No one at the Hill Hotel would have looked twice at a cello in its case sitting on a chair or leaning in a corner of one of the practice rooms.

Go back to the beginning.

David Duntyre's actor-accomplice – call him Mr English – bought the cello. He handed it to Michiko – easy enough: he picks her up in his car; when she gets out she's carrying a cello in a case.

Michiko takes the cheapie cello to the Hill Hotel, walks in quite openly with it, goes down to the basement, leaves it propped against the wall in the practice room next door to the one she and the quartet use.

There it stays until the night of the Bachiana Brasileira. Anne switches all the cellos except Talik's, at the hall. That was to cause confusion. Talik brings home the Emilio; Anne brings the George Duncan cello up from the basement by the back stairs; goes into Talik's room after he's gone down to the midnight buffet. She takes the Emilio out of its case, puts the cheapie in its place. As she goes out she presses the knob in Talik's door so that the door locks behind her. She takes the Emilio down and puts it in the George Duncan case.

Then what? She can't leave it in the practice room. First thing, when the Emilio goes missing, the police will search the hotel. So she . . . she . . . What?

She puts it outside the back door? Where Mr English can pick it up and take it away until it's time to place it on the bench in the crescent gardens?

Crowne had that feeling of satisfaction that comes when you've completed the crossword puzzle. All the white squares filled in, everything cross-matching. He knew he had solved the problem of how the Emilio was taken and put back.

He must speak to Michiko and verify his solution. He knew she would be unable to lie her way out of it if he taxed her with it.

Yet . . . Why should he? The matter of the Emilio was closed. Talik Edder had shaken hands with David Duntyre, the Procurator Fiscal was not interested in taking any proceedings.

Better forget it. To have worked out how the theft was accomplished – that was what really mattered. He had wanted to do that for his own satisfaction.

All the same, Michiko cropped up again in the matter of Anne Gelghorn's death.

Oh, come on, he scolded himself. Just because she helped to steal the Emilio and give it back, that doesn't mean she had anything to do with a death.

Yet he wanted to see what Michiko said when he asked again about that phone call. Though it was late, he went to her room and tapped lightly. No reply. He was almost sure that if he went to Duntyre's room and tapped, he would find her.

But that was the kind of thing one didn't do.

Fifteen

Next day, Saturday, was a heavy day for the musicians. The Kamikura Quartet had engagements both in the afternoon and in the evening. The afternoon recital was Schubert; the evening was the Martinu No. 7 and the Villa-Lobos in E major.

Talik was to play the 'Fantasia for Cello and Orchestra' by Villa-Lobos with the Sinfonia de Méjico. He was practising and rehearsing all Saturday.

Crowne, suitably dressed in a sombre suit and grey silk tie, escorted Angeliza to the office of the Procurator Fiscal to hold her hand and supply Kleenex while she was questioned about Cha-cha.

In his car on the way there, he tried to brace her for the ordeal. 'They had to be told about the cat, because they had to carry out an autopsy on her. But they can't prove you didn't find her here in Edinburgh, Angeliza – do you understand?'

'But I found her in Venice—'

'If you tell them that you'll have to go to court. You'll be fined; you might even have to serve a prison sentence—'

'Prison!' she squealed, thinking of the prisons of her homeland.

'Perhaps not. I don't know the law. But the point is this: all they can prove is that you had a pet cat which died. Do you understand?'

She nodded in wretched assent.

He thought she would go to pieces under questioning. And so she did. And yet somehow it didn't go badly.

'You say it was a stray cat, Mrs Kelly?'

'Yes.'

'Where did you find it?'

'In the street.'

'What street?'

'I forget the name.'

'In Edinburgh?'

She went off into floods of tears, her head nodding as she bowed over herself, wailing, 'Cha-cha, oh, Cha-cha.'

It never emerged whether she had found the cat abroad. Every time the subject was broached she became incoherent.

'You fed it with scraps from the restaurant meals?'

'And with Pussipurr – that has minerals and vitamins also, for the coat.'

'Why did you keep it a secret?'

'It was no secret. Mr McVay knew.'

'Mr McVay buried the cat. Did he know of it before that?'

'*Sim, seguro.*'

'The cat died the same night as Miss Gleghorn?'

'*Penso que sim.*'

'Could we stick to English, Mrs Kelly?'

'I'm sorry. Of course.'

'You had fed the cat from food from the buffet from which all of you ate?'

'Yes.'

'What did you take upstairs?'

'Pieces of fish.'

'What kind of fish?'

She turned to Crowne with a helpless fluttering of her long dark eyelashes. He murmured to her in Portuguese. She gave a little shrug. 'Two or three kinds. I don't recall.'

'The cat ate it all up?'

'Oh yes. He loved these little treats. Poor Cha-Cha.' She sobbed and put a new Kleenex against her lips. 'I didn't mean to give him *a intoxicado*.'

The Fiscal looked at Crowne with raised brows. 'Does that mean drunk? The cat was drunk?'

'No, it means food poisoning.'

'Oh, I see. Well, yes, the cat died of the poison in the fish.'

Angeliza let out a wail of anguish.

'I'm sorry, Mrs Kelly, I can see you're very distressed at losing your pet.'

She burst into a torrent of Portuguese intermingled with sobs. The official frowned, smiled, came round the desk to pat her plump shoulder, then looked helplessly at the prince.

'I don't think we need take this any further,' he murmured.

'Thank you. Come along, Angeliza.'

'We can go?' she asked in Portuguese.

'Yes, we can go.'

'They are not going to put me in prison?'

'No.'

'*Senhor, senhor, obrigada, muito obrigada!*' She made as if to clutch the Fiscal, who retreated briskly.

Leading her out to find a drink in the old High Street, Crowne reflected that, for all her helplessness, Angeliza was a survivor.

He parted with her outside the boutiques in Rose Street, where she was going to seek solace with an investment in knitted silk sweaters. 'I shall buy you also a present, for a thank-you,' she said.

'Please don't – it's not necessary.'

'Oh, *sim*, that tie you are wearing is very dull!'

His next appointment was to arrange for the sending home of Anne Gleghorn's body; her mother in Illinois had decided to bury her daughter in the family plot. Her agent was to meet the coffin at New York. It was all very gruesome and depressing.

A quick lunch, and then it was his duty to drop in on the Kamikura's recital. They were beginning the second

179

movement of the 'Death and the Maiden' when he slipped through the doors and stood quietly at the back. The hall was full. He watched with a feeling of perplexity as they wove their variations, and found it difficult to believe that Michiko had guilty knowledge concerning the death of Anne.

'I am a friend and do not come to punish,' he quoted to himself from the words of the poem that Schubert had set to music. He waited until the *sforzandi* of the third movement before slipping out as quietly as he came in.

Talik was having a break in rehearsal when he called in on him. Angeliza was in the auditorium, plump bosom over-enhanced in a vivid new jersey of knitted and folded silk which made her look larger still.

'Take that female home, Gregory,' begged Talik. 'She came tottering up to me an hour ago asking me to put my arms around her and comfort her, because she was very upset.'

'So she was. An interview with the legal authorities isn't fun.'

'Legal authorities? What is this? She isn't under any suspicion over Anne?'

'She hasn't told you about Cha-cha?'

'Who the blazes is Cha-cha?'

'Her cat. It died.'

'Gregory, I am in the middle of rehearsing a very difficult and demanding work. I don't have time to bother with Angeliza Kelly and her absurd pets.'

'All right, Talik. I'll take her with me when I go. *Tout va bien?*'

The Finn shrugged. 'If this imbecile of a conductor can make up his mind about the tempi, *tout ira assez bien*. But tonight will not be one of my triumphs.'

'Never mind. You can look forward to the Tattoo afterwards.'

He gave a shudder. 'How did I get myself talked into this? I do not at all wish to sit on top of a rock in the cold and watch Scotch people disporting themselves in the dark.'

'You *are* in a bad mood! You know when Hector suggested it you said you thought it very *folklorique*.'

'I must have been out of my mind.' He glanced back at the platform as the conductor tapped politely with his baton to signal that the rehearsal was about to resume. 'Very well, I go to the Tootat—'

'Tattoo.'

'Tattoo – but we must have blankets and cushions and overcoats. I know these *son et lumière* events – always the wind cuts like a knife.'

In the evening the prince took Liz to hear the soprano who had inherited the Schütz recital from Anne Gleghorn. It was a short programme, so they came out of the cathedral by nine. Next came dinner in a new restaurant in Shandwick Place, the kind of restaurant that has shaded candles and a guitarist playing Simon and Garfunkel.

'I have to tell you,' Liz said in an apologetic tone, 'I prefer this to Schütz.'

'That's all right. Not everybody likes seventeenth-century church music.'

She sipped white wine and smiled at him over the rim of her glass. Above her dark silk dress her honey-blond hair gleamed like topaz in the rosy light of the shaded candles.

'It always amazes me that you're so *normal*, Greg.'

'Why should I be abnormal? Or subnormal?'

'Well, first of all you're a prince. Then you do this awful high-brow business with music and musicians. Yet you don't make many waves among ordinary people.'

Crowne laughed. 'It's my life's ambition to sink in among "ordinary people" and just enjoy life the way they do. Being a prince is really no fun. As to the music – well, you only have to look at the crowds who pack the Proms to see that I'm not extraordinary in enjoying it. I think I'm lucky being able to make a comfortable income out of something I enjoy.'

'But you're so bright, Greg! You could do anything – you

181

could make a fortune on the Stock Exchange if you wanted to, run a big corporation—'

He was shaking his head. 'The low profile, the low, low profile, Liz. I can't get involved in politics or anything connected with politics – not stocks and shares, not big business. If you knew how many companies have invited me to join their board of directors, so as to have my name on the letterhead . . . But it's always no-can-do. There's no way of knowing when a business might start getting involved in international politics.'

'Poor sweetheart,' Liz said.

He looked at her with alarm. 'Have you had too much wine, my angel?'

'Are you saying I can't hold my liquor? Them's fighting words, stranger.'

'It's not like you to be so sympathetic.'

'Oh, so I'm not only a drunk, I'm a hard old hag?'

'Ask me after tomorrow whether you're a hard old hag.'

'Why, what's happening tomorrow? I thought we were going to catch some poor dumb fish.'

'That's in the daytime. Night-time is when I make my assessment of your hardness and haggishness.'

'Promises, promises. I bet the phone will ring with some message from Geneva—'

'We'll take it off the hook.'

She was still mulling this over when he drove her back to Murrayfield. 'What time are you coming for me tomorrow?' she enquired as they stood waiting for the door at the side of the dress shop to be opened.

'Six o'clock?'

'You're joking! I thought the Yellow Brick Road was over the rainbow, not beyond the sunrise!'

'All right then, six fifteen.'

Footsteps on the staircase coming down to the door. She kissed him quickly. 'My word, these fish had better be worth it,' she said, and slipped indoors when her friend opened up.

Grinning to himself, Crowne headed back to the Hill Hotel to collect the blankets, footmuffs and comforters deemed necesary for the open-air performance on the Esplanade.

In the hotel vestibule Sergeant Haggerston was talking to McVay, who was already in a quilted coat and a scarf, ready for the Tattoo. As Crowne came in Haggerston raised a hand to halt him.

'Mr Fairmil said if I ran across you to have a word, sir. He thought you'd want to know. We found Togo Noguru.'

'Who's Togo Noguru?'

'The chef at the Lei Restaurant responsible for the Japanese food.'

'Good work! What does he say about the fish?'

'Well, sir,' said Haggerston, with a dour glint that told of a joke plotted and now brought off to his satisfaction, 'no doubt he's had long conversations with the fish, but he's not saying anything to us.'

'Why not?' said the prince, surprised.

'Because he's dead.'

'Dead!'

'He was found off the side of Granton Breakwater this evening with a rope round his ankles.'

'Oh, damn!' A score of questions crowded to be asked. 'What do you think happened?'

'Looks like he couldn't face having to answer for what he'd done, and chucked himself into the sea.'

'First tying his ankles?'

'Och yes, sir. If they want to make sure they don't get second thoughts and try to save themselves, they give themselves handicaps like that. In fact, I think this chap tied himself to an old chunk of iron, then jumped in holding it. But the rope was pretty old and it gradually broke so the body floated up.'

'That's ghastly, sergeant.' The next question was: 'Why should he take it so much to heart – the business of the fish? It was an accident, after all.'

'Well, sir, I hear these orientals set a lot of importance on face. He'd made a muck of things, hadn't he? Caused the death of an innocent lady. And being a stranger in a strange land he felt it all the worse. So he decided to do away with himself in penance.'

'Ye-es. I suppose it was suicide?'

Haggerston raised heavy eyebrows at him. 'What for no, sir?'

'Well . . . Could somebody have done it to him?'

'What, him standing there while somebody ties him to an old iron stanchion, and letting himself be thrown in?'

'No signs of a struggle? No bruises or abrasions?'

'Didn't see him myself, sir, but I gather he didn't have anything more wrong with him than could be accounted for by being bashed against the side of Granton Breakwater for twenty-four hours or so.'

'There'll be a post-mortem?'

'You bet.'

'Um.' Next question. 'What about the phone call to Miss Toshio?'

'I asked her about that. She definitely didn't get it.'

'Did you speak to the switchboard operator?'

'I've just been doing that, sir. As a matter of fact, it's not so easy to track down a phone call by a Japanese caller – she told me that Mr Shige has been putting through calls to Tokyo and receiving calls back. So if a Japanese voice spoke, she wouldn't pay special attention.'

'Of course. I see that.'

'If it'll set your mind at rest about who called Miss Toshio, I enquired at the Japanese Consulate and in fact someone did ring for her, saying he was a cousin of her mother's. Quite bona fide. They told him to try the Hill Hotel. So the phone call to Miss Toshio has no significance.'

'Right.' He felt a great relief. To have suspected Michiko of somehow being in touch with Noguru, that was bad enough. Now that Noguru was dead, it would have been even worse.

'You're all off up to the Tattoo, I hear? I hope you enjoy it, sir.'

'Thank you, sergeant. And by the way, in case Mr Fairmil might worry, I shan't be around tomorrow. I'm going up north to do some trout-fishing. Back early Monday.'

'Good luck with that, then, Mr Crowne, and a guid nicht to you.'

As he left, the others from the Hill Hotel who were going up to the Castle for the performance clustered around McVay. 'Parking isn't easy up by the Castle,' he explained, 'so I've laid on taxis. Those who are here and ready, will you go out and climb aboard? The taxis will come back for the others.'

Talik, in an access of security-consciousness, insisted on locking away his Strad and his Guarneri in McVay's office before leaving the hotel for a longish period of the night. Senhora Kelly hung on his arm. He was being sweet to her, apparently overtaken by an attack of conscience for his bad temper earlier.

They were rather late in arriving at the Esplanade and settling themselves: the massed bands were already marching and counter-marching.

The Tattoo was the usual mixture of the historical, the musical, the martial and the folkloric. To the musicians it was highly entertaining because it was so unlike anything they themselves were involved in. They had a high opinion of the bandmasters who somehow managed to produce a concord of sound in the echoing conditions of the great open arena.

The moment that appealed most to Crowne was when the place was totally blacked out and a solitary piper was spotlit high on the battlements, playing a lament. There was something deeply tragic and heart-rending in the high, keening sound, something from the true springs of folk music from which, in the end, all other music comes.

He thought of Anne Gleghorn, soon to start on the speedy journey to her native land and a small plot of ground that

would be her eternal home. 'No more, no more, no more
for ever,' the piper's melody seemed to say, 'no more shall
music rouse within her.'

The night was fine and clear with little wind. McVay, who
had constituted himself guide, philosopher and friend to the
party, asked if anyone would like to walk a little through
the Old Town to a club where he was a member. Duntyre
seconded it: drinks would be available and a chance to chat
to some of the Fringe performers – 'The cast of my play will
probably be there.'

The older members of the party opted for taxis home
and bed. Crowne would have been quite glad to do the
same, since he was making such an early start next morning for the trout stream. But on the other hand, he might
espy 'Mr English', the man who had bought the George
Duncan cello.

David Duntyre urged, 'Come on, let's take a wee walk.
You should see a bit of Edinburgh that's not neoclassical
and dressed-up Adam. Scotland existed a long time before
the Age of Reason got ahold of it, you know.'

Michiko immediately fell in with the idea. Talik announced
that he wouldn't mind some exercise, so at once Senhora
Kelly murmured that she was greatly interested in Edinburgh
history.

'Can I tag along with you?' Shige asked Talik.

'Certainly. Give your arm on the other side to Angeliza.
Her shoes are too high in the heel for these cobblestones,
she'll fall and break her neck.'

'Listen, Edder . . . About the Guarneri . . .'

'Let us not speak of the Guarneri. Nor about the Emilio.
The Emilio I keep till the day I die. When I get to Vienna,
I make a will that ensures she goes only to a performing
artiste. Also the Guarneri – I had a phone call last night
from Marchier: he is the kind of young cellist I think should
have the Guarneri.'

'No good if Michiko makes you an offer, Talik?' Henry

186

Holt teased. 'The kind of money we're earning now, thanks to Mr Crowne, she might be able to pay you off for it in about three years.'

'Enough of money and business. Come, let us see this old city David boasts of.'

There were seven walkers when they set off from St Columba's, and once again Crowne noticed with regret that Shige was hanging on the outskirts of the group. What a pity his daughter hadn't come to the Festival with him. He had no one to go around with and Michiko, with whom he might have struck up a natural friendship once the misunderstandings of the past had been smoothed away, was totally absorbed in David Duntyre.

The party settled naturally into three groups: Michiko and Duntyre holding hands, Angeliza hanging on to Talik with Shige on her other side, and McVay with Mr Crowne. McVay explained where they were and what they should be looking at.

'This is Milne's Court.' It was a handsome paved area with old stone tenements, beautifully restored, on either side. 'It's a postgraduate centre for the university. Now if you'll just come carefully down these steps . . . They're rather steep . . . Mind how you go, ladies . . .'

Angeliza, who was wearing paper-thin shoes with tittuppy heels totally unsuitable for the cobbled surfaces, had a good excuse for clinging all the more heavily to Talik. At one point she nearly took him tumbling with her, and of course when he 'saved' her they were clutched together in a most satisfactory way.

Good for her, thought Crowne. Perhaps she was going to find consolation for the death of poor Cha-cha after all. Aloud he said to Edder: 'Please don't fracture your skull on these steps. You have a recital tomorrow.'

'Your care for me is touching. But don't worry, I didn't survive the funny fish just to break my neck on a mid-night walk.'

187

'Don't talk like that,' Angeliza protested. 'It's nothing to joke about.'

'I suppose not. It would be a short reunion with the Emilio if I broke my neck a few days after getting her back.'

'You must be careful not just because of the Emilio.'

'Because of you?' he teased, tapping her lightly on the nose with a long finger.

Crowne didn't hear her reply. But it occurred to him that, whether because of Anne's death or not, Angeliza had improved her relationship with Talik.

They moved off together after McVay, who was now asking them to admire the view over Princes Street Gardens and the National Gallery, all of it speckled with streetlamps or gleaming with floodlights.

'It looks like something in a dream, doesn't it?' Crowne murmured.

'Oh, it's real enough,' Duntyre said. 'We're all real, up here in the cold north – we have to be, even though we put on a good show of fantasy for visitors. Do you know the average income is . . .'

What he wanted to say about low earnings was dispersed in the gasping that came as they climbed back to the High Street by means of a series of steep steps. 'This is the way to Lady Stair's House,' McVay panted, trying to address them over his shoulder as he made his toilsome way up ahead of them. 'It's . . . a very *old* building. All of this . . . area . . . here . . . is medieval, you know. Built after Flodden . . . when we Scots were . . . all . . . huddling together . . . for fear . . . of attack.'

'Save your breath,' said Duntyre in amusement. He of course was having almost no trouble, his long legs taking the steps with ease. He even had plenty of strength to help Michiko, but she was of sterner stuff than Angeliza and only needed a hand under her elbow.

'Who was going to attack you?' Shige asked. He too was fit enough to find the stairs little trouble.

'Och, the English, who else?' Duntyre laughed. 'You must realise, Shige the Scots have had a hate–hate relationship with the English for centuries.'

'Only Scots like you!' McVay said crossly. 'People with no real sense of what the world is about these days.' He paused to take several breaths before going on: 'I can see nothing's going to happen over the cello, and Talik's been an angel to forgive you, but the way you bring politics into everything—'

'Who was the lady for whom the house is named?' Crowne interposed hastily to prevent a slanging-match.

Hector turned away from his annoyance to a long explanation about the building. Crowne encouraged him to talk as they stood in the great open court lit by a handsome blue-painted lamp standard. When he returned to the general conversation it was to find Talik joking with Angeliza about the Emilio. 'You must not worry about it, Angeliza, little angel,' he told her. 'I love that instrument and it loves me, but there are some things even a Stradivarius cello cannot do!'

Angeliza giggled happily and Michiko, overhearing, laughed aloud. 'Angeliza, if you think the Emilio is too much competition, get him to give it to me!'

It was the first time Crowne had ever heard her express envy of it. He pricked up his ears.

'No, no – I have already explained, she stays with me for the rest of my life. As soon as it can be arranged, I make a will to ensure she goes to another performer when I die. If you care to wait, my little Michiko, you may have her one day.'

Michiko said, with a straight face, 'How long are you going to live, Talik?'

'A hundred years!'

Hector suspected his sightseers had had enough exercise by now. He suggested he should lead them to the Mercat Cross; from there the nightclub was only down a short slope.

'No more climbing up and down?' pleaded Angeliza.

'No, I promise you – it's just a hundred yards or so along the High Street, down a close—'

'A what?'

'A close, an alley – och, why can't you visitors learn some basic Scots?' cried Duntyre.

On they went, McVay pointing out buildings as they passed. 'The Parliament House . . . the Sheriff Court . . . the Tron Kirk . . .' Politely they looked from one to the other, until there was an interruption at the edge of the group, a sort of flurry.

A lurching figure was grabbing at Talik Edder. Alarmed, Edder pulled himself free.

'Ach, dinna pu' awa' like that, mon!' the man cried. 'Gie's some siller, mister – gie's a wee twicer.'

Talik understood not a word of it. The beggar clutched at him again. 'Gie's a punnote, Jimmy, ye look well aff!'

Talik straight-armed him off, so that he staggered and almost fell. As he scrambled back to his feet he was swearing horribly.

David Duntyre stepped in at once. In the same rapid, fluent speech as the drunk he told him to get up, pull himself together, go away and stop bothering them. He softened the commands by handing him some money. The drunk staggered off, still muttering in resentment.

'Oh dear, oh dear,' wailed McVay, comforting Angeliza. 'Don't you be upset, my dear! He's gone now.' And to Duntyre, 'Really, it's too bad! Those derelicts should be rounded up, they really should, harrassing innocent folk like that!

'Och, the poor souls, they can't help themselves,' Duntyre said with tolerance. 'Come on, let's step it out – that laddie might come back with some of his friends.'

As they moved off at a smarter pace he explained that Edinburgh, like most cities, had its share of drop-outs and down-and-outs, who tended to congregate to the south side of the old High Street. 'There's a centre for them to be taken in care in the Grassmarket,' he said, 'and a place where they can get a meal in Old Fishmarket Close. I hope that specimen didn't alarm you, Talik – they do sometimes get a bit cantankerous, but only amongst themselves as a rule.'

Talik said he quite understood, that Finland had its problem drinkers too.

The club proved to be an agreeable little place where they settled down with suitable refreshments to listen to a flautist playing old Scottish dance tunes. Across the room, a couple at a corner table waved to David. Crowne recognised them as the leading players from the play, *Displenishin'*.

By and by they drifted across to be introduced. The man was Michael, the woman Trish.

'How did the show go tonight?' Crowne asked Michael.

'Not bad, not bad. It's going to be filmed by Scottish TV, you know!' He was justifiably proud and pleased.

'Ach, not a soul will understand my play,' Duntyre said, disappearing into the depths of his whisky.

'You mean because of the message, or because of the Scottish dialect – I mean, the Lallans?'

'We'll tone down the Lallans a wee bit for the telly,' said Michael. 'Eh, David? No sense in making it incomprehensible when we've got a chance to reach a larger audience.'

'I suppose you can do all sorts of accents,' said Crowne.

'Och aye. Edinburgh, Glasgow, Ayrshire, Wester Ross – you name it, I can do it.'

'Oxford English?' asked Crowne.

There was a silence. Then Michael said with a grin, 'I can talk posh, if that's what you mean.'

'Especially when making purchases in antique shops.'

'Eh? Eh? What's that you say? I'm afraid my hearing isn't very good,' said Michael, miming with his hand to his ear.

A Dorsey Brothers tape was put on the tape machine. People got up and began to dance in the old-fashioned way, cheek to cheek. Michael whisked Michiko up and began to dance so as to escape Crowne's questions. Michiko went with his movements, but her eyes remained on Gregory Crowne.

'What were you on about, Crowne?' Duntyre asked with a defiant, amused glance.

'Was he the one who bought the George Duncan cello?'

'Who, Michael? Why would he buy a cello? He doesn't know anything about music.'

'He bought it to exchange for the Emilio.'

'What's that about my Emilio?' Talik said, raising his voice to be heard above the din from the tape-deck.

'Nothing, Talik.' Duntyre turned his back to him and said in a low tone to Crowne, 'Let's keep this between ourselves. He's publicly forgiven me but I always have a feeling he might dot me one.'

'Was Michael the "Englishman" who bought the cello?'

'What if he was?'

'Listen, David, I thought it was a silly thing to do but I'm not trying to make trouble for you. I just want to know . . . Was it your idea, or Michiko's, or Anne Gleghorn's?'

Duntyre pushed his glass about on the shabby little table. He glanced up, met Michiko's anxious eyes, and waved reassurance at her.

'So you think you know all about it.'

'I know how it was done.' He outlined his theory. David said neither yes nor no but something in the smile told Crowne he had it right. 'What I want to know,' he went on, 'is this: was it Anne's idea?'

'As a matter of fact, yes. She wanted to "punish" Talik.'

'And she needed Michiko to help about carrying the substitute cello to the hotel. To get Michiko she had to have a reason – and you and your political cause were the reason.'

'We-ell . . . if you put it like that . . . Michiko came and said Anne had this scheme: would I like to get TV coverage and all that? I jumped at it; who wouldn't?' He finished his drink. 'I think I'll go and hop around a bit with my girl.'

'No, wait, David. One more thing. I'd known Anne over a couple of years. She never struck me as the kind of person who'd work out a scheme like that.'

'What, you mean she was no great brain? It *was* pretty nifty, wasn't it?'

'It was her idea?'

'Oh aye.'

'She came to you with it all worked out?'

'Uh-huh.'

'That surprises me,' said Crowne. 'It really surprises me.'

Angeliza was looking longingly at the little dance floor, and Talik was stolidly ignoring her longing to dance. Crowne felt obliged to ask her. She attached herself to his arm like a bright little Amazonian parrot.

'Happy, Angeliza?'

'Oh, happier than I could have thought, considering that awful interview in the morning.'

'You can put all that behind you.'

'You are so kind, Mr Crowne. Talik, too – he is being kind to me.'

For now, thought the prince. And, looking down at the pretty little woman, he saw the same thought mirrored in her eyes.

'Oh, I know he will change,' she said, as if in reply to spoken words. 'A great musician like that – I am too boring for him. But just for a little time . . .'

The music died; he led her back towards the table. 'Angeliza,' he said, pausing among the dancers, 'the fish you gave to Cha-cha – was there much of it on the buffet?'

'Don't remind me of Cha-cha.'

'I'm sorry, I don't mean to upset you. But you see, the fish that killed Cha-cha comes from a long way off – from the Pacific. There couldn't have been much of it.'

'So it had to come all the way across the world to kill my poor Cha-cha!'

'You scooped up a few pieces, is that right? And folded them into a napkin?'

'Oh yes, I had to be quite quick. The others were eating it up quite quickly.'

'You were keeping an eye on it because you wanted some for Cha-cha?'

'Yes, but people were sampling it – all except Michiko, who said she liked to eat foreign food when she was abroad. She had some Scottish dish, David told her it was good. She recommended it to Mr Shige but he said he liked sashimi and ate quite a lot of the fish. Anne Gleghorn too.'

'The thing is, Angeliza, I'd known Anne for some time and I never saw her eat raw fish before.'

'Oh, you remember, there was this talk about pure food, and she had the idea that this raw fish was the purest thing one could eat. Everybody was trying it, but the pieces I took were for Cha-cha.'

One thing was clear: whoever might have arranged poisonous fish for Anne, it couldn't have been Angeliza. Angeliza would never have done anything to harm the little cat she'd brought all the way from Venice.

He was still turning it over in his mind when he at last went to bed about two in the morning.

What bothered him was this: Anne Gleghorn had acted quite out of character in coming up with a clever plan to steal the Emilio. It seemed to Crowne that someone might have suggested it to her. Someone might have laughingly said to her, 'I know how you could give Talik Edder the shock of his life,' and she would have listened eagerly. The problem was, it was impossible to go to Anne and say, 'Who put you up to it?'

Because Anne Glegorn had died, accidentally.

It had to be an accident, because they had all – all except Michiko – eaten the dangerous fish. Michiko had declined the sashimi, for reasons that sounded perfectly adequate.

194

Yet she and Anne had been together in a plot to take the Emilio and now Anne was dead of a poison that Michiko had taken care not to eat.

Had it been an accident after all?

Sixteen

Gregory Crowne went out into the still-sleeping city next morning to drive his rental car to Murrayfield. As the wheels span under him he had a moment's nostalgia for the BMW he had left in the garage in Surrey – but it would have been tempting providence to leave it in the parking lot at Heathrow. This little Renault was good enough for carting musicians and their scores, their dress suits and their instruments, around Edinburgh.

Liz was ready, clad in tight-fitting jeans by Chipie and one of his own discarded Hathaway shirts. She carried a canvas bag held together with two or three leather thongs, looking as if it had been made by a purblind Red Indian but costing a couple of hundred from an Italian boutique. On her feet were espadrilles from some beach stall in Torremolinos.

As she got in beside him she was yawning enormously. 'I hope this is going to be worth it,' she remarked when her jaw had gone back to normal.

'Of course it is. Look at the sky. It's going to be a gorgeous day.'

'I thought sunny weather wasn't good for fishing?'

'We can always think of something else to do.'

'Oh yes?' she said, yawning again.

'Go to sleep. I'll wake you when we get there.'

The cottage was on the banks of a Perthshire stream that ran through the estate of the Earl of Banteith, one of Grandmama's old admirers. The earl took his angling seriously: he only lent his cottage to others of the same kind.

For this reason he'd taken no pains to make the place look like a 'des. res.' It was a plain, rectangular stone cottage with a slate roof. No roses round the door, although there were raspberry canes in the neglected garden and some unkempt hollyhocks round which the bees were fussing.

'Wake up,' said Crowne, 'we're here.'

'I wasn't asleep,' said Liz, waking up. She stared at the cottage. 'What a funny place. Are you sure you haven't taken the wrong turning?'

The prince gave her a level glance, but refrained from making the obvious retort. He took the key from under a flowerpot by the door. 'This little house has been hallowed by the feet of many devoted fishermen. In this house, Howard Hamilton put a fish on the scales and it weighed out at fourteen pounds.'

'Great,' Liz said, following him in. 'Please don't expect me to cook fourteen pounds of fish for lunch.'

'I don't know why I brought you,' Crowne said, laughing. 'You're totally uncooperative. You do realise this is a serious business, that you're supposed to cheer if I get a catch and weep if I have no success?'

She had wandered into the kitchen, which was surprisingly well fitted. She was opening cupboard doors and looking in the freezer. 'It's all right,' she reported; 'there's steak here if you don't get a bite. In fact, there's a good supply of everything. Which reminds me, I've had no breakfast. Can we eat before we go out after Moby Dick?'

He agreed that it would be a good idea to have breakfast, and to take a steak out of the freezer 'just in case'. In fact, he could foresee the fishing was going to be poor. With the cantankerousness of Scottish weather, the sun was now shining with enthusiasm after three days of muggy drizzle and misty sunlight.

While Liz busied herself with thawing and toasting bread, he examined the angling equipment. The earl's own rods weren't there, of course – he'd have died before he let anyone else monkey about with his darlings – but there were a couple of eight-foot rods of split cane. There was a newfangled salmon rod from America which Crowne picked up and put down. There was a selection of both forward-tapered and double-tapered lines. There were cases of flies, dressed by the earl himself, whose hobby it was: delicate concoctions of feather, silk, deer's-tail hairs, bast fibres, or wool. Crowne was still musing over these when Liz called that breakfast was served.

Love-making should of course occur *before* breakfast, but Liz had other ideas. While the prince was still swallowing the last mouthful of toast and marmalade, she put an arm around his shoulders.

'Mm . . .' she whispered, her cheek against his, 'you smell of oranges.'

'Mm.' He gulped down the sharp-cornered toast just in time to meet her lips.

'And taste of oranges too.'

'Marmalade,' he mumbled, in explanation.

'That's interesting. You know when I put kisses down your spine the way you like it?'

'Mm?'

'You taste of sandalwood then.'

'That's interesting.'

'Yes, isn't it? Don't you think we should pursue the matter? It could be of . . . scientific . . . interest.' As she murmured the last two words, her fingers were creeping between the buttons of his shirt.

'I came here to fish,' he told her, turning to take her into his arms.

'Of course. Angling.'

'Yes.' He was dropping kisses on her hair.

'How about teaching me a few angles, then?'

'Dearest Liz, there's nothing I can teach you.'

She laughed. 'Oh, come on, let's see if that's true.'

The bedroom was as spartan as the rest of the cottage. It

might even have been a fact that the bed was uncomfortable. But for them it was a couch of luxury, a haven of delight. Long limbs intertwined, special curves and creases to kiss and caress . . .

He told her he loved her. She smiled in the dusty sunlight of the room and shook her head. He loved her, she loved him – what did it mean, what *could* it mean? Prince and commoner, rank and class – he said it meant nothing to him, and she knew it was true. But his family . . . his family . . .

So it could never come to anything, but she held him all the closer because it might end at any time, it might all vanish like the magical strains of music that meant so much to him.

At length they were sated, and sat up, laughing at their own mischief, and got up and dressed and started the day again. Liz took some cushions out to the bank of the stream so that she could watch him, so serious, so intent, casting the invisible line over the dappled light under the birches.

It was rather late in the season for trout and no chance of interesting any surface-feeding fish except in the shadows where the angler could merge into the background of trees and bushes. But catching a fish wasn't the point. It was the pleasure of watching the cast whip over the pool, judging whether the fish was interested, letting thoughts come and go in that half-attentive musing that becomes second nature to the angler.

Liz brought out the Sunday papers he had bought *en route*. Propped against a tree, she turned at once to the fashion pages. 'Frilled edges,' she muttered, 'handkerchief hems . . . Quaker collars – oh, no!' When she'd finished disagreeing with the forecasts for winter wear she went gathering wild raspberries.

The prince's musings inevitably began to turn to the events of the past few days.

Last night's conversation with David Duntyre should have set his mind at rest about the theft of the Emilio. He remembered that when he first worked out how it had been stolen he had the same sensation as when he had solved a crossword.

Now he was having the afterthoughts that come to crossword addicts – a nagging suspicion that, though all the letters had fitted across and down, some of the words were wrong. It was like when you filled in 'LOST' when you should have fitted in 'TORT' – two letters fitted and made it appear a correct solution, but a deeper consideration showed you had taken the easy answer.

The wrong letters in this puzzle were his thoughts about Anne Gleghorn. Anne had never been a clever woman. A good singer, sometimes approaching greatness but failing more often through a lack of sensitivity. coached into her interpretations rather than finding her own. Not a thinker. No, not a thinker.

Yet she had come up with this neat and clever plot to get the Emilio. It was so unlike her. It was as if she had given up music and taken up higher mathematics.

And then, after this totally unexpected display of intellectual brilliance, she had died from the accidental ingestion of poison. She had died; everyone else had only been ill. Everyone else, that is, except Michiko Toshio.

Michiko Toshio had not eaten the fish from the Hawaiian restaurant. Very well, just for the sake of supposing, let's say that Anne's death wasn't an accident. Let's say that Michiko was aware the fish was poisonous and refrained from eating it. Michiko knew – they all knew, because Anne had given them the information – that she had had allergies in her youth, cured for her by a teacher who took her health in hand.

So Michiko, understanding the dangers, had let them all eat something that would make them ill but might quite possibly kill Anne.

Why? Why? Why should Michiko Toshio want to kill Anne? He reeled in his line, and as the sun had moved he too moved, following the shade.

All right, try it from another starting point. Taking it as

agreed that Anne's death wasn't accidental, who else other than Michiko would want her dead?

A difficult woman, Anne Gleghorn. Talik had found her so. But Talik wouldn't kill her. Talik had forgiven everyone concerned in the taking of the Emilio. Or so it seemed. Yet even if he still had resentment over that, why pick on Anne? Talik had had no idea Anne was the instigator of the theft. But if Talik had found out about Anne's part in losing him the Conservatoire?

David Duntyre . . . Would Duntyre have wanted to kill Anne? His fellow-conspirator in the matter of the Emilio . . .

But in the name of God, why should anyone want to kill Anne Gleghorn for taking and giving back the Emilio?

Her death had been caused by tetradoxin, the toxin produced by the Tetraodontidae. Apart from Michiko, they had *all* eaten the toxic fish. So her murderer would have to be prepared to eat the fish too, and thereby risk death.

A likely story.

The sun climbed in the sky. September noontide came and passed. The water became so warm the fish all went off for a siesta.

'Nothing doing for now,' he said to Liz. 'Perhaps when the sun is going down.'

'I thought we had plans for after sundown?'

'All in good time, dear girl.'

'Some enchanted evening!' growled Liz, and went indoors with the bowl of raspberries she'd picked.

Despite the idea she tried to inculcate, that she wasn't in the least domesticated, Liz made a good job of grilling the steaks and tossing salad from the few ingredients she could find in the back garden – lettuce gone wild, some elderly radishes, nasturtium leaves. They ate in the living-room, at a fine walnut table on one end of which stood a pile of copies of *Field and Stream*.

Raspberries with thawed clotted cream provided the sweet course. While Liz went to fetch the coffee, Crowne stretched

201

out a hand to pick up a copy of one of the outdoor maga-
zines.

'Trying to find out how to be a good angler?' Liz enquired
as she came back with the coffee pot.

'Humph. You don't get that out of books.'

'You'd think you could, by what's here,' she said, indicating the shelves crammed with books about angling. When
she had poured the coffee she selected one at random. '*Fish
and Fishing in the Himalayas* – there's a bestseller if ever I
saw one. The faded old pictures are rather nice, though.'

She put it back, ran her finger along the rest of the row.
'They need dusting,' she reported.

'Well, you can do that after you've cleared the table
and washed up. It should keep you busy the rest of the
afternoon.'

'Six days shalt thou work and do all that thou art able
And on the seventh scrub the decks and holystone
   the cable.'

'Where did you learn that?'

'My grandfather was in the Navy. He used to say that
cleaning decks in the tropics was the worst form of toil
known to man. But then he'd never done much washing-
up.'

In the end they did it together, then Liz went out with some
cushions to snooze in the sun. Crowne said he'd join her in a
moment. 'Leave some space on the cushions.'

'La, sir, what are your intentions?'

He grinned. She went out laughing.

He drifted towards the bookcase. She'd said you could
learn all you needed to know about fish and fishing from
books. Then she'd talked about her grandfather in the tropics.
Tetraodontidae were fish of the tropics, or at least of warm
waters.

Tetraodontidae . . .

He found a French encyclopaedia of fish. Translated, the entry ran:

> Tetraodontiforms: Known under various names with the connotation of inflation since, if alarmed, the fish inflates until almost orb-shaped or balloon-like. Because of the strong fused teeth (hence the name, which means stone-toothed) they eat crustaceans and molluscs. At certain seasons of the year their flesh is highly poisonous: for this reason there are many deaths on the Indian seaboard and round the Pacific coasts.

Why the devil would anyone import a fish known to be poisonous? Crowne asked himself. He put the book back and found another, a very old volume called *The Natural History of Fishes*. Here there was no coloured plate but, under *Tetraodontidae* he found:

> The Smooth Orb, called the Blower at the Cape of Good Hope. This fish is never eaten because there is a great deal of danger in it, of which the Dutch are very careful to inform foreigners. However, a certain sailor, not believing what they said, had a mind to make a trial and was so hardy as to eat one; but the experiment cost him dear for he fell sick and died not long after . . .

When Liz came in at three o'clock he was sitting at the walnut table with books piled around him, still reading.

'You really do intend to learn how to be a good angler,' she suggested.

He looked up. To her surprise, he wasn't smiling.

'What's the matter?'

'I've got something – an idea, a half-remembered piece of knowledge – trying to come into shape in my mind. It's nearly driving me mad!'

203

She came to stand behind him, and put her arms around his neck. 'What's it about?'

'It's about . . . I think it's about murder.'

'Murder? To come? Or already happened?'

'Both, perhaps.'

'You're talking about Anne Gleghorn?'

'I'm afraid so.'

'You mean it wasn't an accident?'

'It gets more and more unlikely the more I think of it.'

'I could tell something was bothering you,' she said, kissing the light brown thatch on top of his head. 'I don't know anything about fishing for trout, but I could see your heart wasn't in it.'

He twisted his head to look up at her. 'I'm sorry, Liz. I've been poor company, I'm afraid.'

'Don't be silly. Can you tell me what you've been working out?'

'Not till I get it right.' He stood up, and she linked her arm through his as he moved towards the window. After a moment he said, 'What time is it in Japan, Liz?'

'What?'

'The time difference – any idea what it is?'

'You're joking,' she said, looking at him with real anxiety. It was such a weird question.

'Wait. When Shige was going to ring Tokyo he said . . . I think I gathered it was about nine hours ahead.'

'Nine hours ahead. So it's midnight in Tokyo.' She smiled. 'It sounds like the title of a piece of incidental music.'

'No, it's really only two p.m. Greenwich Time here because we're on British Summer Time in Scotland. So it's only eleven at night in Tokyo. That's not too late to ring.'

'Ring who?' she demanded, baffled.

'Just a minute.' He found the telephone behind a pair of waders on the hall table. Phone book there was none. He dialled International Directory Enquiries. After many reconnections he asked for the home telephone number of Takamasa Shige, owner of Orient Paints and Solvents, in Tokyo.

A pause.

'I'm sorry, that number is ex-directory.'

'Operator, this is a very important enquiry. If you like to check with Chief Inspector Fairmil of the Edinburgh Police, he would vouch for me.'

'In that case, sir, couldn't you get the Edinburgh police to make the call for you?'

'They would certainly do so, but it happens that I am the person who knows what to say to Tokyo when I get through. It would be too complex to explain. You could check while the connection is being made if you think I'm leading you on.'

The coolness of the operator's manner was disturbed. 'Oh . . . well . . . yes, I suppose . . . What number are you ringing from?'

He read out the number. 'I'm on the property of the Earl of Banteith.'

'Oh. Who should I say is making the call, sir?'

'Prince Gregory of Hirtenstein.'

'*Oh!* Yes, sir. Just one moment, sir.' There was another pause and then she came back. 'Your number in Tokyo is ringing now, sir.'

'What are you doing?' Liz demanded, waving both hands at him to attract his attention. 'You aren't trying to ring Shige in Tokyo? He's in Edinburgh.'

'Shh,' said Crowne.

The receiver was picked up at the other end. '*Doso?*' said a voice.

The prince said, very distinctly, 'Is that Mr Shige's house?'

There was the fractional hesitation that comes when a good servant is taken by surprise. Then the woman said, 'This is Mr Shige house. Who is calling, please?'

'This is Gregory Crowne, a concert agent, speaking from the Edinburgh Festival. May I please speak to Miss Suso Shige?'

Another hesitation, but of a different quality. 'I'm sorry, Miss Shige can't speak callers.'

'Is she at home?'

'Yes, sir, but not speak on phone.'

'I wish you'd ask her if she'd give me a few minutes. I know it's late at night but I'm interested in offering her an engagement to play—'

A hissing intake of breath. 'Miss Shige can't play any more.'

'She can't? Why is that? I understood from Michiko Toshio—'

The woman in Takamasa Shige's house gave a cry of anger. 'A *bad* girl. Because of Michiko Toshio, Miss Shige is very ill!'

There was a feeling of finality in the way she said it. Crowne said quickly, 'Don't hang up. Are you a relative of Miss Shige?'

'Housekeeper.'

'I handle Miss Toshio—'

'Handle?'

'I get work for her. If she is a bad girl, I need to know. Tell me how she's to blame for Miss Shige's illness.'

'Michiko made Miss Shige do bad things, wrong things!' The woman, though a servant, was one of those who embrace their master's affairs as their own. 'Miss Shige go in factory many times, many times, jump in river many times, breathe in harmful things, swallow harmful water. Some harmful things in chemical industry – everybody knows. Not suitable for young lady like Miss Shige to go there, only silly, but Michiko tell her she must go because her father make harmful things. And now because of her, Miss Shige is very sick.'

'I'm very sorry to hear that. Perhaps when she's better I could speak to her? I'll ring again next week.'

'No, don't ring next week.'

'Next month, then?'

'Miss Shige not here next month.' The voice trembled. 'Miss Shige is dying of *minimata*.'

She put down the receiver on that. At his end Crowne carefully replaced the phone.

'"A death on her conscience",' he said in a low voice.

'What?' asked Liz.

'Takamasa Shige said that Michiko had a death on her conscience. He was right.'

Seventeen

L iz watched him as he picked his Barbour off the old
hallstand where he'd hung it on coming in. He felt in
his pocket for his wallet, to find a card Chief Inspector Fairmil
had given him.

'What are you doing?' she asked.

'I'm ringing the Edinburgh police.'

'What for, Greg? What's up?'

'I can't be certain. I need to talk to Fairmil, get verifi-
cation.'

He was put through in moments. But when he asked for
Chief Inspector Fairmil he was told it was his day off. 'After
all, sir, this is Sunday,' the desk sergeant said.

'I quite understand that, but this is important. Could you
give me his home number?' It was ironic that, though
Tokyo came through clear as a bell, Edinburgh sounded
like outer space.

'Well, I don't know whether he's there, sir, to tell the truth.
I think he said he was taking his kids out for the day to an
amusement park.'

That was understandable. As far as Fairmil was concerned,
the two cases – the hijacking of the Emilio and the death of
Anne Gleghorn – were closed. The Emilio was regarded as
a prank and Anne's death was an accident. So with an easy
conscience he had taken his day off.

'What about Sergeant Haggerston?' he enquired.

'He's out, sir, looking into a couple of Saturday-night
break-ins.'

'Spray-cans?'

'No, sir – it's this line – break-ins.'

'Is there anyone in CID I could speak to? Someone who might know me, for preference.'

'What did you say your name was, sir?'

'Gregory Crowne.'

'Reginald Brown?'

'Crowne, Crowne!' said the prince loudly.

'Just a moment.' After a short pause of hisses and crackles he said, 'I'm putting you through to Constable Dempsey.'

'Yes, sir?' said Jack Dempsey. 'Is that you, Mr Crowne?'

'Jack! Thank God! This is a terrible connection.'

'It's not good. Is there anything I can do for you, sir?'

'Do you know how to get in touch with Mr Fairmil, Jack?'

'He's out for the day with his two boys—'

'Yes, but surely you know how to get hold of him?'

'I suppose I could, if it's urgent. Is it urgent, sir?'

'I think it is. It's about the cello and Anne Gleghorn.'

'What fellow is that, sir?'

'Not fellow, cello. *Cello.*'

'Oh, aye, I'm with you. The cello – which one, sir, the cheapie? If you want it, we've got it. Nobody's claimed it, I suppose you could say it's lost prop—'

'Jack, it's about the Emilio—'

'It's not gone again, sir! Don't say that!'

'Jack, just listen and take notes for Mr Fairmil. It's very, very important. Get him back to the office. I'll come to see him the minute I get to Edinburgh and explain what I'm thinking, but in the mean time—'

'Get the Chief Inspector in on his day off, sir? Och, now, Mr Crowne, it'd have to be something very important—'

'It is important. I think it really is a matter of life and death.'

Jack said something that was wholly lost to Crowne

209

because of the noise on the line. When he was audible again he was saying, '. . . your safety, we could get the local police. Whereabouts are you, sir?'

'I'm in Perthshire—'

'Leicester?'

'*Perthshire* – P-E-R-T-H—'

'Oh, Perthshire. I'm with you. I'll get on to the uniformed branch—'

'Jack! It's not about me! It's about Takamasa Shige!' shouted Crowne at the top of his voice.

'What about Mr Shige?'

'Put a guard on *him.*'

'I don't think there's any activists in Scotland linked up with Japanese leftists, sir – although of course the IRA—'

'This isn't about the IRA, Jack, it's about Anne Gleghorn's death. It was no accident.'

'Sorry, sir, I didn't get that. Miss Gleghorn what?'

'Was murdered.'

'Sorry, sir?'

'Anne Gleghorn was killed by tetradoxin administered on purpose—'

'By getting boxed in?'

'Tetradoxin! Tetradoxin!'

'Oh, I get you, the poison in the fish.'

'Yes, the poison in the fish. It's difficult to explain on this damned phone—'

'You can say that again, sir! I can hardly make out a word you're saying. Anyhow, I'll see to it – I'll get word to Mr Fairmil that you're coming to see him. What time would that be, sir?'

'What?'

'What time will you be here to see Mr Fairmil?'

'About six thirty, I think. And in the mean time, Jack, would you get that expert from the university—'

'What was that, sir? I didn't follow a word of that.'

'Fairmil said he had contacted an ichthy—' He gave up

hopes of getting the word across on the phone. 'An expert on fish. At the university.'

'Oh, aye, Dr Danvers – I'm with you, sir. You want us to get hold of him?'

'Yes, and ask him what he knows about *fugu* fish.'

'Voodoo ships?' said Jack, astounded. 'Would we not be better getting an anthropologist if it's to do with voodoo?'

'Not voodoo, Jack, *fugu* – *fugu fish*.'

'Hoodoo fish – I've got it sir. See you at six thirty.'

The connection was broken. Crowne stood with the receiver in his hand and said some very bad words, first in French, then in German. German was the best language for swearing. Even innocent words sounded bad if you said them with enough venom.

Liz had heard the remarks about getting to Edinburgh by six thirty. She began tidying up the few things they had disarranged. She was rather tight-lipped about it. This wasn't the way she'd expected the day to turn out, not at all.

'I'm sorry,' Crowne said, putting his arms around her. 'I really do have to get back. I don't think I've the right *not* to put my idea in front of the police, however vague it is to me.'

'I quite understand.'

He looked with wistfulness at the borrowed waders in the corner of the entry hall, the rod still threaded with nine feet of brand-new leader, the case of flies. It was hard to leave them, particularly as clouds were rolling over now – there would be rain, and it would have been a perfect evening to go out on the trout stream.

It turned out to be one of those nightmare journeys. Perhaps the crackling on the telephone line had foretold the storm that was coming up, but it took them by surpise. Rain began to sheet down upon the little Renault, wind buffeted it. Up in the hills they found the road blocked by a tree blown down by the rising wind. Nothing he could do would shift it.

Crowne made the mistake of backing the car away from it

to try to bypass it. All that happened was a bogging-down of the wheels in peaty mud. They put his Hennes safari jacket under one back tyre and Liz's sweater under another, but all that happened was that they got ground into the mud.

The hire car wasn't equipped with a telephone. Neither of them had brought a mobile. There was nothing for it but to walk.

An hour later they trudged into a hamlet. Hope rose in them: now they'd be able to find a garage where they could get someone to go out and retrieve the Renault. But no such thing: there was a garage but it was firmly closed. No amount of knocking brought forth any response. Finally an old lady in a cottage across the way came to her door to say, 'Ye'll get nae answer there – he's awa' to the kirk at Bridge of Allan.'

A kindly soul, she offered them hot tea and a chance to dry off. More she herself couldn't do: she had no telephone and no car of her own to offer as transport. But she called in a neighbour, who sent off his son on a bike, and by a complicated system of passing on messages a car was at last produced, complete with driver.

By this time it was getting late, and the old Vauxhall had no turn of speed. When they reached Edinburgh it was mid-evening. Liz, still damp and in a bad humour, was dropped off at Murrayfield.

'I'll ring you later, Liz. Perhaps we could go somewhere nice for dinner.'

'I think I'll take the plane back to London. There's one about nine o'clock.'

'Liz!'

'Well, I have the distinct impression that your attention is elsewhere. You haven't exactly been good company today.'

'I know that. I'm sorry. But one person's been killed, and I think someone else is in danger—'

'Oh, it's all ridiculous, like this fantasy that your grandmother builds up – getting people to put you under protection

212

so that we can't even have a private chat if you *do* happen to have your mind on me! I've had enough of it. So I'll say goodbye for the present, Gregory.'

An angry retort trembled on his lips. Then, to her astonishment, he began to laugh.

'What do we look like?' he said, standing in the rain, surveying their reflection in the dress-shop window. 'Two drowned rats! No wonder you're fed up. Darling, don't go back to London.'

She was wearing his Barbour, but the rain was pouring off the ends of her hair and down behind the collar. Her tight jeans clung to her legs now like long-johns. The prince was in the safari jacket which had been crushed under the back wheels of the Renault and now had only one usable button.

Despite herself Liz began to laugh. But after a moment she sobered and said, 'What makes me cross is that you didn't even *like* Anne Gleghorn very much. But worrying over her has spoiled our day.'

'Liking's got nothing to do with it. No matter how temperamental and touchy someone is, that doesn't mean they can be got rid of like waste paper.'

'No . . . I suppose not.' She pushed her sodden hair back from her brow. 'I think I'll stick to my decision to go home tonight. Presumably you'll be coming to London *en route* to Geneva, by and by?'

'Well . . . yes.'

'Give me a ring. You can collect your jacket and by that time I'll have recovered my sense of humour, perhaps.'

'Oh, Liz . . .'

She kissed him lightly on the lips. 'Bye for now, Greg.'

'Bye.'

He got back into the car. The driver, Mr McDowel from Cantrovach, had watched the exchange with interest. 'Ach, the leddies don't like having their hairdo messed up and their clothes spoiled, sir,' he remarked. 'She'll get over it.'

'Well, it was more than that,' said Crowne with regret.

Mr McDowel set him down at the Hill Hotel. Crowne handed him a Scottish banknote for a large amount. 'Och, no, sir, that's ower much!'

'Not at all, Mr McDowel – you've got to drive back in the rain.'

He telephoned from his room for coffee and sandwiches. While they were coming he showered quickly, put on dry clothes, and was ringing Chief Inspector Fairmil when the food arrived.

'Sorry, sir, we haven't been able to contact Mr Fairmil. He must be on the road somewhere. You know how it is, he's just not actually in any of the places where he said he'd be.'

'Has he a radio or telephone?'

'Not in his private car, sir. And his mobile switched off. Sorry.' Sergeant Haggerston cleared his throat. 'You do make it sound urgent, Mr Crowne. What's up?'

'Nothing, I hope – so long as you did what I asked about Mr Shige.'

'Oh, yes, we made enquiries at once to make sure he was all right, and I'm happy to say he's out for the evening with a friend, so there's no danger there.'

'What?' cried Crowne, choking on a mouthful of smoked-ham sandwich. 'You mean you haven't got someone – what's the expression? – tailing him?'

'We've ascertained that he's quite safe, sir,' said the CID man stiffly.

Crowne gave a groan of despair. 'Never mind. I'll try it from another angle. But if you do find Mr Fairmil, get him to ring me *at once*!' This was said in his princely voice, and the immediate assent from the other end told him it had had the desired effect.

He gulped down some coffee, chewed up the remains of his sandwich and hurried out of the room. His best source of information was Hector McVay – somehow the manager seemed to learn what was going on in his hotel without actual spywork.

Hector was in the foyer, welcoming important guests who were going to dine in the restaurant. He nodded that he would be with the prince in a moment.

'Filthy night it's turned out to be,' he remarked. 'I suppose it sent you home early from the fishing.'

'Don't ask,' said Crowne. 'Tell me, Hector, do you know where Mr Shige went?'

'Out,' said Hector in a voice of gloom.

'Where?'

'I didn't find out and didn't like to ask point-blank. You see, he took Angeliza out to dinner.'

'Angeliza?' echoed Crowne, at a loss. 'That's unexpected, isn't it?'

'From which side? I can quite see that he's looking for someone to chat to. He hangs around the hotel making phone calls and getting phone calls, and if they're about his business I think he must be going into bankruptcy or something because he always looks grim. He had a bit of a friendship going with Miss Gleghorn, didn't he? But now she's gone, God rest her.' Hector sighed. 'He's wasting his time with Angeliza. Short chaps like me and Mr Shige come nowhere in the romance stakes. She only went with him because he promised to take her to meet Mr Edder after his recital.'

Talik Edder was playing Beethoven with Roma Perciavelli at the Reid Hall this evening. Crowne glanced at his watch: by now he was probably into the second half of the programme. If he got a taxi Crowne could be at the artistes' entrance to meet him along with Shige and Angeliza.

That was perhaps the best way to deal with it – with the least fuss and the least danger.

He asked for a taxi. He was told there would be a delay because taxis were busy on this wet evening.

Something in his face told Hector that was a blow. 'Are you in a hurry?' he enquired. 'You can take my car if you like.'

'May I? Thank you, Hector.' When McVay brought the

keys he said, 'I wonder if you would do something for me, Hector? Man the telephone, and if Chief Inspector Fairmil comes through for me, tell him where I've gone.'

'And where have you gone, exactly?'

'I'm going to meet Shige and Angeliza at the Reid Hall.'

Hector frowned. 'It there some kind of trouble?'

'I have a feeling there is. You see, time is getting short for him—'

'For who? Who d'you mean?'

'Takamasa Shige. But after all, he's got someone with him—'

'He's got Angeliza with him,' Hector said with great concern. 'I hope the trouble won't involve *her*!'

'I can't see that she's involved,' Crowne said. 'But if you'll stand by the phone and pass on my message to Fairmil, that's the best thing you can do for Angeliza and everybody else.'

Without another word Hector darted into the area behind the reception desk to be on standby at the switchboard.

Crowne went out into the rain of the parking area. An early darkness had fallen. He got into Hector's neat little Ford and drove away with as much speed as he thought the conditions would allow.

The Reid Hall was in Teviot Place, not too far from the hotel. As he drove round from Heriot's he saw the little eddy of home-going people that told him the recital was over. He congratulated himself on timing it exactly. Once he found them, all he need do was stay with them until he had a chance to talk it over with Chief Inspector Fairmil. Fairmil would catch up with them somewhere, he was sure of that – either at the hall or back at the hotel.

It might be difficult to convince the CID man. After all, there was no real proof. Yet he thought Fairmil would take sensible precautions. The Festival still had a week to run; perhaps in that time it would be possible to get proof. Perhaps among the possessions of the chef from the Lei Restaurant.

216

Hadn't he read somewhere that *fugu* chefs had to have a certificate because of their special qualifications?

He parked without difficulty and hurried through the artistes' entrance of the hall without paying attention to the protest of the old man on the door. The backstage arrangements weren't elaborate. He found a door with a card inscribed MR EDDER, knocked and went in. The room was empty.

'Talik?' he called.

The doorman had caught up with him. 'Now who are you, sir?'

'I'm a friend of Mr Edder's. Where is he?'

'He's gone; he went off rather quickly.'

The door next to Edder's opened. 'Gregory!' said a voice. He went out to the passage. 'Roma! Is that you?'

'Gregory! *Caro mio!* Did you hear us? Were we not stupendous?'

'I only just arrived – I'm glad it went well—'

'*Ottissimo!* He is playing like an engel with his new darling. And how are you, my friend?'

'Listen, Roma – I don't want to seem rude but where did Talik go?'

'Ah, who knows – *l'idiota*, he rushed off, shouting to me to look after his Stradivari. So here I am waiting for him to come back—'

'He left the Emilio? But where did he go?'

'I cannot tell. Someone hurried in the moment we are back after our encore – Talik makes a big exclamation and runs out—'

'Did you hear what was said? Did you see who came?'

'No, I heard the voices, not so that I understood – besides, I was washing the face with cold water, very good after a performance. But I could tell there was a crisis – now wait, Talik said a funny thing! In a frightened voice!'

'What?' Crowne said, seizing her by her muscular shoulders and giving her a shake. 'What did he say?'

'Don't be rough, Gregory – I will tell you! He cried out, "Alcoholics!" and then he rushed out. The other one went too – the one who came – I heard the rush of footsteps.'

Crowne turned to the doorkeeper. 'Did you see someone come in?'

'Not a one, sir.' He hesitated and added, 'But, mind you, I only came on the back door a wee while ago. I was at the front of the hall, opening the doors for the audience to leave.'

'What is wrong, Gregory?' Signorina Perciavelli asked.

'I'll tell you some other time—'

'But where are you going, my dear? And this cello—?'

'Stay there, look after it. I'll send someone.' He ran out.

Alcoholics? It could only mean one thing to Talik – the place they had been last night, when the down-and-out grabbed him to beg for money. But why the hell should that make Talik rush out and leave his precious cello in the care of a colleague? Why should he dash away from a recital like a mad thing?

Useless to take the car on this trip. There was a one-way system that would slow him down and, in any case, once he reached the Royal Mile he would have to be on foot because Talik might be in one of the closes near the Mercat Cross.

He ran through the rainy darkness, telling himself that Talik was probably on foot too and, he hoped, not far ahead of him. Luckily he knew his way about quite well from many trips between concert halls. He sprinted down Candlemaker Row to come out in Cowgate. What had David Duntyre said about the alcoholics? That there was a shelter for them in Grassmarket and a place where they could get food hand-outs in one of the closes.

Grassmarket was on his left, its plane trees writhing in the rain and wind. The broad open place was well lit – he pulled up and gazed across it, but could see no sign of Talik's tall figure, although there were people about.

The other way, then – along Cowgate, which ran parallel with the old High Street. This was deserted, and as he hurried along he was seized with apprehension. Yes, *this* was the kind of setting . . . the ideal setting.

He broke into a long, loping run again.

There were name-boards at the dark entrances to the narrow alleys which ran between Cowgate and the High Street. Some were rather fine old closes, refurbished for present-day use; others were grim and forbidding.

And one of those had a name that caught his eye.

Old Fishmarket Close. That was where Duntyre had said the free food was handed out. He headed into it. The lighting was poor, but he glimpsed, silhouetted by the streetlamps of High Street at the far end, two figures, a very tall man and a shorter, squarer one.

Even as he focused on them, he saw the shorter of the two draw away and lift something high in a swinging movement.

'Talik!' Crowne shouted.

Talik Edder wheeled at the sound of his name. The blow that should have split his head open crashed down on his shoulder. Talik staggered, swayed, fell to his knees.

The weapon was raised again.

'Don't!' Crowne yelled. 'It's *useless*—!'

He was pounding up the steep, slippery cobblestones, desperately trying to narrow the distance before Talik could be hurt beyond remedy. The high stone walls rose up on each side, making a funnel for the rain to pour down. He heard himself shouting against the beat of the rain and the moan of the wind.

Then he heard the smashing of glass as the assailant dropped the bottle. A flying leap over Talik's stooped figure, and the man ran up the close and out into the High Street.

Crowne reached Edder, gasping for breath, taking in mouthfuls of air heavy with the cheap wine which had cascaded over the cobbles as the bottle broke. He crouched over the cellist.

'Are you all right?'

'Ah . . . God . . . my shoulder is wrecked . . .'

But he wasn't dead. That at least he had prevented. And he was able to complain, which meant he was less hurt than he claimed. 'Stay where you are,' Crowne said, and took off after the assailant.

He was just in time to see a compact figure race across the Royal Mile and disappear into yet another of the dark entrances that led who-knew-where. If Crowne stopped to think about it he'd lose contact. He sped in pursuit, throwing himself across in front of a car and reaching the entrance of the close before the driver had even managed to swear in alarm.

The passage he was now in had a roof of some kind – for a moment the rain didn't pour down on him. Then almost at once he was on the edge of a long flight of stairs with a central handrail of iron. From far below he could hear hammering footsteps as his quarry ran down the staircase.

He plunged after, taking the steps in long leaps that could have meant a broken leg if he missed his footing.

He had a vague idea where he was. They had gone headlong down this precipitous passage without a pause to look about, but he thought this close would come out in Cockburn Street. The trouble was, once there the hunt could lead in any direction – there were other closes to right and left, leading back up to the High Street. Or escape might lie in running down the curving incline of Cockburn Street to a road close by Waverley.

He had to catch up. There was no other way of knowing which direction to take. He quickened his furious pace, almost throwing himself down the last ten steps.

The running fox whisked out of the close. There was just the glimpse of a swerve to the left. So! He dived out into Cockburn Street. No sign. That meant the chase was on up the next close on the left.

Steps again – oh, God, how his breath was labouring

now as he tried to run up the staircase. He had a fearful pain in his side but he wouldn't stop. Grabbing his ribs, he ran on. The rain felt like ice on his now burning face.

But he wasn't the only one suffering. The footsteps ahead were faltering. The sound echoed in the wide passage. Crowne shouted again, sparing breath for it, hoping to end the pursuit. The words came out as a gasping cry, unformed, full of his own anxiety and pain.

There was an answering shout – of defiance. The steps ahead went faster. He could see the archway of the close that would take them into the High Street again, and the silhouette that still moved with desperate vigour.

Mercifully there came a few feet of almost level cobblestones, then more steps, then a resting level, two shallow steps which he took in a lunging stride. Out into the High Street.

He saw his quarry already crossing the street. 'Don't!' he yelled. 'What's the use—?'

But there was no let-up. Already the next high-walled, frowning entry was swallowing them up. It was like a precipice, the incline was so steep. There was a handrail, but at the speed Crowne was going it was impossible to catch. He cannoned from one side to the other as he slipped on a worn stone surface glazed with rain and pigeon droppings. It was like a ski run, just as dangerous but without any sticks to guide or brake himself.

He ran out into Cowgate, where the hunt had started. There were only a few yards separating them now. He tried a rugby tackle – and missed; the distance was too great. He landed heavily. He staggered up again, gasping, bruised.

The figure ahead had just disappeared into the fourth of the network of passages between the the High Street and Cowgate. Crowne summoned up a last unknown store of energy and ran.

As he reached the entry, someone cannoned into him. He flailed back, almost measuring his length but saving himself by a despairing grab at the building's corner. Without knowing it, he blocked the way out.

Then he realised he had won. There was a snarl like a cornered animal. The close into which they had just gone was a blind alley.

He threw out a hand in a gesture of appeal. But it was struck aside. He braced himself for attack, wondering if he could block it. To his amazement his opponent turned and made a running leap – at the far end of the little passage.

Crowne gave a cry of warning, but it was no use. The square figure swung itself up the perpendicular face of the building, using the barbed wire nailed there to discourage trespassers or vandals. There were old, grime-blackened windows further up. Did he mean to crash through, and escape through the building . . . ?

Up, up went the climber, with the rain making every surface slippery as ice, the window ledges and every coping grey-blue with pigeon muck.

He watched the hands lose their grip. Torn by the wire, bloody, slick from the rain. They clutched wildly at the slippery granite.

It was like slow motion. The body seemed to take a century to fall. For a moment a barb of wire caught at clothing, but it was a fractional delay.

Fragile flesh and bones upon hard cobbles of granite. A jarring, crushing sound as the skull hit the ground.

For a long moment Crowne didn't move. He stood there, clutching his side, labouring for breath. Two yards away from him the body lay, the unnatural angle of the head on the neck telling its tale.

From what seemed a hundred miles away he heard the police sirens. He made himself move forward to bend over the still figure but couldn't bring himself to touch it.

The flashing lights were reflected off the rain-sodden walls ahead. He didn't straighten, didn't turn. A firm Scottish voice said, 'Now then, what's all this?'

He felt like a very old man as he straightened. He turned. 'Officer, can you get Chief Inspector Fairmil here?'

The young uniformed man pulled up short in the act of passing Crowne. He stared at him in the dimness. 'Chief Inspector Fairmil? What for?'

'Please – try to get him.'

His partner had caught up. Together they edged past Crowne to gaze down at the body. The newcomer knelt, put his hand on the neck. 'He's deid,' he said.

'This yin's asking for Chief Inspector Fairmil.'

'Oh, aye? And who might you be?'

'My name's Crowne. Mr Fairmil knows me.'

'Does he now?' They edged him away from the corpse. 'Just come you out to the edge of the close, sir.' One held him by the elbow; the other went to the car and spoke into the radio.

Time passed – not much, but it seemed to Crowne that the world had gone into abeyance. His head was swimming a little. Elbows and knees, grazed in the ineffective rugby tackle, began to smart. His clothes stuck to him, wet with rain and his own sweat.

The officer who had radioed came back. 'Would you like to sit in the car, sir?'

'Thank you. Is the Chief Inspector coming?'

'Just sit quiet, sir.'

He sat in the back, hands hanging loosely between his knees. He was losing the heat that had been generated by the hunt. He began to shiver.

Soon another car drew up. Fairmil got out, was conducted into the close by one of the patrolmen. They stood out of sight for a few moments. The low murmur of their voices drifted back to Crowne.

Fairmil returned, stooped to look in at the prince.

'Well,' he said bitterly, 'we can put this down to a complete cock-up in communications.'

'I'm sorry. I don't think I made myself clear.'

'Even so, we should have done better.' He jerked his head towards the body in the close. 'So much for our attempt to protect Takamasa Shige.'

Eighteen

J ust at that moment it would have taken more strength than he had for Gregory Crowne to explain.

'Talik Edder is hurt,' he said. 'Further along, the close where the alcoholics go.'

'Hurt?' To the patrolmen Fairmil snarled, 'Where's that ambulance?'

'He's not badly hurt. A broken shoulder, perhaps.'

'What the hell's been going on?'

'We've had a running battle . . .'

'So I gather. People in the houses above the closes reported a fracas, and we got something from a motorist on two men running in the roadway of the Royal Mile. Who was it?'

'Me. And Shige.'

'Who was after you?'

'No,' said Crowne. 'You've got it wrong. I'll explain when I've got myself together, Fairmil. It's difficult.'

It took longer to recover than he expected. He was still shaky an hour later, when Shige's body had been taken to the mortuary and Talik, his right arm in a sling to protect his broken collarbone, was in the Casualty Department of the Infirmary.

They were in Fairmil's office. Crowne had asked that an urgent telephone call be put through to the Hill Hotel.

'What for?'

'To see whether Angeliza Kelly is all right.'

Scowling in mystification, Fairmil made the call. Crowne

225

could hear Hector's voice. 'Senhora Kelly? Yes, she's here – why?'

'Why?' repeated Fairmil, looking at Crowne.

Crowne took the receiver from him. 'She went out with Takamasa Shige to dinner, Hector.'

'So she did, but it came on so wet that Mr Shige said she'd better go on home while he went to meet Mr Edder. Very considerate of him.'

'Oh yes,' sighed Crowne, 'very considerate. Thank you.'

As Fairmil replaced the receiver he said in irritation, 'What's Mrs Kelly got to do with it?'

'Shige took her out to dinner. The story was that they'd go and meet Talik after his recital – of course, Angeliza accepted; the idea of going to meet her hero was gorgeous to her. He sent her home but went himself to the hall, where Talik says he told him Angeliza had been attacked by the alcoholics near the Grassmarket.'

'Shige told him that?'

'Yes.'

'But why?'

'To get him to go with him, alone so that Shige could knock him unconscious with a bottle of cheap wine such as the derelicts drink.'

'Knock him—? What would he do that for?'

'To kill him afterwards. It would look as if Talik had been the victim of an assault by some drunk in a delirium.'

'But hang on – Mr Shige? You said he needed protection!'

'No. I said, "Put a guard on him." I'm sorry. I meant, prevent him from going out and doing anyone any harm.'

Fairmil was shaking his head. 'But Shige's just been killed in an attack—'

'No, Shige was doing the attacking. He attacked Talik Edder and when I interrupted he ran off. I think he was going to attack me, but he changed his mind – perhaps he felt his best chance lay in getting away, putting distance between himself and the scene of the attempted murder. So he tried to climb up to one of the windows in that building blocking the alley – what is it anyway?'

'It's a warehouse, only partly in use.'

'Then he fell, and that was the cause of his injuries.'

'I'll have to have a statement on all this, sir. Are you sure you're saying Mr Takamasa Shige tried to kill Talik Edder?'

'Well, I can say he tried to knock him unconscious. More than that is supposition.'

'And supposing he had knocked Mr Edder unconscious, what makes you think he'd be capable of killing him?'

'Because he killed the chef from the Lei Restaurant. He probably hit him with that piece of scrap iron that he tied on later as a weight.'

'What?' roared Fairmil.

'It's a long story. Can it wait till tomorrow? I'm bushed.'

'I think you ought to give me a statement, sir,' the Chief Inspector said in a frosty tone.

'I'll give you one about tonight. I actually saw Shige strike Edder with a bottle and bring him down. Then he ran, and I followed. Oh, God, why did I do that? Why did I give chase? If I hadn't, he might still be alive!'

Fairmil was taken aback. 'Well . . . I don't think you ought to blame yourself, Mr Crowne,' he said, the frost thawing immediately. 'From what you say, he was attempting a murder and had already committed one. I don't think he deserves much sympathy.'

'But he does. That's the point. But it will take a long time to explain and honestly I don't feel up to it.'

The police surgeon came in at that point. He looked at Crowne, saw bruises forming where his face had hit the ground, saw the raw places on his hands where the iron handrail had grazed them. Beyond that he saw physical exhaustion.

'I think Mr Crowne needs a bath and some rest, chief inspector,' he recommended in the tone doctors use when they mean, 'This is an order.'

Crowne was driven back to the Hill Hotel in a police car. Hector came hurrying out to greet him. 'What's up?' he asked in great anxiety. 'That Sergeant Haggerston was here a moment ago, demanding to be let into Mr Shige's room. And Angeliza is in floods of tears because Talik has come home in a bandage.'

'Mr Shige is dead.'

'Dead!'

'He had a . . . a fall. An accident.'

'Oh, gracious heavens! What an awful thing! And what about *you*, sir? You look as if you've been in the wars.'

'I'm going to bed. Have them wake me at seven o'clock.'

'I'll send you up a hot toddy, sir – you look as if you could do with it.'

Whether it was the toddy, the relaxation brought on by a long hot bath or sheer exhaustion, the prince slept deeply and well. He was stiff next morning, and had to shave with caution, but he was fit for action. He went down to breakfast and found Angeliza hovering. Without invitation she sat down at his table.

'Senhor Crowne,' she said, 'please tell me if Talik's injury is going to prevent him from playing.'

'For a little while, yes. But his collarbone will mend.'

She nodded. 'I thought so,' she said, her eyes brimming with tears. 'Why then was he so angry with me when I said we must be glad it was only a minor injury?'

'Oh, Angeliza . . .' She would never learn how to handle him, never realise that he needed to be cosseted and made much of. She had grown up with the notion that men were supposed to do the cosseting. 'Never mind,' he said, 'he'll get over it. He always does.'

'Speak to him,' she begged. 'Tell him I didn't mean it the way it came out.'

228

But he knows that, he thought. 'I'll speak to him,' he agreed.

Smiling through tears, she searched in her capacious crocodile handbag. She produced a package wrapped in bright blue paper decorated with silver thistles. 'For you,' she said.

'Really?'

'Open it.'

With misgivings, he did so. His misgivings were justified. A truly horrendous silk tie was revealed.

'Much more attractive then those dull striped things you wear,' she said.

'Yes,' agreed the prince, looking at the embroidered unicorns and lions on the pink silk surface.

'Every time you wear it, I hope you'll think of Angeliza Kelly and how grateful she is to you.'

'I certainly will.'

Delighted that he was so impressed with her gift, she left him to his rolls and coffee.

He was on his way out to police HQ when Hector called to him. 'Phone call, Mr Crowne.'

'I'm expected elsewhere, Hector. Take a message.'

At Crowne's suggestion, Chief Inspector Fairmil had asked Dr Danvers of the Department of Marine Biology to join them. A tape recorder was at the ready. 'You don't mind if we record this?'

'Not at all. But I wonder how much of it you can use?'

Shrugging, Fairmil started the machine, announcing the date and time and who was present.

'Now,' he said, 'could you explain what you meant last night when you said you thought the late Mr Shige killed Togo Noguru of the Lei Restaurant?'

'Certainly. But it's better if I go back to the beginning.'

'Which is?'

'The Emilio.'

Fairmil frowned. 'But we dealt with that.'

'No. We worked out how it was done but we never thought about who planned the theft.'

'Anne Gleghorn planned it.'

'No. That was one of my big mistakes. I knew Anne Gleghorn quite well. I should have realised from the outset she wasn't clever enough to have worked out a scheme like that.'

'People can surprise you sometimes,' Fairmil said, unwilling to have the Emilio rear its musical head again. 'Of course she must have planned it – she *stole* the thing!'

'She stole it for someone else.'

'Yes, David Duntyre.'

'No. Takamasa Shige.'

'Shige?'

Crowne put his hands on the desk, leaned back, closed his eyes, and summoned up the logical sequence of events. 'Takamasa Shige was a big wheel – a millionaire with a business to run. Yet he came galloping across the world to buy a Stradivarius cello – himself, in person. That was my first big mistake: I never thought to ask myself why.'

'But we know why. His daughter wanted the Emilio.'

'Oh yes. But that's no reason for a Japanese father to behave the way Shige did. Particularly as, from what we gathered, Suso was somewhat in disgrace. She'd misbehaved in the past, got behind with her musical studies. Nevertheless, Shige turned up here to buy a Strad for her.'

'Well,' said Fairmil, 'in your opinion, what was his reason?'

'He was trying to salve his conscience. His daughter Suso is dying.'

'*What?*' cried Fairmil.

'Of an illness the Japanese call *minimata.*'

'Never heard of it.' He looked at Dr Danvers, who frowned and half nodded, as if the word meant something to him but he couldn't remember what.

'*Minimata* is brought on by the complex mix of poisons

230

from industrial wastes. You remember Michiko Toshio was supposed to have led Suso astray in protest marches against the wreckage of the environment in Japan? Shige's house-keeper told me Suso was very active – I think she said Suso actually jumped in the river into which a factory poured its waste. As a result, she got an ailment for which there's no cure.'

'Yes!' said Danvers. 'I remember – they were trying to bring a case against one industrialist when a score of people died. I think it was mercury poisoning in that case.'

'So Suso contracted this illness. And it was Takamasa Shige's fault. He let his factories spew out these toxins and his daughter was being killed by them. I can imagine that when the illness began and she was showing less ability with her music, he rebuked her – she wasn't studying hard enough, she was a bad girl. And then it perhaps became clear that she wasn't faking, that the illness was real. And the doctors told him they didn't know how to cure her.'

'Is that so? They haven't a cure?' Fairmil asked.

'I believe not,' said Danvers. 'It's difficult to know *which* poison to treat in cases like that. And for some of the modern chemicals, there *is* no antidote.'

'My God.'

'So here is this man,' Crowne said, 'whose daughter is dying. She's dying because she somehow ingested some of the deadly chemicals his factory was pouring out into the environment. He would do anything to assuage the guilt he feels.'

'Hang on,' intervened the Chief Inspector. 'I thought girls weren't thought of too highly in Japanese society?'

'That's no reason to believe that a Japanese father couldn't love his only daughter. All the more if she were wasting away before his eyes – and he is one of the richest, most influential men in Japan. He could pay all the specialists in the world if money would save her. But there's no cure. And *he* did it to her.'

231

'Well, poor soul . . .' Fairmil's face showed he was thinking of his own children.

There was a little silence. Then the prince resumed. 'Suso reads in the newspaper or hears on the news that the Emilio is up for sale. Perhaps she says to him that if only she had the Emilio, she could get well – to have a cello like that would make all the difference—'

'Aw, come on!' exclaimed the detective with a shake of the head.

'You don't know musicians, Fairmil. A good instrument means a lot – and an instrument like the Emilio has something almost magical about it. Besides, this is a sick child – you know how people get strange fancies . . .'

Danvers was nodding. 'She might really feel that this cello could help her. And in any case – I mean, I don't know any of these people, but it's a test, isn't it? Her father tries to show he loves her, but he's been hard and unkind to her up to now. If he gets this cello for her, that's proof, isn't it? He really cares about her.'

'So he says he'll get it for her. He thinks it's only a question of money. He makes her a solemn promise to bring back the Emilio. He knows he has to be quick – she only has a few weeks to live.'

Fairmil got up suddenly, walked to the window, came back and sat down. 'You said last night you felt sympathy for him. I'm beginning to understand why.'

'Yes. But I only understood about all this when it was too late.'

'Go on,' Fairmil urged.

'Shige got here and found the Emilio now belonged to Talik Edder. He tried to buy it from him. I saw him when he arrived – it was a terrible shock to him, I assure you, when of course Talik said no. Shige moved into the hotel. Don't forget he's a businessman, accustomed to seeking advantage where he can. He looked for an "angle" – and soon saw that Anne Gleghorn was full of resentment and anger towards Talik.

'So he worked out the plan to get the cello and used her to put it into action.'

'Excuse me,' Danvers put in, 'I'm new to all this. Why couldn't Mr Shige take the cello himself?'

'An elderly Japanese businessman carrying a cello in or around the Hill Hotel would have attracted attention. But Anne could ask Michiko Toshio to carry the cello in public – no one would look twice at her.' Crowne nodded at Fairmil. 'You know how the theft was carried out. Anne took the Emilio, put the George Duncan in its place, and carried the Emilio down to the basement. I think she was probably supposed not to do that, but to give it straight to Shige in his room.'

'Then why didn't she?' Fairmil demanded. 'Why change her mind?'

'I can't be sure. But I think she just couldn't take the Emilio away from Talik, not for real. Whatever her faults, Anne was a musician. She just couldn't deprive a maestro like Talik of his instrument. Moreover, she'd already deprived him of a position he wanted, and perhaps she felt some remorse. So she took the Emilio down to the back entrance, as she had told Duntyre she would. You must understand that Duntyre and Michiko thought all along that Anne was helping them stage a publicity stunt, nothing more. Anne knew it was a real theft, but she was so angry and resentful towards Talik when it was first suggested to her that she thought – though she changed her mind – that it served him right.'

'The woman scorned,' murmured Fairmil.

Crowne disregarded this cliché. 'The man I think of as "Mr English" came and took the cello, as planned by Michiko and Duntyre – perhaps Anne put it out by the dustbins, I don't know. Anyhow, he took it and kept it safe until it was time for it to turn up in the Hill Crescent gardens.'

'Just a minute. What's Shige doing all this time?'

'What could he do? I suppose he was expecting Anne to tap on his door that night. But she never did. If he had gone to *her* door and shouted to be let in, it would have caused a furore. He could do nothing but wait. And about one thirty Talik and I began a search for the Emilio. It was then he knew Anne had taken it but had decided for some reason not to give it to him.'

'What could he have been planning to do?' Fairmil wondered. 'When we came to search the hotel, we'd have found it in his room.'

Crowne picked up the hire-car key that had been found among Shige's possessions. 'Shige didn't have a car. He kept taking taxis here and there. But here we have a car key. I think this car was parked close to the hotel, and when Anne handed him the Emilio he was going to put it in the boot, and drive the car to some inconspicuous place where it could stay until convenient.'

'But, Mr Crowne, he could never have got it out of the country,' protested Dr Danvers, who had been following the story closely. 'Surely the police would be watching the airports and so forth?'

He glanced for confirmation to Fairmil, who nodded.

'You think it couldn't be done?' Crowne said. 'Let's suppose Shige drove to Cramond. I was there the other night! There are lots of little boats and yachts moored there. Suppose he bribed someone to ferry the Emilio across to, say, Holland or Denmark. Shige flies there, meets the boat at the jetty, takes the Emilio and flies from Copenhagen, or wherever, to Japan. Or let's suppose he buys some samples of British chemicals. That's his business, after all, the making of chemicals. He arranges for the samples to go in a crate by cargo plane to Tokyo. Would you have searched that crate to see if there was a cello in a smaller crate inside?'

The Chief Inspector drew in his breath, let it out, and shook his head. 'Probably not.'

'But he never got the Emilio from Miss Gleghorn,' prompted Dr Danvers.

'No . . . How did she account to him for her change of heart?' Fairmil asked.

'Your guess is as good as mine. But Shige has to accept it – what else can he do? Yet he's driven, chief inspector – driven by remorse and guilt. He keeps telephoning home. The people looking after his daughter say she's sinking. I was told, when I rang, that she wouldn't live out the month. He's *got* to get that cello. It's his proof to her that he loves her, it's to make up for all his anger towards her, it's to make him feel less guilty. But now, if he arranges to have it stolen, Anne Gleghorn will go straight to the police, won't she?'

'Oh, my Lord!' said Fairmil.

No one said anything for a long moment, then Danvers said, 'That's why I'm here, I imagine. The death of Miss Gleghorn wasn't an accident?'

'You're right, Dr Danvers. Let me go back a bit.'

The prince thought back to the evening of the celebratory midnight buffet. 'Hector McVay was asked to put on something special for the buffet. There was to be champagne. He suggested some Japanese fish dishes, said to Shige that he knew of a restaurant where there was a Japanese chef. Now . . . In Japan there is a special dish called *fugu* fish.'

'Ah,' said Dr Danvers.

'I got that as hoodoo fish,' Fairmil said.

'The line was very bad from the cottage,' Crowne said with a profound sigh. 'I couldn't make Haggerston understand.'

'*Fugu* fish? Means something to you, doctor?' Fairmil asked Danvers.

'Yes indeed. A deadly delicacy. There are about a thousand *fugu* restaurants in Tokyo, I was told. Every year about a hundred people suffer from a case of *fugu* poisoning and about thirty of them die. The fish is the globefish, of the Tetraodontidae. If memory serves me, the poison is a lot more virulent than cyanide.'

'But in that case, why didn't everybody drop down dead when they ate it in that whatever-it-was—'

235

'Sashimi,' prompted Crowne. 'Because the amount of poison is usually very small. I can't prove this, but I think Takamasa Shige went to the restaurant and asked the chef to put globefish in that selection of raw-fish dishes. The chef, if he had prepared *fugu* fish, would know which parts to leave out. But even so, there *is* tetradoxin in the fish and part of the heroics is to eat it and know when to stop. I think I read somewhere that when the diner feels his lips going numb, he knows it's time to stop.'

'Good God, it's like Russian roulette!' exclaimed Fairmil. 'You can't seriously tell me that people eat a fish that's going to poison them?'

'I could reply that you can't seriously tell me people ride motorbikes at speeds where they lose control, but they do. You can't seriously tell me that a man will walk a tightrope over Niagara – but he will.'

'It's true,' Danvers agreed. 'The fish is eaten in Japan and other parts of the Pacific seaboard. Of course the intensity of the poison varies from fish to fish, and with the season in which they're caught. But there's always a risk. This man at the restaurant would only provide the dish to another Japanese, who knew what he was eating.'

The Chief Inspector thought about it. To his straight-forward Scottish temperament, the idea was unacceptable. 'Are you telling me that among Japanese people there's a tradition of eating for pleasure a fish that could kill you?'

'Certainly. And I believe I was told, when I heard of it as a student,' Danvers added, 'that in the days of long ago, the warlords would invite their enemies to supper and then serve *fugu* fish. You couldn't refuse – that would have been cowardly. So there they all sat, popping slivers of fish into their mouths, and maybe half a dozen of them felt ill and maybe one or two died – but it was honourable, they all took the same risk.'

'Gosh, talk about supper with the Borgias!'

'In a way, you had a better chance than with the Borgias.

The Borgias arranged for just one guest to be served with the fatal dish. In the samurai tradition, they all took the risk, and maybe that's what Mr Shige had in mind.'

'To Anne Gleghorn the risk was great – in fact, fatal,' the prince took it up. 'Because she had food allergies, a sensitivity to chemicals that she was always talking about. Shige heard her. The tetradoxin she swallowed was enough to kill her. I'm afraid he made sure of that – I remember how he helped her to tasty morsels.'

'But the man must have been mad!' protested Fairmil. 'He might have killed half a dozen people!'

'He might. He might have killed Talik Edder – in which case the Emilio would have been up for sale again, wouldn't it? He might have killed Michiko and Duntyre, he might have killed me or Angeliza – though to do him justice he didn't urge the sashimi on anyone except Anne. He and Anne ate the most.'

'But himself? He might have killed himself!'

'Well, if he had, that would have solved his problem, wouldn't it? He didn't have to face his daughter Suso and say, "I couldn't get the Emilio for you." But to tell you the truth, I think he swallowed just enough *fugu* to have a positive result when the medics tested the urine samples. He'd eaten it before, probably quite often. He knew how his body was reacting – his lips got numb, he stopped eating *fugu*. The rest of us were so drunk on champagne we didn't notice. Except Michiko – she didn't eat any, because she liked to try the food of the country. If *she* had eaten the *fugu* she might have been able to warn us.'

Danvers was nodding agreement. Fairmil said, 'It's damnable. *You* may feel sympathy; I've lost mine, sir.'

'He was in the grip of a tremendous emotion. And your sergeant said something – about orientals not liking to lose face. His pride was involved. He *had* to get rid of Anne so as to take another shot at the Emilio. But after she died, the chef at the Lei Restaurant got worried. He contacted Shige.

237

Shige arranged to meet him, then knocked him unconscious or dead – don't forget, the poor fellow wouldn't be expecting it. Then he tied him up and tipped him into the sea. Bad luck for him that the body broke free of the iron bar and rose to the surface.'

'My heart bleeds for him,' said Fairmil.

'Noguru's death didn't seem any threat to him. No one even thought of it as murder – Sergeant Haggerston accounted for it as a suicide. He thought the man was full of guilt because he had caused Anne's death by negligence.'

'We-ell . . . that was the general view.'

'Did you find a certificate from some Japanese Board of Health, or something of that kind, among his belongings?' Danvers asked.

Fairmil coloured under his freckled skin. 'We found some papers in Japanese. I . . . I never thought to have them translated.'

'People who handle blowfish in Japan have special training. They learn which parts are safe to serve as food.'

'Safe, you say!'

'Well, saf*er*. The poison level is highest in winter,' Danvers went on, 'when the fish tastes best, ironically enough. The fish Noguru prepared had been in cold storage and I imagine it was a winter fish, though there's no way of being sure because it's all gone, every scrap of it gone down the waste disposal. But less than ten milligrams of tetradoxin can be fatal. You can imagine how easy it would be to leave a hundred milligrams distributed through the flesh.'

'How much is a hundred milligrams?' Fairmil wanted to know.

'A hundred milligrams is equal to about one grain avoirdupois, and there are over four hundred and thirty grains to the ounce – so you can see a mere trace could be left and yet cause death. And I imagine Noguru was asked to leave a little risk in the dish, as a favour to a fellow-Japanese. I expect some of the Japanese students here go in for it from

238

time to time, as some sort of tribute to tradition or as a test of their own courage.'

'If this is a delicacy, give me haggis,' muttered Fairmil. 'So now Shige has got rid of Anne Gleghorn so she can't bear witness against him, and also the chef. What's his game-plan now?'

'Time's running short,' said the prince. 'Not only with regard to Suso Shige, but Talik had begun to say that the moment he got to Vienna – where his agent lives – he was going to make a will ensuring the Emilio would go to a performing artiste – in other words, it wouldn't be for sale to Takamasa Shige. Since he wouldn't sell it while he was alive, Shige had to kill him before he left Edinburgh. And last night was the night.'

'Where did he get that idea from – about the wine bottle?'

'We had an encounter with a drunk the previous night. Duntyre actually said we ought to move on quickly in case the man came back "with friends". That gave him the idea. He was going to knock Talik unconscious with the bottle then perhaps break it and cut his throat with the glass.'

'The jugular,' Dr Danvers put in.

'I don't know. Anything that would suit the appearance of an attack by a drug addict or a drunk.'

'But fingerprints, Mr Crowne – he wasn't wearing gloves.'

'He probably only held the neck of the bottle. Once he'd broken it to give himself a killing edge, he'd take the neck part away and put it in a litter bin a long way off. Talik probably wouldn't have been found until later, and who would have thought it odd that only a few pieces of glass were left? The drunk would have run off holding the neck part, that would have been the view.'

'But you spoiled the plan.'

'That's it.' Crowne hesitated. 'I blame myself for what came next. If I hadn't chased him, he'd be alive now.'

'I dunno,' Fairmil mused. 'If you hadn't cornered him in that close – if he'd got away – do you think he could have lived with himself? He must have seen the game was up. We'd be after him for the assault on Mr Edder, and once we got him we'd uncover the rest. I admit he couldn't know you'd worked it all out, sir, but he must have seen that he could never have another chance with Mr Edder. That meant that he'd have to face his daughter, a failure.'

'Yes, he'd have to admit he couldn't get the Emilio for her,' Danvers said, with a sigh. 'And he'd be in disgrace over attacking Edder, at *least*. That's an awful prospect for a man of pride.'

'Seems to me if he'd got away from you he might have thrown himself under the nearest bus,' Fairmil said. 'I wouldn't blame yourself too much.'

A silence ensued. Fairmil stopped the recording machine, glanced at his watch. 'Coffee?' he suggested.

Danvers said he had to go – he had a meeting about university courses awaiting him at ten. When he had gone, Crowne nerved himself to ask the question that had been bothering him all morning. 'Does all of this have to come out?'

'Well, there'll be an inquiry by the Fiscal's office. As you already know from Miss Gleghorn's death, we don't have inquests in Scotland – it all depends on the Fiscal's view.'

'What's he likely to think on this one, Fairmil?'

The Chief Inspector's brows drew together. 'In actual fact, what we have here is an accidental death. Isn't it? Takamasa Shige, for reasons which the Fiscal will consider, climbed up to a window ledge on an old building and fell to his death. His reasons don't come into it, officially.'

Crowne made a sound of relief.

'You're thinking about the daughter, is that it, sir?'

'Well, it's bad enough that her father is dead. To hear what he'd been doing . . .'

'Seems to me there's no reason to go into all that. We'll bring in the Consul. It'll all be done delicately.'

'I should think they won't even tell Suso,' Crowne said. 'Why make her unhappy in her last few days? They'll probably give her messages from her father, the kind he used to telephone to his home. If they do it well, she can die without ever learning the truth.'

'Is she the only child?'

'I believe so.'

'I wonder who'll get all his money? Oh, and speaking of that, sir—' Fairmil grinned. 'You remember you asked me to check on the nephew who might inherit Mrs Kelly's fortune? He's right out of it – he's been on his honeymoon for the last month or so; married an heiress with a lot more money than his aunt.'

'Well,' said the prince. 'There you are.'

The coffee came; they drank it and mulled over the discussion of the last hour. 'I'll send in a full report to the Procurator Fiscal. You'll probably be asked to sign something. You'll still be here?'

'Oh, Lord, yes,' said Crowne, setting down his coffee cup and rising. 'Talik Edder can't play with a broken collarbone. I've got to find a substitute for two performaces, tomorrow and Thursday.'

'Why don't you ask Miss Toshio?'

Crowne was startled. 'Good Heavens no, chief inspector, Michiko is already in the ensemble.'

He left the big detective marvelling at the complexities involved in the making of music.

Nineteen

When at last Crowne got back to the hotel, after a long day of telephoning and bargaining and rescheduling, his card-key was handed to him together with a little collection of message slips.

'Miss Blair rang 8.30 a.m., asks you to ring back.' 'Miss Blair rang 10 a.m., wants to know why you haven't returned her call.' 'Miss Blair rang 11.30 a.m., asks you please to ring back.' 'Miss Blair again 1 p.m., enquired re your health, asks the favour of a return call.' 'Miss Blair again 3 p.m., very anxious you should ring.' 'Miss Blair 5 p.m., *please* ring back.'

He glanced at his watch. Nearly seven in the evening. He went upstairs two at a time, picked up the phone as soon as he had closed the room door and dialled Liz's number.

'Greg?' her voice said the minute she picked up the receiver.

'Yes, it's me.'

'Are you so *very* cross with me, Greg?'

'Cross? What do you mean?'

'Well, you wouldn't return any of my calls—'

'But I've been out all day, Liz!'

'What, since half past eight? Look, if you want me to grovel about how rotten I was to you yesterday evening, OK, I'm grovelling—'

'Darling, I haven't been running a campaign against you.' No, in fact he had forgotten all about her. But he had the good

242

sense not to say so. 'Something bad happened here last night after we parted. Talik was injured.'

'Oh, my God! Seriously?'

'No, but I've had to find a replacement for him and get notices out to the media and so on. I'll tell you all about it when I see you.'

'When will that be, Greg?'

'Well, the Festival ends on Saturday.'

But the echoes of the events would go on reverberating, he thought, as he at last went down to the first square meal of the day. Talik was in the dining-room, sharing a table with a very attractive woman in a rather severe suit.

'Gregory! Dr Simmons, I introduce Gregory Crowne, the concert manager of whom I spoke. Gregory, this is Dr Simmons, who takes care of me yesterday at the Infirmary.' In an undertone he added, '*Charmante, n'est-ce pas?*'

'Talik!'

'*N'importe, elle ne parle pas français.*'

Crowne preferred not to trust in the idea that the pretty young doctor couldn't speak French. 'How is the shoulder?'

'Dr Simmons tells me all will be well. But since I cannot play, I shall be glad to leave for Vienna. This business with Shige has troubled me much. I want to safeguard the future of the Emilio – do you understand my feeling?'

'Perfectly, Talik.'

'And so very luckily, Dr Simmons also goes to Vienna – is that not so, doctor?'

'Yes, a medical conference, it just so happens . . .' She smiled to herself. 'What a lucky break, eh?'

'It seems so,' Crowne said politely, wondering if he should warn her that the lady-loves of Talik Edder came and went with the regularity of the changing seasons.

The last week of the Festival came. The Bachiana Brasileira

243

No. 1 by Villa-Lobos was given two performances by Michiko
Toshio and seven other cellists, among whom was the replacement for Talik, a fiery young Czech called Vaclavek. The
Kamikura finished their programme of Schubert quartets.
The Procurator Fiscal called in Gregory Crowne to tell him
he had decided in favour of discretion concerning the death
of Takamasa Shige and the Japanese chef, a decision in which
the Japanese Consul concurred.

Talik left for London *en route* for Vienna. With him he
took the Emilio and a charming young lady about whom
the newspapermen were very inquisitive. They didn't notice
a plump, overdressed woman among the crowd that waved
him off at Turnhouse.

'Can I give you a lift back to the city?' Crowne asked
Angeliza Kelly.

'Thank you.' She was very subdued.

As they drove out on to the motorway he said, 'You're
staying on in Edinburgh?'

She clasped and unclasped her beringed fingers. 'I think
I will,' she said. 'You know, it is difficult to push myself
where I am not welcome – and Talik has made it clear I am
not welcome.'

'He isn't very kind to his women-friends,' Crowne
acknowledged.

'But Hector has made it clear I shall always be welcome
at the Hill Hotel,' she went on, as if not hearing, or deciding
not to care about Talik's women-friends.

'Even despite the panic you caused him over your cat?'

She gave a little laugh. 'Oh, he was so kind to me over
Cha-cha! He is very kind, you know.'

'Yes, I know.'

They drove for a time in silence. 'I hope you won't find
the northern winter too cold for you,' he ventured.

'Ah,' she said with gentle irony, 'it will be warmer for me
here than in Vienna, no?'

Not bad, he thought. She sometimes showed a surprising

amount of common sense. There was hope for her yet if she could take what Hector had to offer.

For Michiko life was less blithe. White with the pain of parting, she said goodbye to David Duntyre. They shook hands formally in the foyer before she got into the car taking the Kamikura Quartet to the airport.

When the car had disappeared, Duntyre walked back indoors. 'I need a drink,' he said.

'Come on then, let's go in the bar,' said Crowne.

Tam brought them Glenlivet. They drank. 'The place'll seem strange without her,' muttered Duntyre.

'What are your plans now?'

'Well, there's that filming of *Displenishin'* by the telly people. There's some talk of a commission to write something for the National. I dunno. The audience at the National would never understand a word.'

'Perhaps you should try writing in English?'

'Me? Never!'

'Well, you might earn more money that way. Enough to go travelling.'

Duntyre understood the meaning below the words. 'No,' he said, 'when a thing's finished, it's finished.'

So you think, mused Crowne. But maybe Michiko would have different ideas?

For himself, the immediate future was *couleur de rose.* He was going to drop in on Chief Inspector Fairmil to say goodbye, and then he would take the evening flight to London. Where Liz Blair would be waiting to meet him.

But first he must ring his family in Geneva. He went into the booth off the foyer to put the call through.

'Hello, Grossmutti? I'm just ringing to let you know I'll be at the Surrey number from tomorrow morning—'

'Gregory,' his grandmother interrupted in a tone he knew of old. 'What's this I read in the paper about *another* death among the people at the Hill Hotel last week? It's really too bad! You must move out at once, otherwise I

245

shall ask the Foreign Office to arrange for you to have protection again.'

'It's quite unnecessary. I'm going back to London—'

'It's all because of these unsuitable people you mingle with. I want you to give it all up and take that nice job with the Swiss Postal Directorate that I arranged for you.'

They both knew he would do no such thing. The life he led was the one that pleased him.

'I'll be home in about two weeks, Grossmutti. Tell Rousseau I'm coming.' Rousseau was the red setter.

'My child, Edinburgh has really unhinged you if you think I am going to talk to a *dog*!'

With which flourish she rang off, getting the last word as usual.

I'll get my own back, thought Crowne. When I travel home I shall wear that hideous tie Angeliza gave me and startle the life out of her. That'll learn her. Or teach her? Which was the correct English idiom?

I'll ask Liz when I see her, he thought.